Titles by Chanel Cleeton

CAPITAL CONFESSIONS
FLIRTING WITH SCANDAL
PLAYING WITH TROUBLE
FALLING FOR DANGER
FLY WITH ME

PRAISE FOR THE NOVELS OF
CHANEL CLEETON

"Sexy, funny, and heart-wrenching—this book has it all!"

—Laura Kaye, *New York Times* bestselling author

"A sexy fighter pilot hero? Yes, please."

—Roni Loren, *New York Times* bestselling author
of *Off the Clock*

"A sexy hero, strong heroine, delicious romance, sizzling tension, and plenty of breathtaking scandal. I loved this book!"

—Monica Murphy, *New York Times* bestselling author

"A sassy, steamy, and sometimes sweet read that had me racing to the next page."

—Chelsea M. Cameron, *New York Times* bestselling author

"Fun, sexy, and kept me completely absorbed."

—Katie McGarry, author of *Nowhere But Here*

"Scorching hot and wicked smart, *Flirting with Scandal* had me hooked from page one! Sizzling with sexual tension and political intrigue[. . .]Cleeton weaves a story that is as complex as it is sexy. Thank God this is a series because I need more!"

—Rachel Harris, *New York Times* bestselling author

"Sexy, intelligent, and intriguing. Chanel Cleeton makes politics scandal-icious."

—Tiffany King, *USA Today* bestselling author

FLY With ME

CHANEL CLEETON

BERKLEY SENSATION, NEW YORK

**BERKLEY
SENSATION**

An imprint of Penguin Random House LLC
375 Hudson Street, New York, New York 10014

FLY WITH ME

A Berkley Sensation Book / published by arrangement with the author

ISBN: 978-1-101-98696-7

PUBLISHING HISTORY
Berkley Sensation mass-market paperback edition / May 2016

PRINTED IN THE UNITED STATES OF AMERICA

10 9 8 7 6 5 4 3 2 1

Cover art by Claudio Marinesco.
Cover design by Danielle Mazzella di Bosco.

Penguin
Random
House

*To Shakira songs, summer cruises,
and life-changing nights*

Thank you to my wonderful agent Kevan Lyon, editor Kate Seaver, publicist Ryanne Probst, Jessica Brock, Katherine Pelz, and the entire team at Penguin and Berkley for making this book possible.

I'm so grateful to Roni Loren and Laura Kaye for reading and blurbing *Fly With Me*.

Thanks to my awesome Facebook Reader Group and the members of Our So-Called Group for making my days more enjoyable.

And to all the readers and bloggers who have supported my work throughout the years—THANK YOU! I couldn't do it without you.

Big thanks to my family and friends for their love and encouragement, and most of all, thanks to my husband, my real-life hero and inspiration.

This book has been ten years in the making, and I've loved every single one of them. Thanks for asking me to dance.

ONE

JORDAN

There was a time in a woman's life when she had to accept that wearing a headband made of pink—*glittery*—illuminated penises was too much. I couldn't put my finger on the number—and I definitely couldn't do it after my fourth tequila shot—but I figured that at thirty and still single, bachelorettes had ceased to be a fun rite of passage, and had instead become a wake-up call that if Prince Charming wasn't coming soon, I'd have to start exploring my options in the amphibian variety.

Of course, it didn't help that this was my sister's bachelorette—my cute-as-a-button, too-young-for-wrinkle-cream sister's bachelorette. Or that she was marrying my high school ex-boyfriend. I didn't care; I mean we hadn't been together in over a decade, but the fact that my future brother-in-law had once seen me topless added to the surreal feeling of the whole thing.

I took shot number five like a champ.

"I'm getting married!" Meg screamed for what might

have been the fifteenth time that night. Somewhere between dinner at Lavo and partying at Tao, this seemed to have hit her with a vengeance. On anyone else, it would have been annoying; on Meg, it was somehow still adorable.

At twenty-five, she was the baby of the family. A good five inches shorter than me, we shared the same blond hair and brown eyes. We both had curves, but on her, they were bite-size. I was a king-size—tits and ass that could put your eye out—not to mention the pink phalluses bobbing awkwardly on my head.

It had been Meg's idea to dress up, and I hadn't been able to disappoint her. So here I was, thirty years old, terminally single, wearing penises on my head, a hot pink barely there tube dress, and fuck-me Choos that topped me out at six feet. If I ever got married, I was so not doing a bachelorette. Or bridesmaids in hideous dresses. Or arguing with my fiancé over whether we'd serve filet mignon or prime rib. I loved meat as much as the next girl, but the drama surrounding this wedding had my head spinning, and I was just the maid of honor. If I were the bride? I totally got why people eloped.

My parents could do the big wedding with Meg. At least they'd get the budget option with me—if I ever got married at all.

Shot number six came faster than a virgin on prom night.

I wasn't really even tipsy. I could definitely hold my liquor, but this was Vegas, and everything about tonight screamed excess, and as depressing as it was to be the eldest, even worse, I felt like the mother hen to the group of three Southern girls ready to make the Strip their bitch. It was time to up my game.

I rose from our table and headed over to where Stacey

and Amber, my sister's friends from college, were dancing, determined to kick this feeling inside of me's ass.

When I'd look back on this evening, and it would play in my mind on repeat for months to come, this would be the moment. *Freeze it. Remember it.* How often could you say that you could pinpoint the *exact* moment when your life changed?

I could.

If I had anyone to blame for the wild ride that came next, it was Flo Rida. Because as soon as "Right Round" came over the club speakers, my tequila-fueled body decided it needed to move. It was the kind of song you couldn't resist the urge to dance to; it made normal girls want to grab a pole and let loose. Okay, maybe just me. But it felt like kismet, like the song played for me, to breathe life into my sad, old self. So I danced, pink penises gyrating and flickering, hips swaying, hair swishing, until my world turned upside down.

NOAH

"Dibs."

I took a swig of Jack, slamming the glass down on the bar.

"You can't call dibs, asshole. There are four of them."

Easy shrugged with the same nonchalance that had earned him his call sign and made him lethal behind the stick of an F-16. He lulled you into thinking he was just fucking around. He never was.

"Are you saying I can't handle four chicks?"

"I'm calling bullshit on that one."

The guy got more pussy than anyone in the squadron, but a foursome was ambitious even for him.

"Fifty bucks," he offered, knowing my pathological inability to back down from a challenge.

"Fuck you, fifty bucks. You can't bang four chicks."

Easy's eyes narrowed in a look I knew all too well.

"Watch me."

We all gave him a hard time for being a princess because his face was a panty dropper, but he could throw down like nobody's business. Lately, though, this shit had been getting darker and darker. We'd broken off from the rest of the group, Joker had gone back to the hotel to call his wife, and now Easy was drinking like he wanted to die.

The Strip had seemed like a good idea four hours ago, but I was tired and now I just wanted to collapse in the suite we'd booked at the Venetian. I'd flown four sorties leading up to today, each one more demanding than the last. Today's double turn had topped me out at six flights this week, and my body definitely felt it. I was tired, my schedule screwed six ways to Sunday, and right now I was far less concerned with getting laid than I was with getting more than five hours of sleep.

Our commander, Joker, was on my ass for the squadron to perform well at Red Flag—our international mock war held at Nellis Air Force Base in Vegas. As the squadron's weapons officer, it was my job to make sure we were tactically the shit. Babysitting F-16 pilots with a hard-on for trouble? Not in my job description. It was really sad when I was the voice of reason.

Sending a bunch of fighter pilots to Vegas for work was basically like putting a diabetic kid in a candy store. We got as much training done as we got tits and ass. And considering we pulled fourteen-hour workdays? That said something.

"It's a bachelorette party," I ground out, the subject already hitting way too close to home.

The flash of pain in Easy's eyes was a punch to the nuts. Shit. It was worse than I'd thought.

"Screwing around isn't going to change things," I added, trying to keep any judgment or sympathy out of my tone.

If it were anyone else, I would have minded my own business; but it wasn't anyone else, it was *Easy*. He'd been my roommate at the Academy, gotten me through pilot training when I'd struggled, flown out to Vegas when I'd somehow graduated from weapons school.

Easy threw back the rest of his drink. "Be my wingman for ten minutes. I won't go after the bride. Then you can leave."

I'd been ready to leave an hour ago.

"You owe me for the twins in San Antonio," he reminded me.

Shit, I did.

"Ten minutes."

He nodded.

I turned my attention to the group of girls dancing; they looked young and already well on their way to drunk. I was definitely calling in my marker at a later time.

At thirty-three, I was getting too old for this shit. Most of the squadron was either married or divorced, Easy and I among the few single holdouts left.

It wasn't that I was opposed to marriage. I'd thought about how it would feel to land after a deployment to a girl who'd throw her arms around me and kiss me like she never wanted to let go, instead of landing to my bros carrying a case of beer. Hell, I saw the way guys climbed out of their jets, their kids running toward them on stubby legs, looking like it was Christmas, their birthday, and a trip to Disney World all rolled into one.

Even a fucker like me teared up.

I wasn't Easy; I wasn't trying to screw my way through life. I wanted a family, a wife. But I'd learned the hard way that not many girls were willing to stick around waiting for a guy who was gone more than he was around, who missed holidays and birthdays, who came home for dinner some nights at 11 p.m., and other nights not at all. It was hard to agree to moving every couple years, to deployments that stretched on and on, to remote assignments, and *Sorry, honey, this one's a year, and you can't come.*

I got it. It was a shit life. The kind of life that sliced you clean, that took and took, stretching you out 'til there was nothing left but fumes. But then there were moments. That moment when I sat in the cockpit, when I was in the air, up in the clouds, feeling like a god. When the afterburner roared. The times when we were called to do more, when the trips to the desert meant something, when we supported the mission on the ground. The times when we marked a lost brother with a piano burn and a song. I couldn't blame Easy for needing to let off steam, the edge was there in all of us, our faithful companion every time we went up in the air and took our lives in our hands.

We flew because we fucking loved it. So I guessed I already had a wife, and she was an expensive, unforgiving bitch—

Fortysomething million dollars of alloy, fuel, and lube that could fuck you over at any given time and felt so good when you were inside her that she always kept you coming back for more.

JORDAN

As the soberest one in the group, I noticed them first. To be fair, they were pretty hard to miss.

A loud and more than slightly obnoxious bachelorette, we'd run into our share of guys tonight—preppy polos and leather shoes with tassels—some single, some married, all looking like they'd served a stint in suburban prison and were now out in the yard for good behavior. They had that wide-eyed overeager look, as though they couldn't believe their luck—*Look at the shiny lights on the sign. Did you see the ass on that girl?*—and Vegas was their chance to make memories that would keep them company when they were coaching Little League or out buying tampons for their wives.

These two were something else entirely.

They walked toward us, and I stopped dancing to enjoy the show. They didn't look like anyone had let them out for good behavior, or like Vegas was their grown-up amusement park. They looked like this was their world, and they carried themselves like fucking kings.

One was tall and lean, his face—well, fuck, there was no other word for it—he was beautiful. Tan skin, full mouth, blue eyes. Dark blond hair that begged for a woman to run her fingers through. Great hair. Perfect hair.

I admired him for two point five seconds, and then he ceased to exist.

The other one was not beautiful. He didn't have pretty hair, or long lashes, or any shit like that. I wasn't even sure his features really registered all that much before he was just there, standing in front of me, and everything else in the club disappeared.

Dark hair. Dark eyes. Tan skin. Sexy mouth.

He was tall—in my heels we were nearly even, which was saying something considering I was a few inches off of six feet and wearing a wicked pair of Choos. He was broad-shouldered and definitely built. He wasn't dressed up—I doubted this guy even owned a polo—but he rocked his jeans and T-shirt. An expensive-looking, enormous watch that appeared capable of coordinating missions to the moon flashed on his wrist.

His gaze ran over me, his mouth curving as his survey ended at the top of my head. I reached up to see if my hair was out of place and got a handful of something else instead.

My cheeks flamed. The penis headband. *Shit.*

I dropped my hand as though I'd been scalded.

Act cool. Pretend you didn't just grip the base of one of the giant pink phalluses currently bobbing on top of your head.

His lips curved even more as he gave me the full punch of his amusement—gorgeous white teeth and a laugh I wanted to cloak myself in.

He kept coming until his body was a breath away from mine. He was big enough that he blocked out the club around us, the scent of his cologne sending a little shock between my legs. I didn't know what it was about that masculine scent, but some primal part of me that probably harkened back to days when men roamed around bare-chested carrying animal pelts on their shoulders liked it a hell of a lot. His head bent, his dark hair nearly brushing against my blond strands. I got a glimpse of his tanned neck, barely resisting the urge to bury my face there and inhale more of his delicious scent.

I wasn't much of a romantic—not with my track record, at least. I didn't believe in love at first sight, but *lust at first sight?* That was a thing definitely happening all over my body tonight.

"Please tell me you aren't the bride," he whispered in my ear, his lips teasing the sensitive skin there.

I shivered, basking in that voice. It was gravelly, and growly, and I was pretty sure I was drenched.

"I'm not the bride."

Our gazes met, his eyes darkening as soon as the words left my lips in a move that had me sucking in a deep breath, my lungs desperate for air. I didn't know if it was the loud music, or the late night, or the tequila coursing its way through my body, or the stilt-like heels, or the fact that my ovaries exploded as he engaged all of my senses, but either way I was feeling more than a little light-headed and fighting the temptation to reach out and grab on to one of his impressive biceps to hold steady.

He smiled and I might have had a mini-orgasm.

"Thank fuck."

Thank fuck, indeed.

He reached out, tucking a strand of hair that had escaped behind my ear. His hand grazed my cheek as he released me and I swayed toward him.

I wanted to lick him, and bite him, and do all kinds of naughty things to that gorgeous body. Multiple times.

"What's your name?" he asked, interrupting my fantasies.

"Jordan." I held out my hand to shake and then froze, my hand halfway there. *Smooth. You're in a nightclub, not a freaking business meeting.* To say it had been a while since I'd dated was a massive understatement. Plus, I'd have been lying if I didn't admit I had blindingly horrible moments of awkward even on my good days. I pretty much lived in extremes. I either totally rocked it or epically failed, with very little in between.

His mouth quirked up as he held out his hand. "I'm Noah."

Well, now I knew the name I'd be calling out in my dreams.

Our palms connected, his hand warm against mine. I waited for him to let go, already mourning the loss of his touch. But he didn't. He just stood there, holding my hand in the middle of the club, staring at me like I was not alone in these feelings.

"It's nice to meet you," I squeaked. *Really nice to meet you.*

The song changed and the club grew frenzied around us, and then he was pulling me toward him and I was dancing, Noah behind me, his big hands on my hips, fingers laced with mine, his body moving against me.

Yes, please.

For such a tall guy, he had good rhythm. *Really good rhythm.* I loved dancing, but I was more of a dance-alone or with-friends kind of girl. Most guys were pretty terrible dancers, and I hated having to try to match my movements to theirs, unable to let the beat of the song take over. Noah wasn't like that at all. He molded his body to mine, letting me set the pace.

And by the way he rolled his hips against my ass, he definitely had some moves.

Holy hell.

His hand drifted up my side, gathering my hair, fisting the ends. Arousal pulsed between my legs, the beat steady, strong, a slow ache. He pulled me back toward him, his hard cock pressing against my ass. A tremor ripped through my body as his fingers grazed my nape, tracing the skin there, my nipples tightening beneath the thin fabric of my dress.

My body felt overheated, the music and alcohol flooding my senses. Around us, people danced, bodies rubbing against each other, mouths tangling, hands roaming. It was that point in the evening when inhibitions lowered, and it was Vegas—it was a night for letting go.

Head bent, his arms wrapped around my torso, the curve of my breasts brushing against his muscular forearm. Another tremor throbbed between my legs. His lips grazed my neck, brushing over the sensitive curve where it met my shoulder. I bit back a moan.

More.

I leaned into him, reaching out, our fingers threading together, our hands joined. His body behind me called to mind other images—of me naked, on my hands and knees, while he drove into me.

He was easily the hottest guy I'd ever seen, and tonight was quickly ranking up there with one of the more memorable evenings of my dating life.

His hold on me tightened and another mini-spasm wracked my body.

I turned in Noah's arms, my breasts grazing his chest. His hands moved lower, grabbing my ass, hauling me toward him, his gaze on my mouth.

I'd never been happier of my single status than I was now.

NOAH

Dibs had flown out the window. I didn't know which girl Easy wanted, didn't care. This one was mine.

I feasted on her mouth. She tasted like tequila and mint,

her lips soft and plump. Her tongue wreaked havoc on my sanity.

I'd kissed my fair share of girls; drunken kisses in dark club corners weren't anything new. But this—this was mind-blowing.

The second I touched her, she lit up. Her hands pulled on my neck, her fingers threading through my hair, tugging on the ends, yanking me toward her as though she couldn't get close enough. My hands cupped her ass, squeezing her through the thin fabric, loving how she squirmed against me, rubbing herself over my jeans and my hard cock.

She was sex in heels, the kind of body that was all curves, made for a centerfold. The beauty mark just above her upper lip took hot to an all-new level.

I released her mouth, kissing my way down her neck, my teeth scraping her flesh, my dick jerking with the moan that escaped her lips. I nipped her, running my tongue over her skin, the taste of her swirling in my mouth. Jordan gripped the back of my head harder, her body begging for more.

No question about it, not only was she sexy as hell, but she liked to play. I'd just hit the motherfucking jackpot.

I shifted so I was behind her again, my hands on either side of her hips, our bodies swaying in time to the music. The girl was gorgeous—long blond hair, big tits, curvy ass, long, shapely legs shown off by the sexiest pink dress. Absolutely gorgeous. And the second our gazes had locked across the club, her brown eyes had looked at me like I was her favorite meal and she wanted me for breakfast, lunch, and dinner.

Done.

My hands moved higher, pulling her tighter against me. Her neck arched, her head tipping into mine, and one of the pink penises hit me in the face again.

I grinned. Fuck, she was cute.

"Babe, gotta remove the headband. Don't need pink dicks in my face."

Jordan turned to face me, locking her arms around my neck. Her cheeks turned a soft shade of pink and she nodded.

I'd always had a weakness for blondes, and this girl had incredible hair. It fell down the center of her back in a mass of loose waves and curls. I set the headband on the table, my gaze on hers the entire time.

At some point we'd stopped dancing, and now we stood in the club with our bodies plastered together, her arms around my neck.

I stroked her hip, pulling her even closer. We danced for a long time, moving from song to song, our bodies matching each other's rhythm like we'd been dancing together for years. I'd been exhausted, and with one kiss she breathed new life into me.

I leaned down, my lips inches away from her ear, struggling to be heard over the loud music.

"Do you want to get out of here?" I asked, her answer suddenly feeling like everything.

I hadn't come out looking to get laid, had honestly been about to call it a night, but the second I saw her, my plans for the evening became whatever put me in her orbit. I didn't know where this was headed, but right now I was happy to follow her anywhere.

She nodded, and a knot tightened in my chest as she linked hands with me and I led her off the dance floor.

*T*WO

JORDAN

We ended up at the Bourbon Room, a bar in the Venetian that played classic rock hits. It was just after two in the morning when we got there, the crowd caught up in the music, drunkenly belting out songs. It was pretty awesome. Noah's friend, who had bizarrely introduced himself as Easy, entertained the rest of the group as the six of us headed over to the bar.

With two hot guys and three single girls, I wasn't sure how things would go down. Easy had been talking to both Stacey and Amber, so I couldn't get a handle on who he was interested in, but I was definitely sending the message that Noah was off-limits.

We held hands the whole time, our bodies close together, that same chemistry I'd experienced at the club pinging through my body like an electric shock. We grabbed a big table, Noah pulling me back while everyone else sat down, leaving us on the end, partially blocked off from the rest of the group. He released my hand, putting his arm around me, lacing our hands together with his free hand until they rested on his thigh.

His really, really muscular thigh.

Yep, totally wanted to jump him.

I couldn't remember the last time I'd ever been this attracted to a guy right off the bat. I didn't really have a physical type; I'd dated a lot—tall guys, guys I couldn't wear heels around, blonds, dark-haired guys, even a few red-haired guys. But this one? There was a physical energy about him. A raw maleness I'd never seen on anyone before.

He moved with confidence, taking charge of the group, which was almost as sexy as his body. Hell, maybe more. After fifteen years of dating, I was sick of guys who didn't know how to lead, who didn't have their shit together, who made me feel like the man half the time. I was sick of thirty-year-old boys who didn't know how to act like adults, who seemed to be perpetually overcompensating for a small penis. I didn't want a caveman, but I wanted a man who knew who he was, and wasn't afraid to be it.

And so far this guy had hit every single check mark.

Noah leaned down and I got another whiff of his cologne. *Gah.* I had to fight the urge to press my lips to his clean-shaven cheek.

"What do you want?" he asked.

I didn't even bother fighting the smile as I cocked my head to the side, my gaze playful, silence descending between us.

A dimple flashed back at me. The still slightly tipsy part of me wanted to poke him there. It softened his features, giving him a hint of boyishness which was welcome on a face that appeared to have been chiseled in granite.

"I meant to drink." He ducked his head, grazing mine. "But I definitely would like to hear what's going through your mind right now."

I grinned. I could be ballsy with the best of them, but even I didn't have the guts to tell him all the things going through my head right now.

"Bourbon seems apropos."

A waitress came over, Noah ordering for me. While the rest of the group got their drinks, he played with my hand, his fingers exploring my flesh, tracing the lines of my palm, circling my wrist.

I tried to keep my expression neutral, to hide the fact that each touch set off a fire in my body, but it was pretty much useless. He knew exactly what he was doing and how much I liked it.

I hadn't decided if I was going to sleep with him, but the urge to flirt came as naturally as breathing. I leaned forward, the move drawing all of his attention to my breasts. Having double Ds and not using them was pretty much like owning a Ferrari and going the speed limit. Where was the fun in that?

His gaze dipped for a glorious moment, and then he stared into my eyes, a wolfish gleam shining back at me.

It felt as though we were playing sexual chess, each of us making a move that took us closer to getting naked.

His move.

Noah reached out, his fingers connecting with my skin. *Gah.* His flesh was warm against mine, his touch light, teasing, tracing my collarbone, a line of goose bumps forming in his wake.

I froze, held in place by the pads of his fingers, by the whispered promise his touch gave me. I sucked in air, trying not to come undone as I craved more, unraveled by how close his hand was to my breasts and how badly I wanted it to dip lower. My nipples pebbled and another throb pounded between my legs.

I figured thirty was too old to start making out with someone in the middle of a bar at a table with four other people, even if it was late at night, and it was Vegas, but given the temptation in front of me, I wasn't sure the odds of keeping my clothes on trended in my favor.

Noah quirked a brow at me, his gaze knowing, his hands lingering on my bare skin before he pulled back and released me.

I stifled a frustrated growl. Barely.

I struggled to think of nonsexual things like polar bears, and avocados, and whatever random shit flew through my head.

Bananas. Balls. Fuck.

"So where are you from?" I asked, crossing my legs, the movement drawing his attention down again and giving me a chance to roll my tongue back into my mouth.

"Originally, California. I live in Oklahoma now." His hand moved lower, stroking my arm.

My scalp tingled, more goose bumps rising up, my skin flashing hot and cold. Somewhere between the dancing and leaving the club, my buzz had slowly begun to wear off, sharpening my senses, my body humming with awareness.

So much for not panting after him like a horny teenager.

"How about you?" he asked.

Use your words.

"Florida. A small beach town a few hours north of Miami."

He gave me another lazy smile. "How long are you in Vegas for?"

It definitely wasn't a casual question. We both knew

where this was heading. Would this be one night? Two? Were we going to indulge this fire crackling between us?

"Until Monday. We're here for my sister's bachelorette." I pointed out Meg, who was on her phone, probably drunk texting her fiancé.

"And you?"

"Another week," he answered. "We're here for work."

The waitress set our drinks in front of us and I took a long pull of the bourbon. Yum.

"What do you do?" I asked, shifting in my seat. Our legs pressed against each other, my body as close to his as I could manage without being in his lap.

Fuck me. I hadn't been wrong about the muscles.

I considered shopping a solid workout routine and counted chocolate as a major food group. But right now I thanked the fitness gods for the biceps skimming my breasts, the broad shoulders next to me, the outline of his pecs through his T-shirt. His body was a gift I wanted to unwrap.

And then the next thing I knew, Noah's arms looped around me, hauling me onto his lap as though I barely weighed anything at all, my back cradled to his front, my ass in his lap, arms of steel encircling me.

Words failed me.

He reached out, adjusting me slightly, again like I weighed nothing at all—which was a seriously impressive trick considering I was far from dainty—tipping my face up to meet his.

I wasn't ashamed to admit that I pretty much curled into him like a cat waiting to be stroked.

"We're fighter pilots."

I blinked, momentarily blinded by that smile.

After years of meeting guys in bars, hearing lots of *I'm a doctor* or *I'm a lawyer*, that was one I hadn't heard before.

I wasn't one of those girls who was typically turned on by a guy in uniform. I mean sure, I'd crushed on Tom Cruise when I'd first seen *Top Gun,* but it wasn't a *thing* for me. I was more pirates than pilots. I dated nice guys, but I definitely had a bad boy fetish.

I wasn't sure where he fit in.

The military career explained a lot, though. The fine state of his body, for one. The way he carried himself, the rugged air about him. The confidence. Okay, fine, maybe it was a little sexy.

And by the cocky glint in his eyes as he announced his profession, he knew it. And just like that, the attraction I'd felt for him went electric.

Cocky guys were sort of my crack. If you lined up all my exes in a row, the common thread would be that most possessed an overabundance of swagger. Confidence, even to the point of being arrogance, was a major turn-on for me. Not because I thought arrogance was sexy on its own, but because those were the guys you could play with.

I liked a challenge, and there was nothing better than taking a guy who thought he was hot shit down a peg or two. And then reaping the rewards later.

And just like that, I made the decision of whether or not I was going to sleep with him tonight.

Game on, fighter boy.

NOAH

I played the fighter pilot card earlier than I normally did. Some guys like Easy led with it, because it typically led to an easy lay. I usually waited a bit before going in hot, but this girl was a fucking fantasy, so I went with it. I wasn't sure where this going, but I knew where I wanted it to go. Needed it to go.

Her naked in bed. Against the wall. Bent over the couch. In the shower.

Jordan blinked and then a smile spread across her face. It wasn't the smile I expected, the one I usually got from women. The one that led to innuendo and confessions of uniform fantasies. No, her smile had an edge to it, like a cat that'd found a mouse to play with.

She leaned forward again, and my mouth went dry at the sight of her perfect tits thrust forward in her little pink dress.

Why was I starting to feel like the mouse?

"Like *Top Gun*?"

"That's Navy. We're Air Force. We fly F-16s."

Everyone asked about *Top Gun*, so I'd expected that one. What I hadn't expected was the way she asked the question. Her voice as interested as if I'd said, *I fill cavities all day.*

Where were the wide eyes? The shirtless volleyball fantasy? Sure, the reality didn't exactly match the glossy, Hollywood image, but it worked. Usually.

She jerked her head toward the end of the table. "Is that why he introduced himself as Easy?"

Fucking Easy. I was definitely not the only one who'd noticed Jordan. Easy's eyes had gleamed when I'd introduced them, but it had only taken one look for me to lock that shit down. There had been other times when we'd gone after the same girl; sometimes I didn't care and let him swoop in.

This was not one of those times.

"Yeah, that's his call sign."

Call signs, also, usually a panty dropper.

"What's his real name?"

"Alex."

"Why does everyone call him . . ." Her voice trailed off as she watched Easy wrap his arms around a girl on each side. She smirked. "Right."

I laughed. "It's also a flying thing. He's really laid-back in the cockpit. But yeah, his—uh—way with the ladies might have come into play."

"What's your call sign?"

Now we were talking.

"Burn."

I waited for her to say it was hot, or *something*, but all I got was another question.

"So why didn't you tell me your call sign like he did?"

"Because I don't need to lead with my call sign to get laid." I let the promise in my words linger between us.

Her eyes narrowed playfully, her voice silk. "Is that so?"

I leaned in closer, my gaze locking with hers. "My skills speak for themselves."

I expected her to respond with innuendo of her own, but instead she laughed, her eyes twinkling. She met my move and raised the stakes, her mouth brushing my ear.

Finally.

"Aren't you guys supposed to have super-hot-shit call signs?"

I nearly choked on my drink, convinced I'd misheard.

"Excuse me?"

Was she joking? Burn was a hot-shit call sign.

"Like Iceman and Maverick. Something like that."

Was this girl for real? I set my drink down, taking a moment to study her.

I was thirty-three, had been flying F-16s since I was twenty-four. I'd picked up dozens of girls in bars. I didn't go home with all of them; I didn't have a face like Easy's, I struck out a fair share, but the fighter pilot card was magic.

Apparently, she was immune.

And just like that, I realized that what had looked like a casual hook-up just might not be so easy.

"Call signs aren't supposed to be cool," I explained, trying to ignore the feeling that I'd just been shot down. "Most of the time they're given to you because of something you did to look like an idiot. There's almost always an embarrassing story behind them."

"So how'd you get your call sign?"

"That's a story for another day."

"Don't want to mess up your game?" she teased.

I shook my head, feeling like she'd batted me around. "I think I'm going to need all the tricks up my sleeve with you."

Jordan's smile widened and she leaned forward again, her mouth inches from mine, the temptation nearly unbearable. One taste or two was definitely not enough with this girl.

"I'm guessing this fighter pilot thing gets you laid pretty often."

God, I hoped it did the trick now. "It has its moments."

Her brow rose, her voice taking on a distinctive purr. "And you think this is going to be one of those moments?"

I held her gaze, going for honesty when bravado failed me. "You tell me."

JORDAN

The impulse to tell him that he was *definitely* getting lucky was on the tip of my tongue. We were both adults, and it didn't need to be said that obviously we wanted each other. I could climb off his lap, hold out my hand to him, and go upstairs for what I predicted would be a pretty fucking amazing orgasm.

He'd leave me with a hot vacation memory and a story about the time I banged the fighter pilot in Vegas. And likely, I'd be another girl he hooked up with once, maybe even a repeat performance if his body lived up to the packaging.

It wouldn't be a bad ending to the night. I'd had some pretty decent one-night stands, and the odds that this one would jump to the top of the list were pretty high given how turned on I was. I wasn't looking for a relationship with a guy who lived across the country, and I definitely wasn't looking for a relationship with a guy who probably took thrill seeking to extremes.

But ever since I'd seen that flash of cocky, ever since the attraction between us had ratcheted up a notch, the urge to make him work for it had become undeniable.

Because maybe, in some slightly confused part of me, I was curious to see where this was going. I hadn't been looking for anything but fun, definitely didn't need complicated, but . . .

I leaned back slightly, my gaze searching his, my body and mind warring with each other until the decision was made.

I'd had a lot of guys in my fifteen-plus years of dating. There were guys who were fun, the kind of guys who were great for a casual hook-up, a quick and easy orgasm. Then there were the guys who had your mother proclaiming things like, *He's a doctor*, and *He loves kids*, and *He just bought a lovely three-bedroom house*, to all of her friends. The ones you took to your high school reunion. The guys that some-one, somewhere, arbitrarily decided were a "catch."

And then there was the urban legend, Chupacabra-like myth of a man who would fuck you up against a wall while he pulled your hair and then spoon you to sleep after. The guy who would bring you breakfast in bed with an orgasm on the side. The kind of guy who was so masculine that he could get you pregnant just by looking at you.

I'd spent years searching for that guy, only to come up with dud after dud. But this guy? This guy just might be the Bigfoot of the dating world, and everyone knew you did not fuck around with that kind of possibility.

If he was an urban legend, then I needed to make myself one, too—

The Girl Who Does Not Fall for Hot Sexy Fighter Pilots Who Smell Great and Have Nice Voices . . . on the first night, at least. No need to get crazy.

I leaned forward, my body giving a little happy cheer. I kissed him, my fingers threading through his hair, my lips devouring his. And then I pulled back.

His lips were swollen from my kisses, his eyes dark.

"It was nice to meet you, Noah."

He gave me a rueful grin. "Crash and burn, huh?"

I laughed at the *Top Gun* joke. He was definitely more than a pretty face and lickable biceps.

"We'll see how you do tomorrow."

His eyes glinted and I had a sneak peek of how lethal he must be.

"You're not going to make this easy on me, are you?"

I grinned, my mouth brushing against his again.

"Now where's the fun in that?"

I wiggled out of his lap, my body getting a pretty good idea of how badly he wanted me.

I stood and tossed a look over my shoulder, and then I was walking out of the bar, knowing full well that his eyes were on me the entire time.

$\mathcal{T}$HREE

JORDAN

"Are you nuts?"

The words would have been delivered with a shriek if Meg had been slightly less hungover. Instead, they came out with a croak and a wince, as though even that was too much for her.

I grinned, handing over the bottle of pain relievers. "Not the last time I checked."

"He was hot. Really, really hot." She fumbled with the cap until finally I took pity on her and opened it myself.

"He was."

She tossed me a grateful look and swallowed two pills with the big bottle of water next to our lounge chairs.

"So that's it?"

"No, the ball's in his court now. He knows I'm interested."

"But if you were interested, why didn't you go back to his room? You should have seen him after you left. He looked like a kid who'd just had his ice cream cone taken away from him."

I couldn't help smiling at that visual. Some guys would have gone out in search of another girl to take back to their room. The fact that he hadn't bumped him up majorly in my estimation.

I didn't bother explaining my Chupacabra theory. Meg would likely think I was crazier than she already did. She'd started dating her fiancé, Mike, her freshman year of college and they'd been together ever since. She hadn't braved the dating gauntlet and she didn't understand that it was a freaking war zone out there; a girl needed every advantage she could get.

"If he's interested, he'll come find me today. If he's not, it's his loss."

That was the mantra I kept repeating to myself as doubt started to creep in. That said, I'd totally come prepared.

We were lounging at one of the pools at Palazzo, the resort joined with our hotel, the Venetian. It was late February and the weather was unseasonably warm, but even though the pool was allegedly heated, it was a little too cold for a Florida girl to get in the water. But that didn't mean I hadn't rocked my bathing suit "A" game.

I was a beach girl through and through, and owning my own clothing boutique meant I got an awesome discount and my clothing choices were a walking advertisement for the business. Suffice it to say, I had more bikinis than there were days in the month.

Every girl had that one outfit that doubled as her suit of armor—that go-to look that gave her the confidence she needed to kick ass and take names. Thankfully, I'd had the foresight to bring mine to Vegas.

The bikini was white, which was kind of a risky choice, but luckily I spent most of my time at the beach and South Florida had freaking gorgeous weather year-round, so it contrasted with my tanned skin. It was the skimpiest suit I owned, covering the important bits, leaving the rest exposed in between strappy pieces of fabric. I wore my hair down, and as stupid as I'd felt blowing it out and curling it to go lie by the pool, Noah had seemed to have a thing for it last night, and I was on a mission here. No corners would be cut.

I wore a sheer cover-up that exposed more than it concealed, but gave me the right to wear the wedges on my feet that gave my legs the extra advantage I needed.

My makeup consisted of a nude lipstick and some bronzer, a bit of shadow at my eyes, and a swipe of mascara which I never left the house without. I perched a pair of Tom Fords on my face to shield my gaze from the bright Vegas sun.

"Did you even tell him where we were staying?" Meg asked between gulps of water.

The one advantage to having a good forty pounds on my sister was that I wasn't feeling any effects from last night's binge.

"Nope."

"So how is he supposed to find you?"

"Are you talking about the guy last night?" Stacey asked, plopping down next to Meg's lounge chair.

I hadn't seen her and Amber this morning, but Meg and I had left a note in our suite telling them to meet us at the pool.

I nodded.

"He asked us where you were staying."

Meg grinned. "So that's where you and Amber were last night."

Tell me they both hooked up with Easy.

She grinned. "Hey, his friend was hot."

My throat went a little dry. "Please tell me this was a party of three."

Stacey's smile widened. "A lady doesn't kiss and tell. But you'll be happy to know that your guy went to his room alone right after you left. Trust me, he definitely wasn't interested."

Yes.

"So you told him I was staying at the Venetian?"

She nodded. "And I might have added that we planned on coming to the pool today. I didn't tell him which pool, but I figured those were enough breadcrumbs for him to follow. And for the record, if he's anything like his friend, trust me when I say, *you are very welcome.*"

I laughed. I didn't know Amber or Stacey that well, the age difference between us meant I hadn't spent a lot of time with Meg's friends, but they were a lot of fun. A little louder than my sister, but definitely the kind of girls you wanted on a trip like this.

"Thanks. So where's Amber?"

"She's feeling the effects of last night a little more than I was. She said she'd be down in a bit. I think she was going to take a nap."

Meg groaned, using a copy of *Vogue* to shield the sun from her face. "I should probably go join her."

I grinned. "I take it that means you aren't up for a mimosa?"

"I'm never drinking again."

"More for me, then. Do you want one, Stacey?" She nodded. I grabbed my wallet from my beach bag. "I'm going to head to the bar."

There were waitresses patrolling the pool area taking

drink orders, but it was pretty busy, and I figured it would take a while before someone got around to me.

I walked over to the bar, returning a few smiles that were thrown my way by guys I passed, ignoring the catcalls and the invitations to come join them. I had a feeling a lot of people were still drunk from the night before.

I found an empty spot at the bar, waiting while the bartenders filled orders. After they got to me I paid for the mimosas, heading back to the section of lounge chairs we'd commandeered, and stopped dead in my tracks.

Three guys stood talking to Meg and Stacey. I recognized Easy; wearing navy blue swim trunks, he looked even more beautiful than he had last night. He stood next to a hot guy with reddish hair—channeling Prince Harry—who I hadn't met before. And then I saw Noah.

My mouth went dry, and any hope of having a coherent thought fled.

Tanned skin. Abs. Fitness magazine abs. Pecs like you read about. Broad shoulders. Aviators. Black swim trunks. Holy fuckballs.

My Chupacabra dating theory went out the window. Everything went out the window. Hopefully, my clothes would follow.

I was going to make this happen or die trying.

NOAH

I turned and my heart stopped.

I'd dreamed of her last night. The kind of dream that ended with me waking up hard, my hand on my cock. I'd thought it would take the edge off, that when I saw her today, the need that burned inside me would have lessened. It wouldn't have been the first time I'd been attracted to a girl at night only to wake up the next day and find alcohol-tinged arousal lessened by sobriety.

This was not one of those times.

I blinked, half convinced this was a mirage.

She wore white. Some see-through white thing that cloaked her torso and fell just past her hips, baring a lot of leg. Beneath it she wore a white bikini that exposed way more than it covered. And some part of me that had been honed since puberty was pretty sure I could make out the outline of her nipples through the thin top.

I went hard as a rock.

The curves I'd run my hands over last night seemed lusher today, her tits way bigger than a handful, her ass mouthwatering.

Her blond hair tumbled past her shoulders in a gorgeous wave, her mouth full, her lips begging to be kissed. She stopped in front of me, tilting her sunglasses up, her brown eyes dancing, a huge smile breaking out on her face; my heart clenched as though someone had just stabbed me in the chest.

It wasn't exactly a secret that men were visual creatures, and she'd just given me the best image I'd ever seen.

"Hi."

I smiled so hard, it hurt my face. "Hi."

I leaned forward, pressing a kiss to her cheek, holding her to me, my hand against the small of her back, the scent of peppermint and vanilla surrounding me.

I pulled back and pushed my sunglasses up on my head, not wanting anything between me and the girl standing before me.

Jordan handed one of the mimosas off to her friend, but she didn't move from her spot in front of me.

"You found me."

I grinned. "It took a few tries, but eventually, yeah, I did."

Easy walked over, interrupting our conversation. He gave Jordan a head jerk and a smile. "Did you know that the Venetian and Palazzo have several pools?"

A smile tugged at her lips, her words for Easy, but her gaze never leaving mine. "I did."

"He dragged us to each one looking for you."

I didn't even care that he was busting my balls in front of her. I was too dazed to give a shit.

"Is that so?" Laughter filled her voice.

"He was a man on a mission."

I'd definitely be hearing about this one for a while, but it was totally worth it.

Thor came over to where we stood, his gaze locked on Jordan. Hell, given the looks she'd gotten as she'd walked back from the bar, I was pretty sure half of the pool had noticed her.

"Are you going to introduce me to your friend?" he asked, his smile a little too friendly.

I couldn't help it. I put my arm around Jordan, feeling like she gave me the greatest gift ever when her body fit to the curve of mine and her head tipped up to smile at me.

She turned her attention to Thor, wrapping her arms around my waist, leaning her head into my chest.

Fuck me.

"I'm Jordan."

He grinned, the message definitely received. "It's nice to meet you, Jordan. I'm Thor. Now I see why Burn was so intent on finding the right pool. It was definitely worth the trek."

She laughed.

"It's nice to meet you, too. You boys should sit and rest your weary feet after the great pool expedition," she teased.

I tightened my hold on her, my voice dropping for her ears only. "We actually just reserved a cabana over there. Want to come join us?"

Please come join us.

I figured Easy owed me after he'd kept me up last night listening to the sounds of him going at it with the two brides-maids. I was definitely cashing in my marker. I wanted some alone time with her and that bikini she was wearing.

Her smile was another punch to my chest. "I would love to. Let me grab my bag."

We all watched as she bent over and grabbed a giant straw bag, her mimosa in hand. I took the opportunity while she talked to her sister to glare at Easy and Thor. Easy shot me an amused look, as though this girl driving me crazy was solely for his entertainment.

"Fuck off," I growled under my breath.

His smile deepened.

"I think I'm going to head back to our cabana. Can't get too much sun."

I glared at him. "Like hell. You owe me. Hang out here with Thor."

"You sure? You seem pretty nervous. If you need moral support . . ."

"Fuck off," I repeated.

He shrugged, a smirk on his face, shoving his hands in the pockets of his swim trunks. "Fine. Have it your way. I'm just saying. You couldn't close last night; I thought you might need a little extra help."

I stifled a groan. We were bros, had known each other for over a decade, and Easy had been needling me for years.

He was the best friend I'd ever had and he was also a giant pain in my ass.

"I got it, thanks."

Jordan walked back over to where we stood, a smile on her face, holding her free hand out to me. "Ready?"

I nodded, wrapping my fingers around hers, leading her over to the cabana, ignoring the way Thor and Easy grinned at us like idiots.

They could laugh all they wanted; I had everything I needed in the palm of my hand.

JORDAN

I followed Noah to a cabana not far from the lounge chairs, my heart pounding. I was nervous, and excited, and turned on beyond belief, ridiculously relieved that my gamble had paid off. He was definitely still interested.

The cabana was bigger than I'd expected, fully stocked with a flat-screen TV, two loungers, a couch, a couple of chairs, and a platter of food and bottles of alcohol. House music played through the speakers, ivory-colored drapes left open to highlight the view of the pool. I set my bag on the chair, putting my mimosa down on one of the end tables.

More nerves filled me, my body frozen in the middle of the room. I hadn't thought past this moment. I was alone with a ridiculously fine guy I barely knew and some combination of excited nausea rolled through me.

Don't throw up.

I heard him move behind me, and then his hand was at my nape as my eyes closed and I leaned into his touch, my head rolling back to rest on his shoulder, his hips pressing into me.

Gah.

His chest was warm against my back, his body strong. Noah gathered me in his embrace, turning me around until I faced him.

Tension slammed into me, anticipation running through my veins. I tilted my head up the extra inches I needed to put my mouth on his.

His lips parted the second we touched, his hand coming up to cradle my head, his fingers stroking my hair, caressing my scalp. I went catlike again, barely resisting the urge to purr at his touch.

Magic hands.

His mouth slanted over mine, his tongue sliding between us, sending tendrils of fire licking through my body. His other hand slipped down to the small of my back, holding me tight, his erection grinding against me. I might have whimpered the second I felt him hard and heavy between my legs, my hips moving instinctively, wanting him inside me, my clit throbbing.

I figured I'd played hard to get for long enough. Either way, I didn't have it in me for more.

I gripped his biceps, holding on for dear life, my fingernails digging into his skin so hard I'd probably leave a mark. I was too far gone to care.

He pulled away first, his mouth swollen, a sexy grin tugging at the corners of his lips.

Fuck me, I might have just found Bigfoot.

I sat down on the edge of one of the loungers, my legs shaky, that light-headed feeling returning again. This guy should have come with a warning label.

Caution: Kisses will make you forget your name. Proceed at your own risk.

Noah's hands settled on his hips, watch gleaming against his tan skin, the motion tugging the trunks down a bit, exposing dips on either side of his waist.

I died. Holy hell, he had penis cleavage.

Penis cleavage, like the Chupacabra and Bigfoot, was another urban legend as far as I was concerned. I'd heard about it, seen it in magazines, in the occasional movie with an actor that you knew had gone on an apple diet to get a body like that. But I'd never seen it on a flesh-and-blood man.

That was one item checked off the bucket list.

"Do you want a drink?"

I shook my head, the mimosa already discarded, needing to keep my wits about me in the face of all that male magnificence.

"Food?"

I shook my head again. You didn't eat in a bikini like this.

"Drapes open or closed?"

Gah.

"Closed."

Definitely, closed.

FOUR

NOAH

My hands shook as I shut the drapes behind me, blocking out the pool and everything around us. I figured the closed drapes were about as effective as leaving a tie or sock on a doorknob. Thor and Easy would definitely get the message and stay away.

I turned around and my jaw dropped.

Jordan leaned back in one of the lounge chairs, her cover-up on the floor next to her, wearing only the white bikini, which I was pretty sure would prove fodder for quite a few future fantasies.

This girl was unbelievable.

I stalked toward her, sitting down on the edge of the lounger. Jordan slid back, making room for me next to her. Neither one of us spoke. The beat of house music broke the silence between us, tension filling the air.

I lay back on the lounger, rolling over to my side so I could look at Jordan, her body mirroring mine. I propped my head up with my hand, staring down into her face, admiring her brown eyes and pouty mouth. At some point she'd taken her sunglasses off her head, and I couldn't resist the urge to play with her hair, my fingers lingering on the strands just inches away from the slope of her breast.

Her legs brushed against mine, our limbs tangling together, the curve of our bodies two interlaced half-circles.

I swallowed. I couldn't remember the last time, if ever, that I'd been this attracted to a girl. Puberty? Smooth had gone out the window and now I just prayed I didn't make a complete and total ass of myself. Even as my control hung by a thread.

"I dreamed about you last night."

I hadn't intended on telling her, but the words escaped of their own volition.

A pink flush settled over her cheeks.

"Really?"

I nodded.

"I couldn't stop thinking about you. I annoyed the shit out of Easy and Thor this morning looking for you."

Jordan curled into my touch, moving closer, her breasts inches away from my chest.

I threw my leg over hers, my other hand resting on her hip, hovering near the string of her bikini bottoms. Her lips parted, desire filling her brown eyes.

"I wanted to see you, too," she admitted.

I traced her silky skin, my fingers toying with the bathing suit ties at her hips. Each stroke sent a shiver through her body and had her arching toward me. The urge to dip my fingers below the fabric and stroke her made my chest tight, my cock hard.

I struggled to calm the pounding in my ears and heart, to make my touch lazy rather than hungry, drawing out her pleasure.

She held my gaze while I traced the skin at her hip, occasionally fingering the ties there. Her body relaxed even more, her lashes fluttering, her eyes sleepy. Her lips curved, her voice throaty.

"So let's talk about this fighter pilot thing."

I grinned. "I thought you weren't too impressed by that."

She gave me a little shrug and a teasing smile. "Can't let you get a big head."

I laughed. "I wouldn't worry about that."

Jordan shifted, closing the distance between us, her nipples grazing my chest.

I stifled a groan as I felt how tight they were, her arousal egging my body on.

I hooked her leg over my hip, my hand sliding down to her ass, settling her body next to mine.

She bit her lower lip and I lost another bit of sanity.

"So do you guys wear the white outfits?" she asked, a speculative gleam in her eyes.

Fucking *Top Gun*.

I grinned, my hand back to playing with the ties at her hip, the other twisting her hair around my fingers, each touch ghosting across the tops of her tits.

Cute and sexy.

"That's the Navy."

"Oh." She flashed me an apologetic smile. "Those are kind of hot."

I choked back a laugh. "Not letting you around any sailors. Check."

Her eyes twinkled with amusement. I hadn't been wrong last night. She definitely liked to play.

"How about the one from *A Few Good Men*? You know, the black one with the gold and the cool hat."

"Still the Navy."

"Oh."

I grinned. "*Definitely* not letting you around any sailors."

Jordan made a face. "It's not my fault they have better uniforms. So what do yours look like?"

God, she was adorable. I liked her more for busting my balls.

"I wear a flight suit. Green. Zipper down the front. Flame retardant." She gave a little shrug, the move drawing my attention to her boobs, and I grinned again. "Just out of curiosity, do you know anything about the military that doesn't come from a Tom Cruise movie?"

"Nope. You're the first fighter pilot I've ever met." Jordan cocked her head to the side, exposing the curve of her neck.

"What do you do?" I asked, my fingers itching to trace the line there.

"I own a clothing boutique. My best friend, Sophia, and I are partners. We've only been in business for about three years now, but we have a steady clientele and an awesome location by the beach."

So she was sexy and smart. And definitely a risk-taker.

"That's amazing. Have you always wanted to run your own business?"

"I was a business major in college, but it took me a while to figure out what I wanted to do with it. I wasn't really suited for corporate life; I like being my own boss. It's pretty time consuming, especially in the beginning, but I love it. It's really rewarding to see everything pay off. Plus, I work with my best friend all day, playing with clothes. It's kind of my dream job."

"Sounds like it. That's really impressive."

With each moment I spent with her, she hooked me deeper, and I found myself curious to know more about her.

"So you grew up in Florida?"

She nodded. "My family's still there. It's nice getting to be close to them. When Meg and her fiancé, Mike, have kids, I'm excited to be the cool aunt who has them over for sleepovers and goes to their sporting events. We're all pretty close." She tilted her head to look at me. "Do you get to see your family a lot?"

"A couple times a year if I'm lucky. It's hard with work. They're still in California. At least Oklahoma's not that far away compared to some of the other places I've been stationed."

Jordan reached out, her hand tracing my bicep, and I hardened against her.

"How long have you been a pilot?"

I had to think about that one for a minute, no easy feat with her touching me. Counting pilot training . . . it took me three tries to reach the correct number, my concentration broken each time her fingers dragged across my arm.

"A little over ten years," I finally answered.

"Did you always want to fly?"

I looped my fingers under the ties of her bathing suit bottoms, stroking the soft skin there. She bit down on her lip again, her hips rocking forward.

My words came out strained. "Always. My dad was an Air Force pilot. He flew fighters when I was a kid, retired before I hit high school. He used to tell me stories about his assignments. There wasn't anything else I ever wanted to do with my life. I studied aeronautical engineering at the Air Force Academy and got a pilot slot. Went through pilot training, got F-16s, and that was it."

"Aeronautical engineering?" Her brow rose as her finger traveled from my bicep to my chest, her hot pink nails trailing across my collarbone.

My stomach muscles clenched.

"So you're really smart."

I shrugged, releasing her bathing suit ties, my palm settling against her ass, cupping her there, squeezing, my eyes greedy as I watched her arch against my hand.

"I like science. There was a brief period of time when I played around with being an astronaut, but it's pretty much always been jets for me."

My other hand left her hair, drifting down to her waist, lower still, until I grabbed two perfect handfuls. I could die a happy man now.

It was a moment before she spoke.

"So how does it work exactly?" She grinned. "Clearly, I know nothing about the Air Force. Do you have any control over where you go?"

I marveled at her ability to string together a coherent thought. The hard-on raging between my legs was definitely making it more difficult for me to speak. When I finally did, I had to push the words out. It was a miracle I was functioning at this point.

"Officially? Kind of. Certain bases have specific airframes. Only a few locations have F-16s so I'm usually limited to those assignments. Typically, you can list your preferences, but in reality, it's very 'needs of the Air Force.' You go where they want you to go."

The last words came out in a strangled gasp because my throat closed up as she shifted in my arms, and then I was on my back, staring up at her, her body straddling mine.

"I gotta say, this is hands down, the most interesting conversation I've ever had about my job."

She laughed. "I figured it beats the interview-style first date awkwardness."

"Is this a first date?"

She hesitated for a second, a smile playing on her lips. "Yeah, I think it is."

"Does it count as a date if I didn't buy you dinner?"

"I think it's whatever we want it to be."

My eyes narrowed speculatively. "If you have any strange habits I should know about, please spare me and tell me now, because I'm pretty sure in another minute or so, I'm not going to care if you collect creepy dolls or save your toenail clippings."

She cracked up. "That's pretty not-sexy."

"And yet, I'm still turned on."

Her eyes gleamed. "Yeah, you are."

This girl was killing me.

"Does collecting creepy stuffed animals count?"

She could tell me she collected porcelain clowns and I was pretty sure I wouldn't care. I must have made a face, though, because she burst into laughter again.

"You should see your expression. Totally kidding about the creepy stuffed animals. No weird habits that I know of. Of course, if I did have them, I'd probably think they were normal and not flag them as weird at all."

I grinned. "True. I guess I'll just have to take my chances."

"I guess so," Jordan teased.

She brushed her hair over her shoulder, drawing my attention up to her breasts.

"So where have you lived?" she asked.

Apparently, we were back to informational foreplay. God, that answer took me a while to come up with, too, although not entirely surprising considering all the blood in my head had rushed to my lap.

"The whole list?"

She nodded.

"Okay, I was at the Academy in Colorado Springs for college, then I went to Texas for pilot training, then Phoenix for the B course."

"B course?"

She reached between us, her fingers tracing my abs and a few more brain cells died. Being stroked by her was heaven, and I was pretty sure I could lie here all day long.

"Basic course. It's learning how to fly the F-16. Then South Korea, followed by Germany, then a stint in Vegas for weapons school, then almost three years in South Carolina, and now I'm stationed at Bryer Air Force Base near Oklahoma City."

"So you've lived in eight different places since you joined the Air Force."

Her hands went a little lower on my stomach, skimming over my belly button, and I sucked in a deep breath.

Go lower.

"Not including the times I've deployed? Eight places in sixteen years, if you include my time at the Zoo."

"The Zoo?"

"Air Force Academy."

Her touch stilled, her expression intent. My dick protested, but my brain welcomed the reprieve. There was only so much a man could take.

"How many times have you deployed?"

That took a minute, too. "Three. No, four."

"For how long?

"The first two were four months each, the last two six months each. Fighter deployments aren't as long as some of the other deployments."

"And you like this job?" she asked, the doubt in her voice clear.

I grinned. "I guess it kind of makes me sound insane when you put it like that, but yeah, I do."

She remained still, staring down at me, her hands on my stomach, her gaze locked with mine. Emotions flashed through her eyes, altering the tension between us as if a switch had been flipped. I didn't know what had happened, just that something had changed.

I'd have been lying if I didn't admit that I felt pretty far removed from the civilian population. It was hard to explain what my lifestyle was like. That it was difficult to predict where I'd be living in a couple years, or if I was free to go to a family member's wedding even with a year's notice. Dating could be tough considering not many girls liked playing second fiddle to the Air Force. And no matter how hard I tried, I could only make so many promises. Right now I had a job I couldn't quit and a life that wasn't my own.

My original commitment had been eight years out of the Academy. Eight years of service in exchange for millions of dollars of flight training. Then an additional three for weapons school. Now I was eight years away from retirement, a couple years into the next commitment I'd signed. I wasn't sure if I'd stay active duty past the twenty-year mark or if I'd look at my options in the Guard or Reserve, but either way, I planned on sitting in the cockpit until I was too old to fly.

So yeah, bad shit and all, I fucking loved my job.

JORDAN

I reached between us and linked hands, staring down at him, no longer wondering if he was an urban legend.

I was straddling the dating equivalent of the Loch Ness

monster, Bigfoot, and the Chuapacabra all rolled into one, and holy shit, I could die happy if I spent every day with him between my legs.

I'd never met anyone like him. Ever.

I'd dated guys who acted like a two-year cell phone contract was too much of a commitment. This guy had basically given his adult life to serving his country and he acted like it wasn't a big deal. He wasn't trying to impress me or make himself look good. He just answered my questions with nonchalance, as though normal people moved all the freaking time, and went to war, and risked their lives. As if it was easy to sign away large chunks of your life. It gave a completely new meaning to the word "sacrifice."

"How do you do it?" I asked, our hands still joined, my throat clogged with no small amount of awe. The fighter pilot thing might not have impressed me all that much, but his dedication definitely did.

"Do what?"

"All of it. It just seems like you're giving up a lot. Do you ever regret it? Do you ever wish you could do something else or have a little more freedom?"

He shrugged, his stomach muscles rippling with the movement.

Gah.

"It's a job like anything else. There are days that I get pissed off, days that I'm sick of the life. But I do it because I love it. There's nothing like the feeling I get when I'm in the cockpit. I'd put up with anything for that. I joined the military because I wanted to serve, because I believe in the mission. But honestly, it's not that altruistic. I have one of the coolest jobs in the world, and I love it." His eyes darkened, his voice going all husky again. "Nothing else has ever given me the same high I get when I'm in the jet."

God, he was intense, in the best possible way. It would have been easy to focus on the flashy watch, or the cocky glint in his eyes, or the fact that he definitely looked like he had game and was in the market to score. But beneath that, I saw a guy who carried an enormous responsibility on his shoulders.

"You're not just a nice pair of biceps and a six-pack, are you?" I joked as I reached out, my hand resting on his stomach. My mouth went dry as I imagined kissing my way down those abs, licking, biting . . .

His smile uncurled, my nipples tightening with the wicked glint there. "Are you trying to get me naked?"

God, yes.

"Maybe."

He pulled me down toward him, our faces inches apart. He nipped at my bottom lip and a shudder tore through my body.

"Good," he murmured between our mouths.

He kissed me hard, his hand gripping the back of my head, tugging on my hair. His lips weren't soft, his touch definitely not gentle. It was demanding—a kiss that yanked the lust right out of me until I was desperate for more. Our decision to go to Tao last night was beginning to feel like one of the top five decisions of my life.

Noah released my hair, his hands skimming down to my hips again, his fingers hooking under the ties of my bikini bottoms. When he'd toyed with me there before, it had driven me crazy. Now it wasn't nearly enough.

Luckily, he seemed to agree.

His hands moved from my hipbones, tracing the delicate skin above the top of my bathing suit bottoms. His fingers brushed back and forth, each touch sending a tremor through my body that went straight to my clit.

And then he dipped under the fabric and I lost my mind.

His hand hovered there, inches away from where I wanted him to be, his eyes on me, as though waiting to see if he'd gone too far, waiting for some sign to move farther.

"Touch me." I whispered the words, another tremor ripping through me, my nipples tight and aching, my body growing wetter with each second that passed.

Noah groaned, the sound filling the cabana, his fingers dragging down my skin until his thumb hit my clit and I found my nirvana.

He pressed against me, rubbing there, and my body arched forward, my head rolling back as I rode his hand. I'd been so turned on, so ready for this for so long, and with one touch I went off like a firecracker.

He toyed with me, teasing my clit, trailing down, pulling the arousal from my body, slick and wet, and then he slipped inside, his fingers pumping while his thumb rubbed me over and over again, driving me closer and closer to the edge, to the orgasm that lingered just under my skin.

My body was fire, heat engulfing me. My breasts were heavy, my mouth hungry. His touch anchored me, my entire body consumed by the hand that played with me between my legs. This was an appetizer, and as far as sex went, it was mind-blowing. At this rate, the main course might kill me.

I gripped his arms, the need building inside me, the beginnings of my orgasm strumming through my body like the prelude to a perfect note.

And then I shattered.

It was one of those orgasms that you felt from your head all the way down to your toes, aftershocks lingering after I came down, my skin unbearably sensitive. Not to mention, I was pretty sure he'd just given me a sex headache.

So much better than my vibrator.

Noah rolled me over onto my side, speech still eluding me, wrapping his arms around me, hooking a leg over my hip, drawing me even closer.

His lips brushed against my hair as he tucked me into the curve of his body and something fluttered inside my chest. My hands came down to his waist, ready to return the favor, fighting the urge to drift into the nap that was calling my name, my eyelids fluttering as a languid haze filled me, my limbs liquid.

I opened my mouth to speak, but no words came, and instead of taking things further, he just held me until my eyes closed and I slid into sleep, the steady beat of his heart my own private lullaby.

FIVE

JORDAN

"You could have skipped having dinner with us to hang out with Noah. I would have understood."

I swerved to avoid bumping into a group of drunk girls in front of us as we made our way through the Venetian casino. Meg and I walked together, the other two girls up ahead a bit. We'd just finished dinner and were now headed to meet Noah and his friends for drinks and gambling.

"We planned these Vegas reservations months ago. My little sister is all grown up and getting married. Missing dinner wasn't an option."

Meg frowned at me. "We only have two nights left in Vegas."

I was all too aware of that. It figured I would meet Chupacabra-guy on a freaking vacation.

"And that's why it was important that I didn't miss out on your special dinner. We only have a few more of these nights left before you become an old married lady," I teased.

"I would have understood."

"I know you would have. But I would have felt like shit if I'd missed out on celebrating with you over some guy. We came here to help you burn off one of your last single weekends. Not so that I could get laid. I could do that back home."

Sort of. After today's preview at the pool, I definitely wasn't getting what Noah was giving anywhere else. And even though I wasn't willing to ditch Meg for dinner, I had big plans for later on tonight.

Meg made a face. "Nice try, but it didn't escape my notice that you were going through a bit of a dry spell."

Emphasis on the past tense.

I grinned. "Vegas might have changed my luck."

Her gaze narrowed speculatively. "Just how lucky did you get? Did you have sex with him at the pool today?" she screeched.

I laughed. "You know, I don't think they heard you over at the craps table. Maybe we could tell the entire casino the explicit details of my sex life. Or lack thereof."

"I don't care about the rest of the casino. I need more. Spill. Now."

I shrugged. "We just hung out."

"You were with him for a while."

We'd napped together in the cabana, the combination of a night spent partying, a delicious orgasm, the Vegas sun, and alcohol making me unbelievably sleepy. I'd woken up to a smile and an invitation to hang out with Noah and his friends tonight. Which had led to me spending an hour getting dressed earlier.

"Just hanging out. Even I'm not ballsy enough to have sex with a guy in a thinly veiled cabana."

Just let him finger-fuck me until I came. Whatever.

A gleam entered Meg's eyes. "He's hot."

"He definitely is." My voice turned teasing. "Are you

allowed to say stuff like that now that you're practically a married lady?"

Meg's fiancé, Mike, wasn't the kind of guy who was cool with her gawking over other men.

She laughed. "It'll be our little secret. Besides, married lady or not, I'm pretty sure you'd have to be dead to not notice those guys."

"Valid."

"He seems into you," Meg commented.

One of the benefits to having dated a lot was that you learned to read guys pretty easily. And I had to concur; Noah was definitely *into me.*

"Have you thought about keeping in touch with him after we leave?"

I laughed. "Considering I haven't known him twenty-four hours and he lives across the country? No, not really." Okay, maybe once or twice. "I haven't really thought past tonight." Although to be fair, I'd thought about tonight *a lot.*

"I'm just saying it might be something to consider. You guys could keep in touch."

"What, be like pen pals?"

"Whatever works for you."

I gave her some side-eye. "Are you really so concerned about my single status that now you're throwing me at men?"

She grinned. "It looked like you were doing just fine with that on your own."

She had a point there, but I definitely felt no shame. It was kind of hard to regret going after what you wanted when a guy like Noah was waiting for you on the other side, ready to pounce. And with a body like that, he could pounce on me all night long.

I was entertaining thoughts of keeping in touch with Noah, mixed with weird images of lions mating that the word "pounce" had conjured up in my mind, and then we hit the blackjack table and spotted them and I had to catch my breath for a second as the sight of him pushed everything else out.

Tonight Noah wore a pair of jeans that encased his long legs and my fashion eye instantly recognized as Diesel, and a steel gray dress shirt with the collar unbuttoned and rolled sleeves that exposed a nice amount of tanned skin. Easy and Thor flanked him, another guy who looked a little older than the rest of the group, but no less hot, by their side.

Noah laughed at something Easy said, and I watched, a knot in my chest, as Easy nudged him and Noah's head turned, his gaze on me, and the laugh slid off his face to make way for the gleam in his eyes I recognized from earlier when his hand slid between my legs.

Noah left the group without a word, walking toward me, and then his arms were around me, my body enfolded in his, his lips brushing the top of my head.

He pulled back, a soft smile on his face that complimented the gleam. "Hey."

God. That "Hey" melted its way through me, leaving me warm and gooey on the inside, like chocolate melting cake. Hot didn't quite cover it. Nothing covered it. This feeling inside me, like a slow burn I couldn't extinguish, was simply beyond my control. I was thirty years old, I'd been around the block enough times I basically had my own corner with a lemonade stand, and he made me feel fifteen again. Well, fifteen in the body of a thirty-year-old woman who had hit her sexual peak and wanted to take advantage of the hottie in front of her.

"You look gorgeous," he whispered, his words sending a thrill down my spine and validating the hour spent primping in front of the mirror.

I'd definitely brought my "A" game tonight and I liked that he was the kind of guy who seemed to appreciate it. There were a lot of guys who wanted a low-maintenance girl who went hiking, and did marathons, and didn't wear makeup. That girl was awesome; I was just not that girl. Those guys inevitably got upset when it took me an hour to get ready for a night out, or bitched when I pushed luggage weight limits to the max on trips. Those guys said soul-crushing things like, *Do you really need that many pairs of shoes?*

I was fully aware of the fact that I could kind of be a pain in the ass, and I definitely appreciated that so far Noah seemed to like that I was the kind of girl who didn't know the meaning of the word "understated."

'Course, given his friends and his profession, I doubted there was much I could do that would shock him.

I grinned, letting my gaze devour him like a hungry lion faced with a gazelle. "You look pretty good, too. How was dinner?"

He matched my smile. "Boring."

His head dipped, his lips claiming mine. "I was too busy looking forward to dessert," he whispered against my mouth before his tongue slid in and he kissed me senseless.

My arms wrapped around his neck, my chest plastered against his, his hands on my lower back, grazing my ass. He didn't hold back because we were in public, or because we were surrounded by our friends, and considering it definitely wasn't in my nature to hold back, I was greedy for more.

His tongue was tendrils of fire licking through me, his hands sending sparks throughout my body, his lips embers that warmed me, my body humming with need and heat. I'd told myself we would hang out with our friends for a bit and then maybe sneak away. That plan was becoming more untenable with each second he kissed me.

Noah pulled back first, smiling down at me, his eyes twinkling, his tongue sweeping out over his lips as though he wanted every drop of me.

Gah.

His arm wrapped around my waist, pulling me against his body, the thump of his heart beating against my skin. I tipped my head up, inhaling the scent of his cologne, my face buried in the crook of his neck. It took a remarkable amount of willpower to keep from dragging my tongue along the skin there.

Easy cleared his throat loudly, the sound pulling us apart, a teasing smile on his face. "We were thinking of playing some blackjack. You guys in?"

I'd almost forgotten they were all even there. My sister stared at me with wide-eyed curiosity. The other girls looked at Noah like he was the last piece of cake and they all had a wicked sweet tooth. The guys had various expressions of amusement on their faces.

"Do you want to play blackjack?" Noah asked me.

I shrugged. "I'm not great with cards, but I'm up for it if you want."

I didn't want to play blackjack. I didn't want to be in this casino. Right now all I wanted was Noah naked and a room with a bed. And really, at this point, the bed was optional.

He nodded to Easy. "Yeah, we're in."

Totally stupid, but I kind of liked being part of a *we*.

He nodded toward the guy I hadn't met yet. "Joker, this is Jordan. Jordan, this is our squadron commander, Joker."

More melting. It was impossible to miss the fact that he introduced me like I was someone special, someone he was proud of. Impossible to miss the way his arm tightened around me or his voice rose as he made the introductions, as though I was someone he wanted to show off instead of just a casual lay.

I wasn't entirely sure why this mattered, but yeah, it kind of did.

I smiled and held out my hand. "It's nice to meet you."

He returned my smile, his gaze speculative, his big hand engulfing mine. "It's nice to meet you, too."

He wasn't as hot as Noah or Easy, or even as cute as Thor, but he was definitely handsome. He looked to be maybe a decade or so older than the rest of the group, and he carried himself with a calm air the other guys lacked. His cockiness wasn't as in your face and I figured the thick platinum band on his left ring finger had something to do with it.

I wondered what it would be like to be married to one of these guys, but somehow I couldn't imagine it. I was pretty chill in relationships, had never really seen much point in getting jealous, but I figured it had to be weird to be home in Oklahoma while your husband was out in Vegas with guys like Easy. And likely, even weirder that this was a common occurrence.

"He's my boss," Noah murmured as the rest of the group headed toward the blackjack table, us lagging behind. "He's a good guy."

I smiled up at him, so many emotions pinging through me that I wasn't sure I trusted my voice. We'd gone from my wheelhouse to something I didn't know how to navigate.

"Are you okay?" he asked and something lurched in my chest.

It was the same something I couldn't shake. I'd told myself this was a fun weekend, but little by little, fun was giving way to this feeling inside me, this idea that maybe we could keep in touch after this weekend. Maybe it wasn't that ludicrous. We could e-mail or something.

I froze, staring up at him. I didn't know what I was. What I wanted. What I needed. Where this was going. If I even wanted it to go anywhere. I knew nothing beyond the rush of desire crashing into my body like waves over rocks and the feeling that I'd been caught up in the eye of a hurricane, unable to get my bearings.

His gaze darkened, his voice achingly soft, a whisper that trembled through my bones. "What?"

I shook my head and started to walk forward, some part of my brain convinced that I just had to outrun this, fight or flight giving way to flight. I made it a step, maybe two, and then his hand tugged me back. For a moment we faced off in the casino, the sounds of slot machines pinging around us, people yelling, the bright lights flashing around us, the scent of smoke, and cheap perfume, and alcohol adding to the sensory overload. And then it all fell away.

Noah stared down at me, his gaze intent, as if he could somehow sift through all the confusion in my head, as though he could see that I was freaking out, that this had gone from fun and casual to quicksand in the blink of an eye and I didn't know how to deal. He reached out, brushing my hair over my shoulder, his touch lingering on my bare skin, his hands branding me. My throat closed up, my heart pounding, my limbs achy, my body feverish like I had the flu. And then the chills hit me, my nipples puckering, my body flashing hot and cold as desire pushed past the point of want into have-to-have-you.

And then he kissed me again.

He tasted like bourbon, and as soon as his mouth came down on mine, I knew I wouldn't be content to just kiss him.

I wanted more, and unless the Venetian was going to be cool with me straddling him on an empty blackjack table, we were definitely going to need to get the hell out of here.

Noah's arms enveloped me, holding me tight against his body. His hands roamed over my curves, cupping my ass. I moaned, the sound captured between our lips.

"Do you want to get out of here?" he murmured. "We have a penthouse suite upstairs. It has an amazing view of the Strip."

Amazing view of the Strip sounded suspiciously like code for *Let's get it on,* and a hallelujah chorus sounded in my ears.

"Yes."

I wasn't sure I said the word as much as shouted it.

His palm slid into mine, our fingers linking, and another thrill tumbled through my body.

I was a junkie, and tonight didn't feel like enough of a fix. He was a buffet spread out before me, and the desire to gorge myself on him was inescapable. I had two more nights in Vegas, two more nights and then gone. The clock ticked, our time together lessening with each minute that passed us by. And suddenly, playing it cool flew out the window.

We walked over to where most of the group stood near a blackjack table, the guys seated, an impressive stack of chips in front of Easy.

Noah interrupted, taking the lead when I was still too turned on, confused, you name it, to speak. "E?"

His friend stopped talking to Stacey and Amber and looked over at us. Hell, it felt like everyone was looking at us.

"We're going to head out."

Noah delivered the line with way more smoothness than I could have, as though, *We're going to head out* wasn't what we all knew it to be: *We're going to screw like rabbits for a couple hours; don't come up.*

Meg's eyebrows rose while Stacey and Amber looked at me like I'd just won a grand at a slot machine. Maybe two.

Meg pulled me away from the group, her voice somewhere between giddy excitement and sisterly concern. "You're going up to his room?"

I shifted my body so I faced away from the group. "Is that cool? I don't want to bail on the party, but . . ." I made a face that basically said, *Can you blame me?* And honestly, this time the question was merely to be polite. I'd done dinner, but as Noah had said, dessert was definitely mine.

She shook her head, a grin tugging at her lips. "Go get lucky." She nodded toward where Stacey and Amber were pulling out all the stops trying to get Easy's attention. "Besides, I have a feeling you're not going to be the only one getting lucky with a fighter pilot tonight."

I snorted. "Round two?"

"Oh, yeah. I have a feeling all parties involved are more than ready."

I laughed.

"Just be careful, Jord."

"Will do." I gave her a hug. "I'll be back later."

I pulled away and turned my attention to Noah, my heart in my throat. "Ready?"

NOAH

I'd never been readier, arousal mixed with a thin thread of desperation. I didn't know if it was her little black dress, this one impossibly even sexier than the dress she'd worn last night, or the taste I'd had earlier, but either way, I wanted her naked, wet, and moaning.

We walked through the Venetian holding hands, making our way to the elevators that led over to the guest rooms. The idea to get a room on the Strip for the weekend rather than staying in our rooms at Nellis had been all Easy. I'd balked initially, too spun up on Red Flag to even think about partying, and then given up in the face of Easy on a mission and handed over my credit card. I owed him big time.

We got into the elevator and I looped my arm around Jordan's shoulders, pulling her toward me. She smelled amazing again. Not some cloying, flowery smell, but like vanilla and sun, and a hint of the ocean. And apparently I'd become a fucking poet in the face of her ass in that dress, the curve of her tits highlighted by the low neckline.

I shifted our bodies so her back was to my front, shielding the massive erection between my legs from the elderly couple holding hands that looked like they were celebrating their anniversary, and giving the added bonus of her ass against my cock.

Which, come to think of it, made my arousal so much worse.

I buried my face in Jordan's hair, my arms at her waist, holding her against me like I never wanted to let her go. I hadn't been kidding earlier when I said I'd been bored at dinner, that all I had been able to think about was seeing her again. It had possibly been the first time in my entire life that I'd had zero interest in talking about flying. But right now the idea of sliding into the cockpit paled in comparison to the promise of surrounding myself in her warm, wet pussy.

My hands drifted up her stomach, moving closer and closer to the swell of her tits, dancing on the line between appropriate public displays of affection and get-a-fucking-room.

The elderly couple got off a few floors before us, and then my hands went higher, tracing the soft curves under her breasts, my brain somehow registering the absence of a bra before it shut off and my fingers grazed her nipples and I bit down on her neck, her head arching back, a moan escaping her lips.

The elevator pinged and the doors slid open.

Finally.

Six

JORDAN

I stepped over the threshold, Noah behind me, shutting the door, flicking on light switches. I walked over to the window, needing a moment to compose myself, staring out at the bright lights illuminating the Strip. He hadn't been kidding about the view or how spectacular the room was. Floor-to-ceiling windows highlighted Las Vegas in all of its glory. And then I turned, and my gaze settled on him, and the majesty of neon and glitz couldn't hold a candle to the man in front of me.

"Do you want a drink?" Noah asked, his voice gravel, the sound eliciting a pull low in my belly.

I shook my head. The tequila I'd drunk earlier at dinner was becoming a distant memory and now all my senses were coming alive. It had been a long time since I'd had sex, an eternity since I'd had *good sex*, and possibly *never* since I'd had the kind of sex Noah promised every time he touched me.

I didn't want anything dulling that.

I turned back toward the window, and then a second later

the soft strands of music filled the suite. Not cheesy seduction music, but the low, throbbing beat of a house song that set the mood better than anything else could have. I closed my eyes, giving myself over to the tension vibrating between us like a live wire, the music filling my ears and my heart.

This was my favorite moment. Always. That moment right before everything started, when you hovered over the edge, that moment when you existed in the in-between. The promise of intimacy was a game-changer, and yet there was still that tension that lingered, the pause before everything altered. It was that moment when you were in the water and caught sight of a great wave, all of nature hanging in suspension as you watched the beauty of its power and prepared for the ride of your life. It was the possibility of it. Later it could turn out to be a dud, it could fuck you over and disappoint, but now, *now*—

It was magic.

He was magic.

Heat slid through me as Noah came up behind me, pulling me against his body, holding me tight in his embrace like I belonged there. I tilted my head back, leaning into him. He stroked my hair, playing with the strands, his touch achingly gentle. I liked that he didn't rush, that he touched me like he wanted to savor every moment. I liked it, and at the same time, it threw me for a loop. I was happiest when I could put things into tiny little boxes. My personality was chaotic enough; I needed everything else around me to be easily classified or else I just became a fucking mess. And I didn't know what to make of this.

This was a one-night stand. Maybe if things went well, two nights. His touch was supposed to make me come. Instead, it unraveled me until I was quivering each time his flesh grazed mine.

There was something here I wasn't prepared for, a reverence I hadn't expected bubbling up until it became a lump in my throat, blocking out everything else. It had been there between us in the cabana, unbidden, a sense of awe that filled me. Hell, maybe it had even been there that first night I saw him, simmering underneath the urge to take off our clothes. Or maybe I was wrong to try to separate the two. I didn't know what I was anymore.

Noah stroked the back of my neck, a shiver rippling through me. His touch was light, his fingers teasing. He slid forward, tracing the curve of my neck, skimming my collarbone, my entire world focused on the pads of his fingers. Each part of my body that he touched felt remade, born again to something new, something I'd never imagined. As though I gave those pieces to him, losing myself at the same time I found something I'd never expected.

There was so much beauty here that it hurt. I'd wanted dirty and quick and I'd gotten the slow death, death by one thousand strokes.

I loved every single one of them.

I sucked in a deep breath when Noah reached the center of my chest, hovering there, inches away from my cleavage. He turned me to face him, his other hand tipping my chin up so our gazes locked.

My mouth went dry.

His eyes were night, dark pools I couldn't read, his breath ragged as though he'd gone to war and barely come out the other end. I drank his sighs as though they were water and I was dying of thirst, wanting, needing to take each part of his body into mine.

This wasn't sex. It was worship.

And then his lips closed over my earlobe and I forgot everything as I succumbed to the deep pull of lust that assailed me and gave him my body even as I clung to my heart, as if I could hide it away from him in some secret place he couldn't touch.

I wasn't a romantic, far from it. And I hadn't confused sex with love in a very long time. But I'd never gotten this before. Never felt such a strong link between my body and someone else's, never felt the kind of cause and effect that meant that he did and I felt.

Until now. Until Noah took fifteen years of hard-won dating knowledge and flung it back at me as though it were nothing, and suddenly, I felt a different kind of naked. Like my bravado, and sass, and all the armor I put on had failed me. I went from the driver's seat to just-along-for-the-ride with a few caresses, and hell, I was all too willing to follow him.

He nipped me, his mouth hot against my ear, paying homage to another part of my body as if each curve of flesh was a stop on his own personal pilgrimage and I was his hallelujah. I'd never thought of my ears as particularly erotic, but holy shit, Noah proved me wrong.

His fingers stroked my skin, moving lower until he reached the top of my dress. I arched forward, my body craving more, laying myself at his altar.

"Touch me," I whispered, my voice hoarse and needy, my plea sounding suspiciously more like a demand. I wanted to cloak myself in the promises his body gave me, sink down on his cock until he filled me. I wanted the memory of this night to sustain me long after the magic had gone, when I was back to my ordinary life and dates that ended with too-wet kisses on my doorstep and a pint of Häagen-Dazs after.

This was one of those magical nights I'd read about, dreamed of, but never experienced myself. And now that it was here, I was overcome with the desire to both draw it out and rush to the best part.

Noah's hands settled on my hips, holding me in place as his gaze all but devoured me with the same fervor as a condemned man given his last meal, and another ache filled me. I didn't feel like some interchangeable girl like I had with other guys, like I was just the means to an end for a guy chasing his next orgasm. I felt like he chased *me*.

"I never want to stop touching you," Noah whispered, his voice throaty and low, my legs quivering as the words cloaked me in heat. His hand skimmed up the curve of my waist. "It feels wrong to be near you and not touch you. My hands turn greedy around you. So fucking greedy. I can't get enough. There are too many places on your body that I want to touch, kiss, lick, fuck."

Yes, please.

I'd never been shy about my body. I would never be called skinny, but it wasn't lost on me that there were plenty of guys who liked boobs and asses, and thankfully, I had both to spare. And by the way Noah looked at me like I was a present for him to unwrap, I figured they worked for him.

Not to mention, I had a pretty awesome view myself . . . and a whole lot of fantasies.

I reached between us, my own fingers turning greedy, fumbling with the buttons on his shirt, the need to have him naked and on top of me—or under me—eclipsing all else.

Noah stilled as I reached his stomach, my hand slipping down to stroke his abs through the thin fabric of his undershirt. His muscles flexed reflexively beneath my touch, my mouth dry, body wet. I wanted more of what I'd seen at the pool today. I wanted to gorge myself on him until I was happy, and sated, and too full to move.

My movements went from hesitant to hungry, racing

through the buttons, tugging the shirt off his shoulders until all he wore was the V-neck white T-shirt that looked like it had seen more than a few washes.

The knot in my stomach tightened.

I didn't know what was in the Vegas water, but whatever it was, there was something about his ruggedness, his I-don't-give-a-shit, this-is-who-I-am, fucking-deal attitude that turned me on completely. This wasn't a guy I would be able to manage; there was little softness to him. He was a handful in a way I'd never experienced before. A man who lived by a code of his own, one I still didn't completely understand. And where I'd never thought I was the kind of girl who appealed to a rugged guy, the evidence to the contrary stood right in front of me.

I pulled at the hem of his T-shirt, my fingers sliding over satiny smooth skin. I yanked the fabric higher, the hiss that escaped his mouth singing in my blood. Our hands collided as we both struggled to get it over his head and then his shirt hit the floor and I sank to my knees.

I was tall enough that my lips leveled with the bottom of his stomach, tantalizingly near the indents on either side of his hips. I could write poetry about those two gaps. I kissed him there, inhaling his scent, my tongue hitting the dips just above his jeans. He groaned as I licked him, rocking forward, his arousal heavy and hard, inches away from my mouth.

The moment hovered suspended between us, his body vibrating with need. And then my hands grasped his belt buckle and we careened toward release.

I unbuckled his belt, the sound of the metal clinking together crackling between us. I pulled the leather through the denim loops with a snap, the belt falling from my fingers as I attacked the buttons at his fly, another groan escaping his lips as I stroked his cock through the denim. I was a woman possessed, whatever we'd created here between us finding a home inside me.

I slid the jeans off Noah's hips. He jerked away to remove his socks and shoes, working the pants down his legs until he stood before me wearing black boxer briefs—*yum*—and a wicked smile. I tilted my face up, our gazes locking, my heart a steady drum. His hand reached out and stroked my hair, his fingers wrapping around the strands like a rope that bound me to him.

Noah's eyes went onyx, his voice hoarse. "I wanted you like this the first second I saw you. Imagined you on your knees, that look in your eyes, while I fucked your face."

My clit spasmed.

I'd never been a flowery-sex kind of girl. My enthusiasm for phrases like "making love" and "joining" was tepid at best. I'd never cried during sex, preferred the lights on, and nothing got me off like the filthy words that fell from a guy's lips while he fucked me. So on every single level, this was working for me. A lot.

"Your mouth . . . your lips . . ." He groaned. The fist in my hair tightened, pulling my head back, dangling me somewhere on the precipice between pleasure and pain until it hurt so good. "You have fuck-me lips, a mouth made for sex. Full, soft, plump . . ."

I figured it was the only time a guy would ever get away with using the word "plump" in a sentence referring to my appearance without getting kneed in the balls. But he was right, my mouth did feel swollen, my lips sensitive, my tongue itching to lick him from base to tip.

Noah reached between us, the pad of his thumb brushing my lower lip, pressing down on the skin, opening my mouth.

His fingers slipped in and I sucked them deep, the little bit of himself he gave me not nearly enough. I kept my gaze on his the entire time, the approval filling his eyes heating me from the inside out. Somewhere along the way this had ceased to be about what I wanted and instead became about pleasing him, about giving him a night he'd never forget. I'd already checked that box off for myself.

I drew the boxer briefs down his legs, each inch of fabric sliding down sucking more and more air out of the room until I could barely breathe.

He was beautiful. Big. Thick. Absofuckinglutely perfect.

Definite Chupacabra territory here.

I leaned forward, dragging my tongue along the underside of his cock, tasting him, his hands gripping my hair even harder, his hips canting toward me, a shudder rocking through him. His reaction fed me, satisfaction coursing through my veins. I swirled my tongue around the tip, sucking him deep between my lips, the groan that reverberated through his body the best sound I'd ever heard.

I'd never felt more feminine in my life. This was power, madness, glory. This was a complete and utter shattering of his control and mine. I was the one on my knees, but it was impossible to feel anything other than the sense that I held his world in the palm of my hand.

NOAH

I'd never experienced anything that gave me the same kind of high I found in the cockpit. Until now.

She took me into her mouth and I forgot my fucking name.

I hadn't been wrong in all my fantasies about her pouty lips—the girl gave magnificent head, made even better by the fact that she clearly got off on it, too. There was nothing worse than a girl who went down on you like it was a chore, but this girl licked and sucked my cock as though each stroke of her tongue, each bob of her head, took her closer and closer to finding her own brand of ecstasy.

Her tongue swirled around the tip, a shiver trembling down my spine, drowning in the silky wetness and hot suction of her mouth, the urge to come between her lips.

Maybe "magnificent" wasn't a strong enough word.

I pulled back, my hands on Jordan's hips, lifting her up and carrying her over to the couch in the living room. One of us had entirely too many clothes on and I couldn't wait until I had my mouth on her, until I learned if she tasted as sweet as she looked.

I settled her on the edge of the couch, my hands spreading her wide, sinking down on my knees. Jordan stared down at me with the same dazed expression that I was beginning to recognize as her sex-face, her fuck-me mouth swollen from our kisses and my cock.

It was like someone had dropped a fifty-pound weight on my chest. And then squeezed.

I opened my mouth to speak, words flooding my mind, all of them praise I wanted to lavish on her that fell short before they even left my lips.

I didn't know how to describe the feelings pounding through me. Didn't know how to quantify the sensation that from the moment we'd crossed over the threshold, fuck, from the moment I'd seen her, everything I'd known to be true had rolled and turned into a world I no longer recognized.

"This is better than a DCA sortie," I muttered with a groan.

"What?" Her lips came down on my neck, sucking at the skin there. My dick throbbed.

I hadn't even realized I'd said the words out loud. "It's a good thing. A really fucking good thing."

I slid my hand up under her dress, skimming my fingers along her inner thigh, caressing her. I'd never felt anything as smooth or as seductive. The image of me fisting my cock, coming all over her pretty skin, filled my mind.

That would definitely be better than anything I could find in the cockpit. Hell, the image alone was heart attack inducing and I was *thisclose* to coming. Foreplay went out the window.

"How do you get this thing off?" I asked, tugging at the bottom of her dress.

Jordan grinned, her voice a breathy whisper. "Quickly."

She slid away from me, fumbling with the back of the dress and then she lifted her hips and pulled it over her head, the fabric hitting the floor, her body bare but for her heels and a sheer black thong that highlighted more than it concealed.

I went a little light-headed, the pain in my chest intensifying.

She sat back down on the edge of the sofa, her legs spread, no shyness between us. Motherfucking jackpot. Her confidence was hot on a whole other level. I liked that she didn't insist on the lights off, that she didn't shy away from me looking at her, committing every inch of her body to memory. I had big plans to lick and suck her later, after I'd had her once or twice, to cover her skin with marks from my lips and teeth, to have her moaning as I drove her crazy with need.

The pieces of her body that I'd gotten earlier had been pretty amazing, but the whole picture was something else entirely.

She had the most perfect tits I'd ever seen in my entire life, hands down, no contest. They were the ultimate handful—hell, more than a handful—her nipples a pretty shade of pink I couldn't wait to get my mouth on. I cupped her breasts, my thumbs rubbing against her flesh, hardening the points until I couldn't take it anymore and I leaned forward, capturing her nipple between my lips.

Yes.

She tasted sweet. Melt-in-your-mouth sweet. Addictive. No way was one night going to be enough with this girl.

I tongued her nipple, my teeth grazing her flesh, tugging, my cock hardening as her body responded to my touch, with the soft sighs that escaped her lips. I moved to her other breast, my fingers replacing my lips.

When this had started, my primary concern had been to feel good. To make her feel good. We'd passed by good a long time ago and the mission had changed.

I was a good pilot, hell, a great pilot, because I was relentless, my focus single-minded when it needed to be. When I had a contact on my scope, I didn't let go until that fucker was dead. One night wasn't enough with this girl, and good wasn't what I wanted anymore. I wanted to see her again, beyond Vegas, beyond this night. Getting shot down wasn't an option.

I reached up, pulling her thong off until she was naked before me.

She was fucking gorgeous.

I stood, my hands hooking under her hips, carrying her with me, wrapping her legs around my waist. My mouth went back on hers, my tongue thrusting inside and out, mimicking the motion my cock was desperate to make. We hit the bedroom, her hands scraping over my skin, her core rubbing against me, slippery and wet, throbbing around me.

I set her down on the bed and released her, reaching over and scrounging through my bag for a condom, my heart pounding. My fingers closed over the little foil packet, a silent shout of triumph rushing through me, and then I was ripping it open, my hands shaking as I slid the condom onto my cock.

Jordan lay on the bed, her gaze on me the entire time.

I opened my mouth to speak again, to say something, *anything*, but nothing came. Instead I found myself striding toward the mattress, and then I was between her legs, the head of my cock teasing her entrance, cursing the latex barrier between us, and then with one smooth stroke, I slid inside her, pressure building at the base of my spine.

So fucking good.

Jordan sighed as I filled her, her body clenching down around my cock. For a moment I stayed still, seated to the hilt, the feeling too good for movement, for anything.

Her hands trailed down my back, heating a path down my skin, and then I couldn't *not* move, and my hips began pumping in a familiar rhythm that was as natural as breathing, instinct taking over when my brain failed to work.

My mind went blank, my entire world reduced to the in-and-out, thrust-and-release of my body inside hers, of the shudders that traveled through her to my cock. Sweat pooled on my brow, my body straining as I rode her, as I reached for a release I couldn't yet grasp. Not until she came.

And then it built inside her, coming on strong, and Jordan shattered beneath me, her head thrown back, the look of utter abandon on her face the hottest fucking thing I'd ever seen. And as I watched the last remnants of her orgasm slide out of her, I took the embers, and tilted my hips, increasing my pace, thrusting in and out, harder, faster, bringing the next one on like a one-two punch.

When her second orgasm hit, when she shrieked my name, her body closing down on me like a vise, I let go, finally giving in to the release I craved until I saw stars.

Nothing had ever come close to my hand on the throttle, in the clouds like a god, going Mach 1.5, the world below me nothing but a memory. But now, my cock surrounded by her wetness, her body shuddering around mine as her pussy clenched down, the wave of her orgasm thrusting her tits forward and arching her back, my balls tightening as I succumbed to my own release, I preferred fucking to flying.

$\mathcal{S}$EVEN

JORDAN

Noah hooked an arm around my waist, tucking me into the curve of his body, my cheek resting above his heart. His hand trailed down my side, lazily stroking my hip, squeezing my waist.

I resisted the urge to purr. Barely.

My eyelids fluttered, another yawn hitting me. It was late. Or early, depending on your perspective. We'd dozed on and off, our naps interrupted by intermittent, grade-A fucking. I'd lost count of how many rounds we'd gone, orgasm after orgasm sliding together in a mindless blur. But while the sex had become a haze, the *after*, the postcoital cuddling, sharpened everything.

I didn't know what I'd expected exactly, just that it hadn't been this. He touched me the entire night—twisting my hair around his fingers, his hips against mine, a hand grazing my legs, waist, back, my face buried in the curve of his neck, his lips ghosting across my skin. His scent covered me.

The sex had been the best I'd ever had. The *after* was awe-inspiring.

You're in Vegas. What happens in Vegas stays in Vegas.

I repeated the words to myself over and over again, cloaking myself in them like a security blanket. I had no problem with no-strings-attached sex. Hell, sometimes I preferred it. But there were freaking strings everywhere I looked here.

Time to go.

I tipped my head up, pressing a quick kiss to his lips.

"I should let you get some sleep." I made my mouth twist into a smile, ignoring the weird pounding in my chest and the confusion in my mind. "Thanks for the orgasms."

I moved out of his grasp, rolling over to my side. My legs reached out to hit the floor, already mentally preparing for the walk of shame, when suddenly I was on my back again, a large, aroused body on top of me.

Gah.

I stared up into Noah's face, the satisfied, sleepy look in his eyes replaced by something a lot sharper that had a knot tightening in my stomach.

Definitely intense.

"So that's it?" His voice scraped over me.

The knot got bigger.

I shrugged, trying to be the girl who didn't make a big deal out of sex, the cool girl, the girl who wasn't lying here feeling like there was nowhere else she wanted to be. His eyes got flinty and I figured I failed.

Noah pulled back, my body going cold. I watched, my mouth dry, as he walked naked from the bed—spectacular back and ass on display. He grabbed a pair of exercise shorts from his suitcase, tugging them up over his hips, those freaking indents teasing me again, and my resolve to be cool-girl sort of went out the window as I tried not to drool.

We stared off against each other, the bed-of-many-orgasms between us.

I grabbed the sheet, tucking it under my arms, covering my body, ready to flee at any moment. I could tell he was pissed, or on his way to pissed, at least, but I wasn't sure how this would go. And I really didn't know what I wanted when I got there.

I swallowed and dug deep.

"What else is there? It was good. Really good. But you have to get back to the base for work, right? And I should probably check in with my sister."

Noah's gaze narrowed, his tone silky. "Good?"

I rolled my eyes. I had a difficult enough time with the regular male prima donna attitude; my enthusiasm for fighter pilot prima donna attitude was pretty much nonexistent. It had been off-the-charts mind-blowing, and yeah, I was kind of being an asshole for ducking out—though legions of men had certainly done so before me—but that didn't mean I was in the mood to inflate his ego.

"I saw stars."

My tone might have dripped with sarcasm, but I'd have been lying if I didn't admit that there was a kernel of truth to my words. And by the look that flared in his eyes, he definitely knew it.

His arms crossed over his chest, his stomach muscles rippling.

I was an idiot.

"You're freaked."

He didn't bother posing it as a question; I figured the wide-eyed panic settling over my face said it all.

"I'm not freaked," I sputtered.

So totally freaked.

His head snapped to the clock next to the bed. "So you normally flee hotel rooms at 4 a.m.?"

I sighed. He had me there. Time to give up.

"Look, I can appreciate that you aren't one of those guys who's a dick about a girl staying the night, but I'm also not the kind of girl who's going to be a clinger. Tonight was amazing, but haven't we sort of reached our natural conclusion here? Where's it going to go?"

Where can it go?

"Where do you want it to go?" he returned, his tone even, his gaze impossible to read.

"I don't know."

That was the problem. I wasn't trying to be difficult; I really was that confused. He didn't fit into any box I'd come up with, and now I was coloring outside the lines, imagining all the possibilities of where this could go if I threw caution to the wind. And I was *really* good at throwing caution to the wind. Hence why it should be avoided at all costs.

"Do you want to know where I want this to go?" Noah asked, his voice going husky, his eyes soft.

I swallowed, my nipples tightening in anticipation because I just knew his answer was going to be really, really good.

"Maybe."

I was pretty sure whatever answer he gave me, I wasn't prepared to hear it, even as I craved it. I was right on the edge, the desire to be reckless delivering a melody that called to me like a siren's song.

"I want you on your knees while I fuck your mouth. I want to feel your pussy tighten down on my cock when I'm filling you up. I want to sleep with my arm hooked around your waist. I want to kiss that mouth of yours—sweetest fucking thing I've ever tasted. I want more nights with you, and days, too."

When he put it that way, I was pretty sure I fell off the fucking cliff.

"I want to make you come over and over again. Want to hear you scream my name. Want to play with your tits until you're writhing and moaning over my cock. If you want that, I'm game."

I considered the fact that I refrained from fanning myself to be a testament to my willpower. I so did want that. All of it, over and over again, with a few moves of my own thrown in.

"You live in Oklahoma. I live in Florida," I repeated slowly, as though saying the words would convince me of the insanity of all this.

He nodded. "Yeah. And I'll just be totally honest with you, my job doesn't leave a lot of time for dating. If we do this, we take it one day at a time. But this doesn't have to be good-bye."

Part of me wanted that. Part of me was greedy for more nights with him. And part of me was thirty years old, already past the point when I'd thought I would have met *the guy*, and own *the house*, and have the two point five kids I was supposed to drive to piano lessons and soccer camp. I could literally feel the cobwebs gathering on my eggs, the reality that if I didn't meet *the guy* soon, I was slightly fucked.

I'd always figured I would date a guy for a year or two before we got engaged. And then a year for the engagement so we could enjoy it and plan the wedding and just revel in being in a committed relationship without having to endure fights about whose turn it was to take out the trash or why no one had changed the roll of toilet paper. And then I figured another three or four years of being married to do married-people things before we added in a miniature person to take care of. And considering I wanted, like, three kids?

Way behind the power curve here.

I didn't really have time for a no-strings-attached fuckfest—however appealing it might be.

But the problem was, it wasn't just appealing, it was roll-your-tongue-off-the-floor earth-shattering. And maybe he wasn't the settle-down kind of guy, but it wasn't like I'd met a lot of that guy, either. And cobwebs or no, thirty was the new twenty, right?

And if he really was the dating Chupacabra . . .

"So this fuckfest you're proposing?"

He choked back laughter. "Fuckfest?"

"That's kind of what it sounds like."

Noah's lips twitched. "Not going to say no to that."

"Is this a monogamous-but-don't-expect-a-ring sort of arrangement?"

This time he didn't bother hiding his smile. "You're a little neurotic, aren't you?"

"Only in the fun way."

His smile deepened. He moved toward the bed, his body hovering at the edge. "I wasn't planning on sharing. Or looking at anyone else."

"So you're not going to fit the fighter pilot love-'em-and-leave-'em stereotype?" I teased.

He knelt on the bed, prowling toward me. "Babe, we gotta expand your knowledge beyond *Top Gun*."

I leaned back, letting the sheet fall down to my waist, my breasts bare before him.

"So expand my fighter pilot knowledge."

His smile went from playful to intent. "Is this another one of your conversation-foreplay sessions?"

I grinned, my eyelids fluttering, hair flipping, sliding into full-on flirt with ease.

"Maybe."

He leaned over me, his big body hovering inches away, his mouth close enough that if I just leaned up, I could put my lips on his.

"I'm beginning to see how fun you could be in briefings, babe."

Okay, maybe the uniform thing would be kind of hot.

I reached out, my fingers stroking his back, tracing the ridges of his spine all the way down to his spectacular ass. I tugged on the workout shorts, sliding them off over his hips. He made a growly sound in his throat that told me he liked it—a lot.

I leaned up, my lips grazing his ear, unable to resist the urge to let my tongue stroke his lobe. The shudder I felt against my hand at the base of his spine told me he liked that, too.

"So tell me fighter pilot things. Is there a password? A secret handshake?"

He slid down to his elbows, his chest pressing into mine, his cock settling into the curve of my hips, his hand pushing the sheets away until there was nothing between us.

"Cute."

I ground my hips up toward him, feeling another rush of satisfaction as his body stiffened and jerked against me. He wasn't the only one who knew how to get what he wanted.

"Seriously. Teach me."

He groaned. "You can't say things like 'teach me' when you have your legs spread beneath me and expect to actually have a coherent conversation."

"Am I distracting you?" I teased, sliding my hand between us, cupping his balls.

Another groan.

"Definitely distracting me."

"Tell me fighter pilot things. I'm seriously disappointed if there isn't a secret handshake."

He tilted his head to look at me, another smile tugging at his lips. "You have my dick in your hands and you're still busting my balls?"

"Pretty much."

He sighed, as if resigned to his fate. "No secret handshake. Shit ton of traditions—songs, things we say, things we don't say, things we do, things we don't. It's its own code."

I was beginning to figure that out, just like I was beginning to realize that he was definitely his own man. And I liked that a lot.

"Okay, give me an example of the lingo."

I circled his cock, stroking and squeezing, loving the feel of him jerking against my palm.

He was silent for a moment and I wasn't sure if he was thinking of an answer or succumbing to the feel of my fingers working him over.

"Vocabulary." He pushed the word out. "We don't say 'box,' we say 'container.' And we don't say 'head,' we say 'cranium.'"

I blinked, my hand stilling. "What?"

"We don't say 'box.' We say 'container' instead."

"You just said 'box.'"

"To explain it, yeah. But otherwise, no 'box.'"

What?

"Why?"

"Think about it."

I thought about it.

"Once again, why?"

He lifted himself up on his elbow again, his hand reaching between us, his fingers stroking me much as I did to him, teasing my clit. "We don't say 'box.'"

I took a second—probably because he was already stoking the fires of arousal within me—and then the totally juvenile, sexual joke hit me.

"You have got to be kidding."

The last word came out with a squeak as his finger dipped lower, sliding into me with one smooth thrust. I tilted my hips up, wanting it deeper, and he gave it to me, plunging a second finger inside.

He flashed me a boyish grin, entirely too pleased with himself and still hot as fuck. "Nope."

My eyes narrowed even as my breath hitched and he did a twisty thing with his fingers that had my head falling back.

"And cranium?" I ground out.

"We don't say 'head.'"

I got that one a little faster, despite the fact that he'd definitely just hit my G-spot. "That is the dumbest fucking thing I've ever heard."

"You going to lecture me on fighter pilot vocabulary, or are you going to come your brains out?"

I opened my mouth to give him a sassy retort, but then he hit that spot *again*, and a moan escaped instead.

His head came down, his lips brushing against mine as he whispered, "Definitely going to come again."

He wasn't wrong.

NOAH

I woke early, a week of being on the day train with early brief times catching up with me.

Part of our job was dealing with the sheer unpredictability of our schedules. Some days I showed up at 3 a.m. and came home at 4 p.m. Other days I was in at noon and home at 2 a.m. It made getting on a consistent sleep schedule challenging, to say the least. So even though I'd barely slept all night, my hands, mouth, and cock full of Jordan, I was up now, lying on my side, my arm draped around her waist, watching her sleep. Watching her sleep and trying to get my shit together.

I figured it was the combination of tits, ass, and attitude that had me hooked. Not to mention the hair. And the laugh. She had a great fucking laugh, one that reverberated all the way to my dick. She felt tailor-made for me, my type to a T. My type in a way I hadn't found before. So yeah, I was definitely not letting her walk away without seeing how this would play out.

She stirred, her body stretching out, a lazy yawn spreading her lips.

"Morning."

Her eyes fluttered open, giving me a sleepy smile. "Good morning."

I reached out, my finger trailing down the curve of her cheek, her skin silk beneath my touch.

"I like waking up to you," I whispered, my voice tight as I gave her more than I'd anticipated.

The knot in my throat only got bigger as I watched the pretty pink spread across her cheeks. It had been a long time since I'd woken up with a girl in my bed, since I'd had a night like last night—hell, I wasn't sure I'd *ever* had a night like last night. And yeah, maybe I was more than a little lonely. Or maybe it was just how good she felt beside me.

My last girlfriend, Heather, and I had been together for

a year, only to break up when she'd wanted four little words and a ring, and I'd given her four very different little words—*I'm going to Afghanistan.*

Maybe she would have handled the short-notice deployment better if a diamond had accompanied it, but even as I'd thought about it, I couldn't make myself pull the trigger. It hadn't been a commitment thing; it had been the feeling that we were interchangeable to each other. I'd liked her a lot, but that was a pretty shitty basis for a marriage, especially one that would be tested as much as a military marriage would be. And considering she lived in the same town where I was stationed and had already been through her fair share of fighter pilots, I was pretty sure I was little more than a patch and a pair of wings.

Nothing about the girl next to me felt remotely interchangeable.

"Me, too," Jordan mumbled, her voice a little sad.

She sat up, staring over at the alarm clock on the nightstand. It was just after 10 a.m. I'd been watching her sleep for two hours, which was one hour and fifty-five minutes longer than I was comfortable with. I wasn't a player by any stretch of the imagination, but I also wasn't the kind of guy who watched girls sleep. But it had taken that long for me to figure out where I wanted this to go, to plan my next steps with the same level of attention I gave to a mission.

"Come back to Nellis with me."

I said the words like they were an impulse and not what they really were—the result of two hours of mulling over what the hell happened next and how to handle the unexpected conundrum of meeting a girl I really liked in Vegas, of all places, the home of one-night stands and no-strings-attached fun.

"What do you mean?"

"We have to be back at the base this afternoon. I have to mission plan for a sortie Monday morning. Come back with me. You could stay in the hotel if you want." My heart beat a little faster. "When does your flight leave on Monday?"

"Afternoon. Three or four."

"I should be back from my flight by then. I could say good-bye before you leave. And we'd have tonight together."

She was quiet for a moment, and I held my breath, waiting to see what her answer would be.

"I have plans for brunch with my sister and her bridesmaids in an hour at the Wynn. What time are you going back?"

"As long as I can get back by six, whenever works for you."

I didn't say the rest of it, the pleading part of my brain that desperately wanted another night with her in my arms. I figured this was the moment when I would find out if everything between us had been enough to keep her interested, enough for her to be willing to take a chance on this. She'd been uncertain last night, and fuck if I hadn't done everything I possibly could to convince her, and still I didn't know if it was enough.

It felt like an eternity, but finally she gave me the answer I needed.

"Okay."

The surge of triumph that filled me had me pulling her body under mine, taking her mouth, my hips rocking against her core.

"How much time do you have before you have to start getting ready for brunch?"

Jordan wrapped her legs around me, her hands grabbing

my ass, pulling me even tighter into her body, and I took that for her answer.

I made her come twice before she left to meet her sister, a wide smile on her face and her hair a messy tumble that unmistakably said she'd just been fucked.

EIGHT

JORDAN

We held hands as the cab made the forty-five-minute drive from the Strip to Nellis Air Force Base. We didn't speak.

Maybe it was stupid, but I was nervous. So much more nervous than I'd been going up to his room, the kind of nervous that came with venturing into uncharted territory where boundaries were murky and undefined.

I kept questioning the decision to come with him, doubting my sanity, cursing the impulsive streak that had me hitching my wagon to a guy I knew next to nothing about. But no matter how many times I tried to wrap my head around how I'd gotten here, I couldn't get to a place where I didn't see myself sitting next to him, my hand clutched in his.

So I gave up and just went along for the ride.

"Are you hungry?" Noah asked, breaking the silence between us.

I shook my head. "I'm pretty sure I'll never be hungry again. That buffet was *intense*."

He grinned. "Yeah, it's my favorite. Definitely the best buffet in Vegas."

I'd considered not gorging myself on the eclectic fare for like a second, but the lure of so many of my favorite foods had been too powerful to ignore. Hopefully, I had a bit of time for the food baby in me to subside before we were naked and horizontal—or vertical considering the added food poundage he'd have to support if he did me against the wall again. Or in the shower. He'd had some amazing moves in the shower this morning.

"How long do you have to go into work today?" I asked, hoping that would buy me enough of a reprieve.

"An hour or two? It shouldn't be long. I just have to finish up the mission planning I started on Friday."

Friday. The day we met. The day all of this had started. It had only been two days and yet it felt like so much more.

"We can go out and get a drink after or stay in if you want," Noah added.

I squeezed his hand. "I think we should stay in."

He raised our joined hands to his lips, my pulse racing as he kissed my knuckles, his voice rumbling over my bare skin. "Sounds good to me."

This guy was so freaking hot.

"So am I going to get to see some planes while I'm here?" I squeaked, trying to get my bearings back.

He grinned. "Do you want to see some planes?"

I'd never really thought about it, but it'd be cool to see what he did all day.

"Yeah, I do."

"We can check out the flight line, then. There should be some jets out for you to look at."

I nodded like this was a normal, everyday occurrence, when really it felt like I was in a movie or something. The whole thing was just surreal. I mean, a few days ago, I'd been getting ready to board a flight to Vegas. Now I sat next to this fascinating guy whose touch set off fireworks throughout my body. I'd never imagined my life could change so much in just a few short days, and even though this was still new, and I wasn't even sure what *it* was, that feeling that I stood on the precipice of something unexpected was inescapable.

We drove to the Nellis Air Force Base gates and Noah took me to the visitor's center to get me checked in with a pass that would let me stay on the base for the night. The whole thing was way more intense than I'd expected, and silly though it may be, I felt like I was entering a whole other world. I cracked a joke about being in a spy movie that made Noah hook his arm around my neck and press me into his side for a kiss that left me breathless.

I watched as people in uniform saluted Noah, and while he was nice to everyone, it was impossible to miss the air about him that stated unequivocally that he lived in a world where he commanded a great deal of respect. And that was undeniably sexy, too. Maybe it was the fact that he was confident without being an arrogant dick. Or even more, the feeling that he'd earned every inch of the deference that he was given.

We walked the rest of the way to the hotel and he pointed out things on the base, holding my hand the whole time. As much as he gave off the cool, tough guy vibe, I loved that he didn't shy away from being sweet with me, that he didn't care who saw. Every moment I spent with him made me like him a little bit more, unveiling a side that was even more intriguing.

He took me up to his room and we dropped off our bags

and then he grabbed his wallet and a lanyard with an ID card on it and held his hand out to me.

"Come on, I'll take you to see the flight line and the squadron."

I fucking melted.

I wouldn't have protested if he'd led with sex; hell, food baby or no food baby, I'd been ready to jump him again for a while now. But he wanted to show me where he worked. And he genuinely looked excited to do it.

I really liked him.

He took me on a short tour of the base as we headed to the flight line, his arm draped around my shoulders, pointing out the various sights. I didn't know what I'd expected a military base to look like, but I walked around wide-eyed as he gave me a crash course in how the base operated. We walked over to the building where he had been working while he was at Nellis for the past couple weeks and he pointed out the flight line across the street, showing me the row of F-16s.

"There's no flying on the weekends, but you'll hear them taking off tomorrow morning. They're loud."

They looked loud. They were huge, gray, intense. The guy who I'd spent the night with felt even more like a mystery. I couldn't quite wrap my head around what it would be like to sit in the cockpit and fly one of these things. What it would be like to go to war in one, to do the kind of maneuvers he described now, to fire *missiles* or drop *bombs*. He said his primary mission was suppression of enemy air defenses, and while I had no clue what that meant, it sounded badass in a way that was far out of the realm of badass I'd previously measured all other things by.

"It means we're the first ones in during a conflict," he

explained. "We take out the enemy's air defense systems to protect the other planes."

And suddenly badass began to sound really fucking dangerous. I swallowed, reconciling this new part with all the other ones I'd learned about him.

Noah flashed a badge at some scary-looking security guys with some serious weaponry that had me sidling up closer to him, and then we were standing next to one of those giant metal beasts, and I once again struggled to get my bearings. As much as I stood out, he looked like he'd been born to be here, that feeling that I'd first gotten when I saw him at the club coming back to me.

This was his kingdom.

Noah stroked the metal with a gleam of pride that was both paternal and loving as he explained to me how the planes had the base and squadron they were from painted on their tails, as he threw out complicated terms and palmed the training missiles affixed to the jet. We walked along the row of F-16s, and he pointed out the one with his name, rank, and call sign painted below the cockpit.

He answered all my questions, explaining what the training missiles were and how they worked. He told me that part of his job was teaching guys how to fight in the air, and given the way he went through the process with me—clearly and methodically—I totally got how he would be really amazing at it.

"What's it like?" I asked as we began walking off the flight line.

"Flying?"

I nodded.

He was quiet for a beat and I realized he wasn't with me anymore, that he was somewhere else, up in the sky.

"It's the ultimate rush. Everything fades away when I'm in the jet. For an hour or so, my entire world narrows to this cockpit. In one moment, it feels like I have the world in the palm of my hand, and in the next, it's fucking terrifying and I'm putting out fires to make sure I don't crash. For sixty-plus minutes, I'm consumed with getting my ass on the ground in one piece. It's both heady and humbling. Best job in the world."

I leaned into him, pressing my lips to his, giving him all the feelings crashing through me like a wave carrying me away. Then and there, I knew, whatever happened between us, wherever this headed, I would always share a piece of him with this jet.

I understood, or thought I did, at least, but that didn't mean it wasn't a little scary, too.

NOAH

I exited the airspace in a four-ship formation, descending, my eyes on the Strip as I approached the runway, the big hotels gleaming in the Vegas morning sun. I hit a visual approach to initial, five miles from the runway, my jet two thousand feet above the ground.

Almost home. Almost back to Jordan, who I'd left curled up in my hotel room bed, her body calling me back as I'd headed to work long before the sun came up.

I keyed the mic and checked in with the tower, looking out the left side of the jet, the runway beneath me. Almost there. I executed a left-hand bank turn, slowing the jet, the gears coming down like clockwork. I looked over my left shoulder, made the radio call, waiting for the tower's clearance to land, and then I began descending in the turn, slowing my airspeed. I slipped the power back to idle and I flared it off, wheels touching the ground, bringing the nose of the jet down.

I put on the speed breaks to slow the F-16 to a taxiing speed, exiting at the end of the runway, the motions I went through each time I flew nearly as familiar as breathing.

I taxied in to de-arm the jet, maintenance doing a quick check of the systems to make sure it was good to taxi back. I called the ops desk, notifying them of my status, and then I taxied the F-16 until I hit the parking spot and put it in park. I flipped the canopy switch, the canopy rising as I shut down the jet, going through the motions that were rote.

I began unhooking hoses, my com cord. I released my harness, then my lap belt, followed by my seat kit and G-suit. Each movement was a little faster than normal, still methodical but definitely spurred on by my desire to get back to the room. Grabbing my helmet bag from behind the seat, I disconnected the cord from my oxygen mask and removed my helmet, the dry Vegas air hitting my face. I picked up my gear, handing it off to my crew chief, then stuffed my classified materials in my G-suit pocket.

Almost home.

I stood in the cockpit, swinging myself to the canopy rail to avoid standing on the seat. I climbed down the ladder, unhooking my harness, letting the boys breathe, doing my postflight walk-around, running my hands on my jet, stroking the metal. I finished everything up, an edgy energy filling me as I went back to the squadron and rushed through the debrief, struggling to concentrate with the knowledge of what awaited me on the other side.

I went home to the girl waiting for me in bed.

JORDAN

I heard the sound of the key card sliding into the electronic lock, my heart pounding with anticipation.

Noah had to wake up early this morning so we'd gone to bed at 10 p.m. last night. Well, he'd gone to bed. I'd lain awake, a million thoughts running through my mind on loop, struggling to get it together, to figure out how I was going to get on a plane and fly back to Florida leaving all this behind me.

Yeah, I still didn't have an answer to that one.

I had to get back. My partner, Sophia, was working the store and watching my dog, Lulu, but it was only a temporary arrangement. It wasn't like I could duck out on my responsibilities. Even if I wanted to.

I'd spent the morning packing, waiting for Noah to come back from his flight before I headed to the airport, and now he was here, and holy hell, I was not prepared for the sight in front of me.

I'd been asleep when he'd gone to work in the morning, so I'd missed the opportunity to see him in a flight suit. Now that I'd made up for that and experienced him in his full glory, I knew it was an image I'd likely never forget.

Noah opened his mouth to speak, staring at me kneeling on the bed, and I held up a hand in the air, cutting him off.

"I'm gonna need you to just stand there for a moment."

He cocked his head to the side, a gleam entering his gaze.

"You know how guys get off on pictures of topless girls with their legs spread and like a cherry hanging from their mouth?"

His eyes went dark, a delicious tension filling the air around us as he nodded slowly.

"This is my version of a *Playboy* magazine and you're basically Miss February."

Noah's lips curved. I wasn't kidding.

I came up on my knees, crawling to the edge of the bed, sinking back on my heels, his body close enough that I could reach out and touch it if I wanted to. Which I didn't. Not yet, at least. Right now I wanted to burn this image into my brain.

He wore a green flight suit covered in patches and Velcro and all kinds of interesting zippers and pockets that hugged his tall frame in all the right places, his legs seeming longer, his shoulders broader. His sleeves were rolled up to expose tanned, muscular forearms, his wrist adorned with the watch I had previously thought capable of conducting missions to the moon, and now knowing what he did for a living, probably wasn't that far off.

His feet were covered in rugged green boots, a blue hat in his hand, which I figured was another part of his ensemble. His flight suit was unzipped a bit, exposing a khaki-colored T-shirt underneath, the zipper that ran down the entire front of his flight suit, from neck to crotch, a temptation I couldn't ignore.

His eyes locked on to me like he was devouring me, even as he stood as I'd asked him, his lips firm, his jaw tight, his hair just a bit messy.

I rose up on my knees, crooking a finger at him, beckoning him closer, my nipples already pebbling with the promise of what was to come.

Noah stalked toward the bed, his gaze intent on me dressed in his T-shirt, which I'd slept in the night before. He stopped so close that our bodies touched and I swayed a bit toward him, unsteady on my knees as I reached out and stroked the patch on his shoulder, a gold leaf-looking object.

"What's that?"

"Major rank."

I trailed my hand down to his chest, tracing the stitching on the patch with his name, Noah Miller, and his call sign, Burn. I moved over to his shoulder, to the patch with the lettering that said "Aces Wild" and had a picture of an F-16 on it.

"And this one?"

"Squadron patch. Our squadron is the Wild Aces."

I touched the patch on his other shoulder, reading the words there.

"This one?"

"It says that I graduated weapons school." He grinned. "And yes, as much as it pains me to admit it, it is kind of like the Air Force's version of *Top Gun*."

My eyes gleamed. "So you're kind of a badass."

His hand reached out, skimming under the hem of the T-shirt, palming my ass, squeezing, molding me against his cock.

A hiss escaped my mouth.

He quirked a brow at me. "If I said yes, would it help me get laid?"

I gave him a teasing smile, my eyes smoldering. I leaned in closer, my lips grazing his ear, my words a whisper.

"You were always going to get laid. The flight suit, and the patches, and your general badassness just mean that later on, when I'm by myself, turned on and needing relief, it's going to be your face I see when I have my hand between my legs."

He groaned, his grip on me tightening, and then the next

thing I knew, my back hit the mattress and six feet, two inches of aroused fighter pilot mounted me and took the fantasy to a whole other level.

He still smelled like Noah, but there was another scent there, too—a combination of gasoline, sweat, and metal that was sexy as hell. His flight suit felt scratchy against my skin, my fingers fumbling for the zipper between us, tugging it down until I had a hand in his boxers, stroking him, and he groaned again, burying his face in my neck.

There was something different in the way he kissed me this time, how his hands pulled my hair, and he nearly ripped the shirt off me. It was in me, spurring me on as my heels dug into his back, as I gripped the open sides of his flight suit, hauling him toward me so I could feast on his mouth. My fingernails scraped at his skin, my hips seeking his, every part of my body desperate to collide with him.

There was no foreplay here, no laughter, no sweetness.

There was desperation.

Need and want sharpened to a knifepoint that stabbed me over and over again until I ached.

I wasn't ready to walk away from this, wasn't ready to let go. And yet, somehow, I had to get on a plane and leave all of this—him—behind.

Zippers and Velcro dug into my skin, and I craved the bite, wanted the marks to last on my skin. Wanted to remember every single second of this when I feared it would soon all feel like a dream.

Noah reared back, leaving me spread open on the bed, chest panting, skin flushed, mouth swollen. He grabbed a condom, sliding it on, his flight suit unzipped, boxers open, *gah*.

He pulled me to the edge of the bed, his fingers stroking my clit, dipping into the wetness there, and then he replaced his touch with his cock as he thrust into me, hard, his hands coming to rest on either side of my hips, holding me in place as he began fucking me in earnest.

I came undone.

There was nothing to do but hold on for the ride, nothing to do but get swept up in Noah. When I came, I came hard, my arms and legs wrapped around him like I never wanted to let go.

NOAH

I stood outside the base hotel, Jordan's bags on the ground next to us, taxi waiting, staring down at her face, our bodies entwined, my feet lead, every instinct screaming at me not to let go.

I felt raw inside after the sex we'd had, although "sex" seemed too tame a word for it. I felt scraped, and scratched, and hollowed out. Like I'd gone a round with the centrifuge and lost.

I ran a finger down her jaw, tracing her face, ending at her mouth, my thumb brushing back and forth against her fuck-me lips.

"When can I see you again?"

I wasn't fucking around. Not after everything, and *definitely* not after what had just happened between us in bed.

Her lips curved against my fingers.

"When do you want to see me again?" she asked.

"What are you doing this weekend?"

A beat of silence passed and then her smile widened.

"You?"

Relief flooded me. God, I adored this girl.

"Unfortunately, I can't get leave with such short notice, but if I bought you a plane ticket, could you come out to Oklahoma? For the weekend?"

She hesitated for a second. "The store's open, but between Sophia and the staff, we could probably cover it."

"So you'll come?"

She nodded, her gaze on me. "I'll come."

Yes.

I captured her mouth, putting everything I had into the kiss, giving her the kind of good-bye that I hoped would keep the memory of us alive until I could see her again. When I couldn't stall any longer, I pulled back, unable to resist the urge to stroke her hair.

"I'm sorry I can't see you off at the airport. Stupid meeting."

She smiled. "It's cool. You more than made up for it with the send-off you gave me."

"Let me know you landed safely, okay?" I murmured against her mouth. "I'll call you tonight."

Jordan leaned up, pressing a soft kiss to my cheek, her lips cool against my skin.

"I will. Be safe, Noah. I'll see you Friday."

I squeezed her hand and then released her fingers, watching as she got into the cab, as the door shut behind her. I stood there as the cab drove away, farther and farther, until it was nothing but a speck on the landscape.

And then it was gone and the knot in my chest grew, until I reminded myself that even though this felt like good-bye, it was something else entirely. It was the beginning.

Just four days and then I'd have her back again.

$\mathcal{N}$INE

JORDAN

I felt like a different person getting off the plane in Florida. It was strange—parts of me were still the same and yet they felt so altered. It was like everything was divided into halves—the *before* and the *after*. And Noah was somewhere in the center, turning my world upside down.

I walked into my boutique, The Sassy Seahorse, the next morning, coffee in one hand, a bag of croissants from the bakery next door in the other.

We had the best location, one Sophia and I had spent weeks searching for. It wasn't cheap, but it gave us amazing foot traffic from tourists and locals. Our town, Seaspray, wasn't big, but it had the cutest beach area that drew a crowd during Florida's nearly nonexistent winters and postcard-like summers. Little shops lined the streets, all locally owned boutiques with colorful awnings and cute names that incorporated alliteration and some form of marine animal and catered to a mix of wealthy locals and tourists who were so filled with gratitude to be out of snow and below-freezing temperatures that they happily parted with seventy dollars for a bathing suit.

Our boutique sat a block from the beach, so close that you could smell the salty air, sandwiched in between The Coral Cupcake, a bakery known for incorporating cute beach-themed designs on some of the best baked goods in the world, and The Preppy Pelican, a kid's clothing store that I'd already mentally spent a small fortune at in preparation for Mike and Meg eventually having kids.

The front door swung closed behind me and the sight of brightly colored dresses, metallic sandals, and bikinis with funky prints hit me full-force. It might have been late February, but it was Florida and the tourists were already coming in droves, flocking toward one part of the country that wasn't besieged by winter. It was early, but it was already shaping up to be a very good year.

I set my bag down behind the register, going through the motions of opening the store. Sophia had closed the night before so there wasn't a ton of straightening up to do. Just turning on the register, flicking on lights, making sure everything was neat and in its proper place.

We were open six days a week, from ten in the morning until six in the evening. We'd fidgeted with our hours before finding the perfect combination that worked with our sleepy town. This part of the state wasn't the get-drunk-and-take-your-top-off Florida that you saw on news programs lambasting the debauchery of spring break. No, this was quiet Florida, the home of the early bird special, the kind of town where families moved because it was a good place to raise kids.

My parents were third generation, and I'd never considered living anywhere else. I'd gone away for college, but my family was here, and I was a Florida girl through and through. I'd figured I'd meet some guy and we'd get engaged and then married, and settle down here, and it would be the perfect place to raise our kids. I just hadn't planned on how long I'd be searching, or considered the fact that while this was a great place to raise kids, it was a really shitty place to be single. There wasn't any nightlife to speak of, and more and more of my contemporaries were heading farther south in search of better jobs and a more affordable cost of living.

Making my dating pool even smaller.

I finished tidying up minutes before the seahorse-shaped clock on the wall hit ten. I walked over to the entrance, flipping the sign in the front window and propping the door open.

They came in droves.

The awesome thing about living in a small town was that it genuinely felt like a family. I'd known most of our customers since I was a kid, and we had a loyal base that came to stock their wardrobes. And everyone knew we'd been to Vegas, so of course, they all came in wanting details.

I was telling my fifth person about Meg's bachelorette when Sophia strolled in with my dog, Lulu.

Best part of owning your own boutique?

The ability to bring your dog to work whenever you wanted.

Lulu's entry was accompanied by the usual noises and exclamations that came whenever anyone saw her. She was quite possibly the cutest dog I'd ever seen, and while I might not have been the most impartial source considering I loved her like a child, the attention she garnered confirmed my feelings.

She had short legs and a squat body that looked like a cross between a pug and a dachshund. Her face was all beagle, her fur covered in black and white spots that made people ask me if she was a mini-Dalmatian. Her tail was possibly her best feature. It wagged constantly in an enthusiastic thump that had been known to whack you if you got too close. She wore a pink rhinestone collar that gave her a stately look and an air of royalty.

She was pretty badass.

I crouched down and she ran toward me, hopping up on her hind legs, her paws on my thighs, covering my face in doggy kisses.

I seriously loved my dog.

"I missed you so much," I crooned, making ridiculous baby noises that had her tail beating even harder.

I picked her up, wincing a bit at her increased heft. She loved treats, and Sophia definitely had the indulgent aunt role down.

I hugged Sophia. "Thanks for taking care of her. And for holding down the fort. The store looks amazing."

Sophia grinned. "No problem. It was my pleasure." She leaned forward and gave Lulu a kiss. "Next time, I might not give her back, though. She's the best sleeping buddy I've ever had."

"Yes, she is." I made more kissy noises that had Lulu squirming in my arms trying to give me another few licks. Finally I set her down on the floor, watching as she waddled over to the pink velvet pillow Sophia had bought her for Christmas last year. She plopped down, curling her body up so that she could keep watch on her humans and on the store that had become her domain.

"So what did I miss?" I asked, heading behind the cash register.

"We got in that new bathing suit line we ordered. The striped bikinis? They're cute, right? I grabbed one."

They were cute. A little preppier than what I normally

wore, but definitely Sophia's style. I trended toward kitsch and she was more elegant, but it gave the store an eclectic feel.

"Anything else?"

"I think we might need to hire some extra help before the summer if things keep going the way they are. At least for Saturdays."

We'd kept our staff pretty small in the first couple years to minimize expenses. Sophia and I were both single so it hadn't been that difficult for us to work all the time. Little by little, we'd grown the business to include a manager and five part-timers.

"I'll put out some feelers and see if anyone is looking."

Sophia grinned. "Okay, enough business talk. Let's get to the good stuff. How was Vegas?"

I'd always been that girl. The one who bitched about guys with her friends over drinks. The one who sent frantic texts from the bathroom on dates with messages like, *He invited me back to his place, but it's only our second date, HELP*. Sophia knew every single detail of my dating life; nothing was off-limits. So I was shocked when I heard myself respond with—

"It was good."

"That's it? Good?"

Good didn't even begin to cover.it, but I didn't know where to start—although I was going to have to say something soon because I definitely needed her to cover me this weekend.

"It was a little better than good," I hedged.

I didn't know why I was being so weird about this. I could have just said: *I met this really hot guy, and he was amazing in bed, and I think I like him. Like* really *like him.* But I didn't. I wasn't ready for the questions; for the first time in my life, I didn't want to dissect our every conversation or the meaning behind whether he held my hand or not. I just wanted to enjoy it.

I cleared my throat, ready to come up with some excuse for why I needed the weekend off, when two-dozen pink roses did it for me.

Our gazes whipped to the front door and the man walking into the store in a delivery uniform, holding a stunning bouquet in a vase. My heart clenched, unable to look away. I didn't need to read the card to know who they were from.

Definite Chupacabra.

The deliveryman stopped in front of us. "Is there a Jordan Callahan here?"

I could feel my cheeks flaming, my stomach fluttering like a flock of geese had permanently taken up residence in my gut.

"I'm Jordan," I squeaked, Sophia's stare burning a hole through me.

I took the flowers and set them on the counter next to the register, my fingers itching to open the little white card in between all that pink and green.

"Good, huh?" Sophia's brow rose. "I think you left a few things out."

"Maybe a few."

I couldn't wait any longer; impulse control had never been one of my strengths. I snatched the card out of the bouquet, tearing open the little white envelope with the impatience of a child opening gifts on Christmas morning. I stared down at the writing, my heartbeat kicking up another notch.

I miss you.

It wasn't poetry. It wasn't even the most romantic thing

a guy had ever said to me. And still, somehow, those three words *did* feel like the most romantic thing ever. Maybe it wasn't about the words; maybe all that mattered was who gave them to you.

I turned toward Sophia, a smile on my face. "Can you cover for me this weekend?"

NOAH

She'd only spent one night in my hotel room at Nellis and yet she'd left her mark. When I walked in the door, I felt a pang of disappointment to not see Jordan sitting on the bed smiling at me. Housekeeping hadn't changed the sheets since she left and I could still smell her shampoo on the pillow, her perfume surrounding me. Maybe it was those taunting scents that had made me send her that card with the flowers.

I'd debated whether it was too much to tell her I missed her this soon; it had only been a day, after all. But I did miss her. And while I'd spent plenty of years keeping my distance in relationships, not wanting to lead a girl on or create the impression that I was ready to give more than I could, it felt different with Jordan. Maybe it was getting older and being a little tired of dating, but I didn't want to play games anymore. I wanted her, wanted to see where this was going, and I didn't want to fuck around.

I sat on the edge of the bed, unlacing my boots, pulling them off, another wave of exhaustion hitting me. My socks came next, and then I unzipped my flight suit to the waist, shrugging out of the top half, the familiar pull of the zipper conjuring images of Jordan kneeling in front of me in bed, the curve of her ass barely visible beneath the hem of my shirt.

I figured it would be a while before I could put on or take off my flight suit without thinking of fucking her in it. I might have been tired, but other parts of my body decidedly were not.

I pulled my cell out of my flight suit pocket. It was late in Florida, but I'd promised to call Jordan when I got back from my sortie. I pulled her number up in my contacts and hit Call, hoping it wasn't too late.

She answered right away.

"Hi."

My chest tightened a bit at the sound of her voice—sleepy and adorable. We'd only spent two nights together, but I could still imagine her curled up in bed, her hair fanned out over her pillow.

I leaned back against the headboard, settling in to the image of Jordan doing the same.

"Hi, babe. Did I wake you?"

"No. I was just lying here waiting for you to call."

It felt good. Really good. Most of the time I came home from work to an empty house; occasionally, I found Easy in front of the TV. It felt good to have someone to talk to, even if there was a country between us. Even when I would have preferred her next to me, tucked against my side, her tits and ass cuddled into me.

My balls tightened.

"How was your day?" I asked.

"Good. Someone sent me the most beautiful flowers."

I grinned. "I'm glad you liked them."

"I loved them. You were the talk of the town this afternoon. Word spread like wildfire and people kept coming into the shop to ask me about the man who sent me roses."

I laughed.

"I'm not kidding. I sold like two dresses and three bathing suits off of flower foot traffic alone. I probably owe you a commission."

"I could think of a few things I'd rather have instead."

Her laughter filled the line, throaty and sexy, and I came to terms with the fact that while I might have been exhausted, my dick was wide-fucking-awake and ready to play.

"Really?" she teased.

The word escaped with a purr.

Jesus.

Part of me didn't want to get my hopes up and assume phone sex was on the menu, but I was starting to think *phone sex was on the menu.*

"You have no idea how badly I want to fuck you right now," I half whispered, half groaned.

Her breath hitched on the other end of the line. "Tell me. How do you want to fuck me?"

Dead. This girl slayed me.

"Spread your legs."

I shifted onto my side, holding the phone between my shoulder and ear, my hand slipping beneath my boxers, fisting my cock.

"What are you wearing?"

"A lace camisole and a thong."

Instant visual. I could practically see her tits straining against the fabric, the outline of her nipples so tight, could imagine taking one into my mouth and sucking hard, watching it flush with color as I teased her, could see the outline of it, shiny with my saliva. Marked.

I stroked up and down, my cock jerking against my palm.

"I want your hand between your legs."

She gave a breathy sigh.

"Stroke yourself over your thong. Finger your clit."

I closed my eyes, imagining her lying there, her legs spread open as though she were waiting to be fucked, playing with herself.

"I want to watch you like that one time. Just want to sit in a chair and watch you get yourself off. There's nothing like you coming. Most beautiful fucking thing I've ever seen."

"God, Noah."

"Play with your nipples with your free hand."

I heard Jordan adjusting in the bed, imagined her in a similar position to me. I'd learned enough about her body in the short time we'd been together to visualize her back arching as she played with her tits, could imagine her writhing as she fingered herself. The visual was . . . fuck me. My hand pumped harder, my teeth sinking down on my lower lip with a sharp bite.

"Are you wet?"

She gave another breathy sigh that I felt in my dick.

"Yes."

"Slide your hand under your thong. I want to hear you fucking yourself with your fingers. Want to imagine you lying there, playing with your clit, all that heat."

I remembered the feel of her perfectly—slippery and wet, so fucking warm.

"If I were there right now, I'd have my mouth between your legs."

Jordan groaned.

"Even if I wanted to, I wouldn't be content to just sit there and watch. I'd have to taste you. I'd bury my face in your pussy, licking every drop. You'd be amazing. So fucking sweet. I'd want to savor your orgasm on my tongue, watch you shatter against my mouth."

She groaned again and I increased my pace, images of fucking Jordan flashing through my mind, the memory of squeezing her ass in my hands, of her sinking down on my cock, riding me, her body milking mine as she took what she wanted, bringing me closer and closer to my own release.

"I'm so close," she whispered.

"Are you going to come for me?"

I needed to hear it, needed to give her that. Needed to know she'd fall into sleep sated from the orgasm I'd wrung from her.

"Y-yes."

"Good."

We stopped talking, the only sound between us the quickening breaths and muffled beats of us chasing our orgasms. And then she moaned, and I listened as she found what she was searching for. I came a minute later, imagining it was her body surrounding me, her hands, her mouth giving me the release I craved.

I fell asleep drowning in her and woke up the next morning with a smile on my face.

TEN

JORDAN

Get up. Get up.

I stared at the woman sitting next to me, willing her to rise from her seat. She ignored me.

Ahead of us, rows and rows of people began deplaning; behind us, another line waited with no gap in sight. If she didn't claim her place in the aisle to exit the plane, we'd be relegated to the very last ones off, which normally I wouldn't care about, but considering who I had waiting for me . . .

I cared a lot.

I waited, waited . . . *fuck*. We were going to be the last ones off.

It was literally a difference of a few more minutes, but even with the phone sex—which seemed to get better each night—this week had already felt like an eternity. I wanted to see Noah, and considering patience was not a virtue I possessed, I wanted to see him now.

She turned to face me with a conspiratorial smile.

Yes, get off the plane.

"People these days. Everyone's in a hurry. I'd rather wait until the plane is totally empty. No need to rush and push."

No. No. No.

I'd had a lifetime of Southern gentility drilled into me, and while a lot of it didn't take, some of it was inescapable. Like always being polite to strangers.

I flashed her a smile, despite the voice screaming in my head.

Let me off this plane.

I sat patiently, or as patiently as anyone could with their foot tapping a mile a minute, until finally it was our turn, and we were indeed the last ones off the plane.

And then impatience gave way to nerves. Lots and lots of nerves.

What if my memory was better than the reality? What if this was a mistake? What if we didn't have chemistry this time? What if he wasn't attracted to me? Did my outfit look okay? Should I have worn my hair up? Did I have too much makeup on? Did I have too little makeup on?

Commence freak-out.

Everything about this was making me a little nuts all of a sudden. I'd flown across the country to see a guy I'd known for, like, three days. And by "known," really I was talking biblically. I didn't even know him all that well. And given my track record, the odds of me fucking this up were not small.

What was I thinking?

Fuck. Fuck. Fuck.

I cursed in time with my steps, profanity flitting through my mind each time my sole touched the floor until it became a catchy little tune in my head.

The arrival area loomed closer and closer, and I searched the crowd for Noah, remembering that he'd said he might have to pick me up straight from work, wondering if he was running late . . .

And then I saw him.

Flight suit. Big fucking smile. Roses. Nerves gone.

I launched myself at him, my purse flailing inelegantly behind me. He didn't shy away, didn't act like he was embarrassed to be seen with the girl who had no concern for appropriate behavior. Instead, he caught me mid-laugh, my arms wrapped around his neck as he gripped my waist, hauling me toward him. His mouth came down on mine and my lips parted instantly and then his tongue was inside me and it took every inch of willpower I possessed to keep from hopping up and climbing him like a vine on a wall.

I settled for a kiss.

I had not been wrong. This kiss lived up to every memory of us I had. This kiss was unreal.

We broke apart what felt like minutes later, Noah's lips swollen, his mouth curved in a satisfied grin. His hand settled just above my ass, possessive, teasing, hot as hell.

He stared down at me, his eyes dancing. "Hey."

Maybe it was the phone sex, but his voice triggered some feelings in my lady parts.

"Hi."

We both stood there like idiots, grinning at each other, and then he took my hand and propelled me toward the baggage claim.

"In a hurry?" I called after him, his long strides eating up the carpet.

He flashed me a grin. "You have no idea."

I followed Noah over the threshold, my gaze taking in all the little details, all of the pieces that made up his life.

He lived in a one-story house in a quiet subdivision with brick homes and decent-sized lots. It had a family-friendly vibe to it, which wasn't what I would have predicted for a single fighter pilot, but it definitely impressed me. I'd seen my share of gross boy apartments, and while his artwork tended to have a single-focus—pretty kick-ass framed photos of planes at various stages of flight—there were no dirty clothes on the floor, no empty beer bottles on end tables.

"Hey, Jordan."

I spotted Easy sitting on a leather sectional in the family room, watching a movie on a ginormous TV. Noah had mentioned that he owned the house and Easy lived with him.

"Hey."

Easy rose as I walked toward him, enfolding me in a quick hug. He gestured to a spot on the sectional.

"Sit."

I kind of wanted to go bone Noah in his bedroom, but Southern manners and all . . .

I sat down, Noah not bothering to cover up the groan that escaped his lips as he sat down next to me, placing my suitcase on the floor.

Easy looked down at my luggage and shot me a teasing grin. "Planning on staying awhile?"

My cheeks flamed. Yes, maybe I had overpacked. It hadn't been easy deciding what to bring. I had a mixture of sexy dresses that were basically a nuclear arsenal in and of themselves, casual jeans and sweaters that were designed to convey the image that I wasn't trying too hard or anything, and a fortune in lingerie that was definitely trying too hard, but I was pretty sure Noah would appreciate a hell of a lot . . . if Easy ever let us go.

Noah shot him a look. "Like you don't spend a fucking hour getting ready in the morning."

Easy winked at me. "He's jealous. He wishes he could be this pretty."

I snorted. The guy totally owned how full of shit he was. You had to appreciate that, at least.

Noah wrapped an arm around my shoulders, pulling me against his body. I felt ab ridges.

Gah.

He ducked his head so that his lips tickled my ear, his words loud enough for Easy to hear. "You look amazing in whatever you wear, babe."

I went a little melty.

Easy laughed.

"So how was the rest of your Vegas trip?" I asked, wanting to get off the subject of my gargantuan suitcase pronto.

"Good," Noah answered. "We had a few jets break getting back, so some guys are stuck out there still, but not exactly a hardship. There are a lot worse places you can get stuck."

Easy made a face. "I'm still pissed about getting stuck in the desert." His gaze shifted to me. "I had to make an emergency landing in a neighboring country when we deployed to the Mideast. It was intense." He gestured toward Noah. "Meanwhile, these guys got back and took leave and went diving in the Caymans."

"Does that happen a lot? Uh, jets breaking?"

I knew nothing about planes, but that kind of sounded like a big deal.

Easy snorted. "We're flying planes that were built when some of us were born, so yeah. It happens. Not to mention, the maintainers have to do their part. Maintenance has been on its ass since we left for Red Flag."

"So when you say jets break, are you guys flying them when this happens?"

Noah answered. "It depends. Sometimes it breaks before we take off and we have to step to another jet. Other times you can have a problem when you're in the air."

"What do you do then?"

"Depends on the problem. We have a checklist and procedures we go through in the event of an emergency. Some stuff isn't a big deal; other stuff is a lot worse. Our job is to make the right judgment call and decide whether we should stick with the mission, fly home, divert to the nearest runway, or eject."

I didn't like the sound of "a lot worse." Or "eject." I didn't like the sound of any of this. Or the way they casually discussed the plane "breaking" like it wasn't a big deal. I guessed it came with the territory, but that didn't make it any less intense. My idea of risk-seeking behavior was eating more cookies than the recommended serving size or making out with strangers on a dance floor. It wasn't this casual disregard for personal safety.

"Have you ever ejected?" I asked Noah, not sure I wanted to hear the answer.

He shook his head.

My gaze drifted to Easy. "You?"

"Only if she isn't cute." He grinned. "Sorry. Pilot humor."

Wow, it was surprising that he could fit in the cockpit with a head that big.

Noah squeezed my leg. "I'm going to go change, okay? I'll be right back."

I was a little sad to see the flight suit go, but I nodded.

Easy jerked his head toward the kitchen. "Do you want a beer?"

I hesitated and then nodded again, feeling like I needed the liquid courage. I didn't know what it was, but I had a hard time feeling comfortable around Easy. Maybe it was how hot he was or the fact that he so clearly knew it and knew that everyone else knew it, too. Noah was hot, but in a less obvious, cocky way. Easy was in-your-fucking-face. And some part of me had been trained since puberty not to trust a guy who was too good looking. I found it hard to believe that Noah would be friends with a guy who was a dick, but the verdict was still out on Easy.

He got up from the couch, his long legs encased in worn denim, wearing a ratty-looking navy T-shirt, striding to the kitchen. A minute later he returned with a beer dangling from his hands. I wasn't a huge beer drinker, but I didn't really want to stand out as being high maintenance. Or more high maintenance than I already appeared to be.

My outfit, for one, was admittedly a little over the top. I'd channeled my motto of "go big or go home" when dressing for the flight. I'd ended up with a tight pair of ripped jeans, in a look that was basically, "I did a drummer last night," and had gotten me some side-eye as I'd strutted through the airport—justifiably so. They were also a little tough to walk in considering I could barely breathe, but hey, fashion was pain, right? Because I apparently didn't give a fuck, I'd paired the jeans with stiletto boots that walked the thin line between high fashion and hooker. I wore a low-cut sweater and I'd teased my hair out into fat curls that spilled down my back. It was totally over the top, but it was also kind of me, and given the appreciation that had flashed in Noah's eyes, it was definitely the look I was going for.

I took the beer from Easy, taking a sip, silence yawning between us. It was the kind of silence that spoke volumes, and I figured he knew I didn't like him. I also figured he didn't give a shit. Okay, maybe that wasn't fair, and maybe I was wrong to judge a book by its cover, especially considering mine sort of screamed bimbo.

I took a sip of my beer. "Sorry to show up last minute. I'm sure you're tired from being gone for so long and it's probably a pain to have someone staying here right after you got back."

Easy shrugged. "It was important to Noah."

"You guys are really close, aren't you?"

He nodded. "We were roommates in college. We've been close ever since. He's like a brother."

"He seems like a really good guy."

Easy smiled, and without the smirk, he appeared a little more approachable. "Yeah, he is."

I searched for something else to talk about, but came up short. I figured it wasn't great if I alienated the best friend, but for some reason I couldn't relax around him. And I couldn't tell if he approved of me or not. There was something shrewd in his gaze that gave the impression that his devil-may-care attitude was more show than anything else.

Yeah, the verdict was definitely still out on Easy.

"He likes you a lot."

I opened my mouth to speak—no clue what I was going to say—and then we were interrupted by Noah walking back in the room, wearing jeans and a T-shirt.

He shot Easy a look that made me wonder if he'd heard our conversation—*so awkward*—and then he was back on the couch next to me, tucking my body against him.

We sat there for a few more minutes, half watching the movie Easy had playing, half chatting, and then Noah leaned down and whispered in my ear.

"Do you want to go to bed?"

I nodded, not sure I trusted my voice to speak.

Easy gave us a knowing grin that had my cheeks flaming again—*fucker*.

Noah pulled me up from the couch, taking my hand and

leading me down a hallway with more airplane pictures, which I was beginning to think were some form of guy porn. We passed by a few closed doors, my heart picking up with each step we took.

"I'll give you the grand tour tomorrow, okay?"

I nodded.

Noah opened a door at the end of the hall, stepping back so I could enter first, and then the door closed behind us, and I was in his arms, my back to his front, his hand sweeping my hair away, his lips grazing the sensitive hollow between my shoulder and my neck.

My head rolled back and the rest of my nerves slid away.

NOAH

I descended on her like a ravenous man presented with his last meal. And if she were food, she'd be a fucking filet mignon.

The jeans were something beyond hot, showcasing her long legs, hugging her ass. Her tits were high and perky, and I'd been dying to get my hands on her all night. Not to mention the hair, and the heels, and the way she'd strutted through the Oklahoma City airport like she was a fucking rockstar.

As great as the body was, the attitude was everything.

I was seriously hooked by this girl.

She smelled amazing—her scent different than what I'd remembered in Vegas, but somehow the perfect complement to the bombshell look she had going on.

I was going to fuck her all night long.

Jordan pushed back against my body, grinding her ass against my cock. I was already hard as a fucking rock. I groaned, nipping her skin, my tongue following my teeth, the movement tearing a shudder from her body. My hand found the top of her sweater, slipped under the cup of her bra, and then I was squeezing her breast, rolling her nipple between my thumb and forefinger, getting off on the little throaty moans she made, the way her hips arched against me like she was as desperate as I was.

"I can't go slow now. I'll go slowly later. Promise."

I ground out the words, my hands already taking over, tugging at her sweater, pulling it off, cupping her breasts, *fuck me*, sliding down the soft skin, down her stomach, until I reached the snap of her jeans, fumbling with the button before dragging the zipper down and slipping my hand inside her thong.

I found her clit, stroking her, once, twice, before going lower, needing to fill her up. I slid a finger inside her, the friction not nearly enough, my cock jerking as she rode my hand. She turned in my arms, attacking my clothes like a woman possessed, sliding down my body, her mouth following the path her hands took.

It all became a haze, sharpened by random sensations— her teeth on my pec, her nails streaking down my back, the rasp of a zipper, the soft thunk of clothes hitting the floor.

Somehow we got naked and then she was bent over the bed, her palms on the comforter, feet on the ground, ass in the air, looking like every fantasy I'd ever had. Hell, I was pretty sure this image would be burned in my brain for eternity.

I grabbed a condom from my jeans' pocket, tearing open the foil wrapper and sliding it on, my hands shaking with the movement. And then I was sliding inside *her*, my hands on her hips, pulling her closer while I fucked her hard.

It felt like forever, and at the same time, like the blink of an eye. There were no words, nothing but the joining of our bodies speaking a frenzied beat. And then she was coming, and I was coming, and our bodies collapsed in a heap on the bed, and I knew without question that she had ruined me for all other women.

$\mathcal{E}$LEVEN

JORDAN

It was ridiculously ironic that when I was twenty, my body was capable of sexual acrobatics, only to be relegated to partners who came after a minute and whose repertoire didn't extend past missionary. Now that I was thirty, I'd found a man whose art was fucking, and of course, my body felt like it had been run over by a truck. Twice.

I'd possibly done something to my back. And there was a kink I couldn't work out of my neck no matter how hard I tried. And I was hobbling. Sort of. If you looked up the phrase "Rode hard and put up wet," you'd see a picture of my wincing face, my torso slightly hunched over to take some of the pressure off my aching back.

Death by orgasms.

It was the kind of thing I normally would have found hilarious, except I was beginning to realize there was nothing funny about sex injuries. And I probably needed to haul my ass to a gym.

I padded to the kitchen, following the smell of coffee, not sure I was ready to face Noah, but definitely sure I couldn't handle getting pounced on again. I figured the odds of Easy walking in on us would help keep us away from each other.

Fingers crossed.

I hit the kitchen and caught sight of Noah leaning against the countertop, draining a giant sports drink, his Adam's apple bobbing in a way that had my gaze going straight to his tanned neck. And then lower . . .

Jesus, take the wheel.

Apparently he'd gone for a run—was he human?—and lost his T-shirt somewhere along the way. His chest was bare, a pair of low-slung athletic shorts clinging to his thighs. A glimmer of sweat coated his skin.

I took a step back.

Another round would kill me. We needed space. And public places.

Noah set the drink down, his gaze settling on me, a slow smile spreading across his gorgeous mouth. He took a step toward me.

I took another step back. I lifted a hand in the air.

"No more sex."

He stopped, his hands on his hips, head cocked to the side, a different sort of smile playing on his lips.

"What?"

I shook my head. "I need a sex break. A moratorium. A hiatus. A chastity pact. And you need to stay in your corner." I gestured toward the cabinets. "Space, good. Touching, bad."

The smile widened. "You're sexy as fuck when you're being neurotic."

No. No.

"I'm serious. I think you broke my vagina." And my back. Not to mention my freaking neck. And there was this twinge in my hip . . . maybe that was what the hobbling was about.

Noah exploded into laughter, and in a flash his arms were around me, burrowing me against his muscular, sweaty, *fuck* . . .

"Do you need me to kiss it and make it better?" he whispered in my ear, his voice teasing.

I groaned. "I need you to not have sex with me for twenty-four hours. I mean, twelve. Okay, fine, eight."

He pulled back, his eyes dancing with amusement. "How about I jump in the shower . . ."

Roll tongue back into mouth.

"And then I take you to breakfast. There's a really good pancake place a few miles up the road."

My gaze drifted down the impressive abs, held, and then back up to his face again. "You eat pancakes?"

This time he leaned into me, brushing my hair off my face, pressing his lips to the top of my head.

"No, but you do. And if I can't keep you satisfied with the tools at my disposal . . ." He flashed me a wicked grin that brought a little spasm between my thighs. "Extraordinary times call for extraordinary measures."

His lips were on me again, all too brief and fleeting, and then he was gone, walking down the hall to take his shower. I stood in the kitchen, my gaze glued to his back and the ass that I kind of wanted to bite.

It really was a snowy day in hell when pancakes were starting to look like the consolation prize.

They so were.

NOAH

I held Jordan's hand as we walked toward the restaurant, our fingers linked, the same smile I'd had since I saw her this morning still on my mouth.

I couldn't remember the last time I'd dated a girl that I'd smiled this much around, if ever. Or that I'd felt this way about. Maybe it was fast, but I knew without a doubt that I wanted to move this into the relationship zone.

She was fucking hilarious. Smart. Sexy as hell. Gorgeous. Kind. She was everything I could have ever wanted in a girl and a few things I hadn't realized I wanted, but now that I had them, I wanted to hold on tight.

I had no idea what the future held, but this was the kind of girl I could see myself having a future with. The kind of girl who would greet me when I returned home from deployments with her arms and legs wrapped around me. This was the kind of girl that if you were smart, and played your cards right, you changed your life for.

I held the door open for her, unable to resist admiring the view despite her no-sex edict. She'd gone for casual, but considering the way she filled out her jeans, casual made a statement.

The restaurant was packed when we arrived, and I went up to the hostess station and gave my name, and then we stood in the corner of the entryway, waiting for our table to become available.

I squeezed her hand. "Hungry?"

Jordan nodded. "Starving." She tossed me a quizzical look. "So what do you normally eat for breakfast?"

I shrugged. "Oats. Fruit. Yogurt."

She grinned. "Way to live dangerously."

I matched her grin, my voice becoming a parody. "That's right. I am dangerous."

She burst out laughing at the *Top Gun* reference. "Cute. I thought you hated that movie."

"I don't hate the movie. I thought it was the coolest thing I'd ever seen when I was a kid. I couldn't figure out why he wanted to spend so much time with that girl, though."

"And now?" she joked.

"Now that I've been inside you, I can see the appeal. Apparently some things are better than flying," I answered, my tone completely serious.

Her cheeks turned pink.

"You totally can't say things like that to me in public."

I grinned, unable to resist the urge to kiss her.

Jordan pulled back with a breathless sigh, her arm tight around my waist. I stared down into her brown eyes, a pang in my chest as I realized that she would be leaving tomorrow, and I had no idea when I'd see her again. I literally had months of vacation days accumulated, but taking leave was another thing entirely. We were always busy, seemed perpetually undermanned, and even when I gave plenty of notice, there was always some commitment that came up and prevented me from leaving. Joker was a good guy, and he definitely appreciated the importance of taking care of your personal life, but I wasn't sure he could spare me so soon after Red Flag. Especially since we had a TDY to Alaska coming up.

I wanted to go to Florida. Wanted to make an effort to see her, wanted her to know she was a priority. I'd been here before. I mean not *here,* not with someone I liked as much as I liked her, but there had been other girls I'd wanted to date, other attempts at starting relationships that had crashed and burned because no matter how hard I tried, work always came first.

What I hadn't told Jordan was that I'd gotten my call sign in part because of an emergency I'd had in the jet, but also because I was shit at relationships. When I was younger, it had been easier to shrug it off, to tell myself it didn't matter, that I had plenty of time to meet a girl, start a family. And now I felt like an idiot. I was thirty-three, and my life wasn't that different from what it had been a decade ago. Still going out to bars and clubs with Easy, looking to get laid, still spending holidays in front of the TV with crappy takeout on the years that I couldn't make it to California to see my family.

And now there was Jordan. And even though it hadn't been that long, and I had no idea how things would play out between us, she was too perfect for me to ignore the twinge that told me that if I fucked this up with her, the odds of me finding a girl like her again were pretty much nil.

She nudged me. "You okay?"

I nodded. "Yeah." I hesitated, wondering when I'd become the guy who initiated the relationship conversation. Maybe it was a side effect of growing up. Or maybe it was the fear of losing out on this chance.

"I can't believe you have to leave tomorrow."

"I know. It's been a short visit."

I squeezed her hip. "So when am I going to see you again?"

A hesitant smile played at her full mouth. "You want to see me again?"

"Yes."

The smile got bigger. "Good."

I felt like a teenager again, but it was the truth, and somewhere along the way I'd made the conscious decision not to play games with her.

"I like you. A lot."

She beamed back at me, squeezing my hand. "I like you a lot, too."

"I know this is tough with our schedules and everything, but I want to try to make it work." I couldn't believe I was having this conversation in the entrance of a pancake restaurant, but at the moment I couldn't be bothered to care all that much. "I want to see if there could be a future here."

My heart pounded. On the one hand, we were both definitely at that age when relationships implied settling down. On the other, honestly, I'd been here enough times to be hesitant to make promises I couldn't keep. And she seemed like she understood about my job, but other girls had before her, only to end things when an unexpected deployment came up or I missed the holy trifecta of Valentine's Day–birthday–anniversary.

Jordan leaned toward me, wrapping both of her arms around me, pressing her face to my chest. Her words were muffled there, but I heard them anyway.

"Me, too."

JORDAN

It was way too soon for me to admit this. Way too soon for me even to be feeling it. But I did.

I liked him. A lot. And despite the logistics of it, my heart could definitely see a future with him, even as my head struggled to figure out how to have a future with him without giving up something that mattered a lot to me.

We spent the day doing touristy stuff, Noah showing me around Oklahoma City. I didn't know if it was the fact that he'd basically exhausted me or what, but the sexual tension between us settled to a more manageable level since the first time I'd met him, and instead of thinking about how much I wanted to jump him, I spent most of the day just enjoying his company.

He was really fun and smart. He made me laugh constantly. And he was sweet, affectionate in a way that tugged at my heart.

He held my hand as he led me around the city. When he drove us places in his big SUV, his palm rested on my thigh, not in a sexual way, but like he wanted the reminder that I was next to him. Like he needed it.

With every hour that passed, I fell deeper, harder, and I freaked out a little bit more.

For dinner, he took me to a hole-in-the-wall barbecue restaurant that had amazing brisket.

We were *that* couple—we sat next to each other in the booth, his hand on my thigh. I'd never understood why couples sat like that and even mocked my fair share for looking like they were Velcroed together, but now that I was in the same position, I totally got it.

And liked it. A lot.

"So what does March look like for you?" Noah asked, his fingers stroking my leg through the denim.

Ever since he'd broached the subject of wanting to see me again, I'd thought about my schedule, wondering how many more weekends I could ask Sophia to cover for me and watch Lulu before she got annoyed. I'd definitely done my share of weekend shifts for her, but still, I didn't want to be *that* girl—the one who met a guy and let him take over her life. I'd worked too hard to build my business and was too proud of the store to start flaking.

"Spring break is always busy for us, so the store will

probably be pretty hectic. And my sister's getting married at the end of March."

And I still didn't have a date.

I thought back to our earlier conversation in the pancake restaurant, wondering what exactly Noah meant when he talked about seeing if we had a future. Were we a couple now? It seemed kind of fast, but everything he'd said sort of gave that impression even though he hadn't exactly said the words.

It had been so much easier when I was younger. If I liked a guy, we had the whole boyfriend-girlfriend talk and got it over with. But in my thirties, calling someone my boyfriend just sounded kind of weird, and all the other euphemisms never really sat well with me.

So, yeah. Awkward.

Noah was silent for a second. "I'd like to try to come visit you in Florida."

"I'd really like that."

He smiled. "Good. I can talk to the guy who handles leave for the squadron on Monday and see if there's time for me to get away. Worst case, maybe I can just come in late on a Friday after work and then leave Sunday."

My next question made me nervous, but I couldn't resist the opportunity. I already felt kind of like a loser considering I was an unmarried bridesmaid in my sister's wedding. Having a smoking hot fighter pilot for a date? That'd make up for it.

"Would you want to be my date for my sister's wedding?"

I sort of blurted it out, my heart pounding in my chest. Maybe it was too fast. Maybe he would think it was too much pressure—I mean, my family would be there. He'd already met Meg, but my parents were another matter. I could see him being freaked. I would be freaked.

"If you don't think it's too soon or anything," I added, unable to stave off the word vomit escaping from my lips. "It probably is too soon. And you totally don't have to go. I was just thinking—"

"Jordan?"

I stopped talking.

A smile played at his lips. "I'd love to take you to your sister's wedding. I'll check with the squadron, but I don't think we'll have anything going on around that time so I should be good to go."

The fact that he wasn't scared off by meeting my family filled me with all the warm and fuzzies. Definite Chupacabra.

I gave huge mental thanks to Meg for not dressing us in poufy lime green dresses or something equally hideous. Hopefully, my parents would be too busy marrying off their younger daughter to embarrass their older one. And really, I was pretty sure Noah didn't need to see my parents to get a glimpse of the embarrassing sides of me. I did a pretty good job of that on my own.

"Do I need to wear a tux?"

I nodded.

Meg's wedding was taking place at this gorgeous country club in town. It was black tie, and they'd been planning it for, like, a year. I had no idea how much my parents had spent on it, but I figured a lot. I also figured they were so excited to get a daughter married off and on her way to giving them grandkids, that they hadn't batted an eye at the expense.

"Do you think you could come out again for a visit in March?" Noah asked.

My heart thumped and my voice squeaked with excitement.

"Yeah. Maybe not for a couple weeks so that I can be at the store for the spring break rush, but I should be able to make it happen once things settle down."

He grinned. "Good."

I hesitated, and then went all in.

"So are we dating?"

He laughed. "Yeah."

"Exclusively?"

His gaze sobered. "Do you want to be exclusive?"

So freaking much.

I nodded.

He smiled again.

"Then yeah, we're exclusive."

It wasn't every day that you got a hot wedding date and a boyfriend in one fell swoop. Apparently, my romantic luck was changing. Finally.

$\mathcal{T}$WELVE

JORDAN

The next few weeks were every bit as chaotic as I'd antici-pated. The spring break crowd had come in droves, and while the town had been bursting at the seams, thankfully so was our bank account. Sophia and I extended our normal hours, our lives utterly consumed by the shop. Between that and helping out with last-minute plans for Meg's wedding, I'd barely had time to talk to Noah. He was swamped with work, too, and even though we still talked every day, the conversations were shorter than either one of us liked. It wasn't just difficult to juggle the distance; the time differ-ence and the erratic hours we both worked made finding time to talk even more challenging.

Long distance sucked balls.

"Are you really bringing a date to your sister's wedding?"

I looked up from the bathing suit catalog I was flipping through. My mother stood in the entrance of the store, a slightly manic look on her face, dressed from head to toe in

Lily Pulitzer. She and Meg were pretty much preppy twins. I was the one who totally stuck out like a sore thumb.

"Hi, Mom."

She came over to the register, giving me a quick hug, her gaze running over me as though the existence of a wedding date had somehow altered me physically.

"Who is he?"

So Meg hadn't totally spilled the beans to our parents. I appreciated that, at least. I wasn't entirely sure how to make, *I met a fighter pilot in Vegas a few weeks ago and now we're sort of dating even though he lives across the country,* sound any less crazy. Although, to be fair, I figured they'd be so excited for me to be in a relationship that they wouldn't care too much how it came about.

"He's someone I'm seeing," I answered, keeping my tone evasive. If years of dating had taught me anything, it was not to get my parents' hopes up. Sometimes it seemed like they handled my breakups worse than I did.

"Is he local? I didn't recognize the name."

Ugh. "No, he lives in Oklahoma."

Her brows rose. "And he's coming all the way here to be your date for the wedding?"

Yeah, I'd never get tired of hearing that. I'd had guys that were too lazy to pick me up for dates and suggested that we meet at the restaurant instead, so the fact that one was willing to fly across the country to take me to my sister's wedding was pretty epic.

"Yep."

"How did you meet him?"

I stifled a groan. It was going to come out eventually. "We met in Vegas."

"For your sister's bachelorette?"

Ugh.

"Yes."

"Why didn't Meg tell me that?"

Because likely Meg wanted to spare me the interrogation headed my way. I loved my mother, but she definitely could get a little too involved in my life. Especially my romantic life. She'd married my dad at nineteen and they'd been happily married for like a billion years, so she struggled with my perpetual singledom.

Why can't you just meet a nice boy? was a refrain commonly heard in our house. And now that I had definitely met a nice boy, I wasn't ready to share him with anyone. I didn't want to hear all the ways Noah probably wasn't right for me, because I didn't doubt that they weren't going to take the news that he was a fighter pilot well.

It wasn't that they weren't patriotic, they were; it was just that we were a close-knit family. They wanted their kids in the same town, never expected us to leave. And the inescapable truth was that any future I'd have with Noah would likely involve my leaving Florida.

I hadn't quite wrapped my mind around that one, either.

"Meg's wedding is in less than a month; I imagine she has more important things on her mind than my love life."

"So what does he do?"

I hesitated, trying to think of a way to spin it that wouldn't freak my mother out. And then I realized I was thirty years old, had left the nest over a decade ago, and this was kind of ridiculous.

"He's a fighter pilot."

There, I'd said it. The world did not explode.

"Like in the military?"

Her voice rose on the last word.

I nodded.

Her mouth tightened.

"Don't you think you should be settling down, Jordan?"

I blinked. "What do you mean?"

"You aren't getting any younger. Don't you want to have children one day? Why don't you want to date someone who would offer you a solid future?"

Did such a person exist? Besides, I loathed the saying "You aren't getting any younger." As though I were somehow unaware of the intricacies of the aging process. And kids? I did want to have children. Eventually. I definitely wasn't there yet, and some part of me feared that I should be, but whatever.

"Yeah, I'd like to have kids someday."

"Don't you think you're getting a little old for someday? For wild hair?"

Wild hair?

I made a face. "I'm not following you."

"I just don't see why you would indulge in a fling right now. It doesn't make sense. I'm sure this boy is nice, but where's the future in it? You live in different states. You run your own business. You can't just take off whenever you feel like it. You have responsibilities here."

Inwardly, I winced. Noah wasn't exactly a fling, but at the same time, her words hit a little too close to home.

"I don't know. I hadn't really thought about it. We've known each other for a few weeks. I wasn't exactly hoping for a proposal."

She shook her head, disappointment flashing in her gaze. "It just seems reckless. Do you want to spend your life following some man around the world? What about the store? I just don't understand what you're thinking."

Annoyance filled me at being taken to task like I was a child. "Hold up. I've known him *for a few weeks*. I like him.

It's not a fling. But it's also not a freaking lifetime commitment. I don't have answers to any of those questions, but I don't think I need them. We're dating. Getting to know each other. Why is that a bad thing?"

"Because there's no way this will end well for you. What if you fall in love with him and then his job takes him away? Or what if you decide he's what you want? Are you really willing to throw your entire future away? Everything you've worked so hard to build?"

My head spun.

"You've been giving me a hard time about being single *for years*. I thought that was the whole point; thought you wanted me to prioritize relationships."

"Not with someone who's going to take you away from your family, your home, your career. Someone who won't be able to offer you any kind of stability."

I didn't want to fight with her in the middle of my store, but I was starting to get pissed. Really pissed. I was close with my family, but I was an adult. It was my life, not theirs.

"Look, Noah's taking me to Meg's wedding. We like each other. We're dating. It's exclusive. He's a great guy and I could see myself falling for him, and I think he really likes me. Beyond that, I don't know. And I'm not going to stand here and freak out about it."

"Jordan—"

"No. I love you, but I'm done with this conversation. It's been a long time since I've been this excited about a guy. Honestly, I'm not sure I've ever been this excited about a guy. So while I appreciate that you love me and are just worried about me, I'm not going to get into this. My relationship with Noah is private."

She gave me the disappointed look again, one I'd seen

over and over again throughout my childhood. I knew my parents loved me and I felt the same way about them, but it wasn't lost on me that I was definitely the "difficult child," the one who never seemed to play by the rules they wanted me to follow.

She stood there for a second, as though she were warring with herself to say more, and then she simply nodded, gave me another hug, and said good-bye.

If only the fears she'd planted in my head left as easily as she did.

NOAH

"Hey, beautiful."

I heard the smile in Jordan's voice through the phone. "Hi, handsome."

I leaned back against the headboard, stifling a yawn as I looked over at the clock. It was fairly early here—just after 8 p.m.—but a week of early show times had caught up with me, and considering the fact that I had to wake up at three tomorrow morning, I was ready for bed.

"How was your day?" I asked, settling into our nightly routine.

I'd called her every day for the past two weeks. Sometimes we talked for only a few minutes, but we filled each other in on what had happened during the day. She talked about her store; I mentioned things I was worried about at the squadron, talked about the pilot upgrades I was in charge of overseeing right now. It wasn't anywhere near as good as having her physically here, but it helped me to feel connected to her, even when she was so far away.

It was quickly becoming one of my favorite parts of the day, even though the distance made it tough at times.

"It was good," Jordan answered. "Busy. We're definitely still getting some of the spring break crowd. We've already hit our March sales targets and we're only halfway through the month."

"That's awesome, babe. I'm so proud of you."

"Thanks."

"Are you still okay to come out this Friday?"

It had been two weeks since her last visit and I was already dying to see her. I'd never had a great experience with long distance in the past, and I didn't know what it was about her, but if anything, the time apart had brought us closer. Maybe it was the phone calls. When your relationship was reduced to talking on the phone, you got to know each other in a way that had nothing to do with sexual attraction. We still had phone sex—and an unforgettable video chat—but the bulk of our time was spent learning each other's personalities and quirks. Talking on the phone stripped away the distractions, making it easier to just concentrate on each other.

"Yeah, I am. I'm excited to see you."

"Me, too," I replied. "I'm sorry I can't pick you up. I tried to move this guy's IPUG cert but there was no way to make it work in the schedule and we really need to get him through before we go TDY to Alaska. I'll try to duck out of work early, though, so we can spend some time together."

"IPUG? TDY?"

I grinned. I was quickly becoming her little Air Force dictionary.

"Instructor upgrade. If he passes this ride, he'll be qualified as an instructor pilot in the F-16. And, uh, TDY is a temporary duty assignment. Kind of like a civilian business trip."

Except our training usually involved blowing shit up.

"Do you think he'll pass?"

"He was a strong flight lead, and he's only hooked a couple rides in the IPUG, so yeah, I think he'll be good. The debrief will take a while, though. Are you sure you don't want me to see if I can get someone else to pick you up from the airport? Easy's probably free."

"It's cool. I'll just take a cab and meet you at home."

Silence filled the line as her last words settled between us.

I was surprised at how much I liked the way she described my place as "home." It had always just felt like a house—an investment opportunity that I'd probably rent out when I got my next assignment. The idea of her there made it feel like home.

"I meant your house," she sputtered.

"I liked it the first way better," I answered softly.

More silence.

If these past two weeks had taught me anything, it was that there was so much more to my interest in her than just the physical. In a way, the distance was a blessing of sorts. It sucked, but it highlighted the parts of our relationship that were easy to miss when you were in a constant state of arousal. Not being able to have her when I wanted had taught me to appreciate the other parts of her—being able to talk to her after a long day, telling her about frustrations at work, listening to her talk about her dreams and plans for the store.

"There's a squadron function at the O-Club on Friday. Do you want to go?"

"O-Club?"

"Officers' Club. The squadron will be there and families

will come out, too. No kids, but there should be a lot of wives there."

Everyone at work had heard about the girl I'd met in Vegas, and thanks to Easy being Easy, Jordan was kind of a legend among the guys. He'd finally stopped when I'd told him to fuck off after he'd described her as being "stacked like a centerfold." I hadn't shared that particular tidbit with Jordan considering it hadn't escaped my notice that he wasn't her favorite person.

"Like meet your friends?"

"Well, yeah. I've told everyone about you and they're dying to meet you."

"Is there a dress code or something for this?"

"It's after work so we'll all be in flight suits. You can wear whatever. It's casual."

"Okay."

I couldn't wait to show her off. I hated that our schedules and lives were so intense right now and I couldn't take her to California to meet my parents and the rest of my family. At least this way, she'd get a chance to meet my military family.

"Joker's wife, Dani, will be there. You'll love her."

I knew Jordan was apprehensive about the whole military thing, but I figured if anyone could show her how to navigate the lifestyle, it was Dani. As the squadron commander's wife, she was in charge of a lot of the Wild Aces social functions, and even though she was almost ten years younger than Joker, she acted as a de facto mother to all of us.

"It'll be fun. Promise."

*T*HIRTEEN

JORDAN

I left Florida first thing in the morning Friday, my flight arriving in Oklahoma City in the early afternoon. I took a cab to Noah's house, struggling to get my bag up to the front door, lifting the mat for the key he'd left there. I found it and unlocked the door, hauling my bag over the threshold and shutting the door behind me with a thud.

I walked back to Noah's room, setting my suitcase down, checking my cell to see if he'd texted. He'd mentioned that if he finished up with his debrief, he'd try to come home early and spend the rest of the day with me.

I couldn't wait to see him. Nearly three weeks apart from each other was way too long. I didn't know what it was about this relationship that made the distance so tough. Maybe it was that we were just starting out. We were still in that honeymoon, can't-keep-my-hands-off-you phase, which only made the time apart seem even longer. And it was also the fact that this was our norm. It wasn't like he was on a business trip; our relationship was defined in so many ways by being apart. By me being the one who came to see him. Our relationship was shaped as much by the time together as it was by the absence of each other.

I started rummaging through my suitcase, setting my toiletries in the bathroom adjoining Noah's room, hanging up the outfit I'd planned for tonight to avoid wrinkles. And then the door swung open and I turned, my gaze landing on Noah.

I opened my mouth to say, "Hi," but the word got lost somewhere between our lips as he devoured me, his hands running over my body, kissing me until I went dizzy. God, I'd forgotten how good he could kiss. Forgotten how amazing his tongue felt, the slight nip of his teeth, the hair against my face . . .

Wait. What?

He leaned back, his arms still wrapped around my waist.

I froze at the sight of my man, tall and lean in his flight suit, aviators in hand . . . mustache.

What?

"God, I missed you," he groaned. "You look gorgeous."

I'd woken up at 3 a.m. just so I would have time to do my hair and makeup before I arrived. Given the thing on his face, clearly he hadn't been as concerned.

I couldn't look away. "Mustache" wasn't the proper word. Mustaches were trimmed and groomed, and while definitely not my favorite thing, there was symmetry to a mustache. This was just like a forest of hair had moved in, bushy and unruly, and invaded his upper lip.

What the fuck?

"Sorry, but I have to go back to work."

I tore my gaze away from the mustache, focusing on the words coming out of his mouth.

"I thought you were home."

He shook his head. "Sorry, but we had a last-minute flail with the schedule and they need me to lead a four-ship."

He'd taught me that a four-ship meant a formation of four planes.

"I'm probably not going to make it back before the party starts tonight, so can you catch a ride with Easy? He's coming back and can get you on base."

My mind sped as I tried to dissect all the things being thrown at me. I was nervous enough about going to this squadron thing without the added pressure of now going with Easy, who I wasn't even sure liked me. I wasn't going to know anyone there; I'd sort of been counting on Noah to be there. And I really wasn't excited about the fucking forest on his face.

I'd flown across the country expecting the Noah who was sweet on the phone with me, and instead I'd gotten Grizzly Adams. Grizzly Adams mixed with a bad 1970s porn star. I'd sort of thought he'd be excited to see me, too. No, I didn't expect him to get up at 3 a.m. to do his hair and makeup, but was personal hygiene too much to ask for?

My eyes narrowed as I gestured at that thing. "What's going on?"

"I told you. Flying tonight. I'll be home late. Sorry." He stepped back, releasing me. "I gotta go."

Wait. What?

"I mean what's on your face?" I blurted out, figuring that was the easiest and most obvious place to start. I gestured toward his lip, not really wanting to touch it, already mentally cringing over the fact that it had brushed my face.

I had a thing about hair. On anyone. Boyfriend or not, I always landscaped for myself. So to say I was not thrilled to see a mustache on my boyfriend's gorgeous face was the understatement of the year.

"It's March, babe."

That was his explanation? I stared at him like he was delusional—no, scratch that—I stared at that thing on his face. It was like a hairy caterpillar had crawled up and taken residence over his lip.

Ugh.

Tell me the mustache wasn't a permanent thing and I'd just met him on a brief hiatus. We'd met in February. Last time I'd been out here had been the last weekend in February. And our video sex chat had been a few days after that and the quality hadn't been all that great. Sure, I'd seen some stubble, but not this.

"You don't shave in March?"

He gave me a look like I'd just said "fuck" in church. "It's Mustache March."

I blinked. "What?"

"Mustache March."

"What the fuck is Mustache March?" I asked, my foot tapping now. Meg was getting married *next weekend*. No way I was taking him to my sister's wedding with that thing on his face. No fucking way. A whole month? Those pictures would last forever. How could he not mention this? I didn't mean to be superficial, but he looked like a total perv.

He just stared back at me like we spoke a different language. Maybe we did. He was clearly speaking Fighter Pilot and I was speaking Girl Who Is a Bridesmaid in Her Younger Sister and Ex-Boyfriend's Wedding.

"We grow mustaches."

He said this proudly, as if mustaches were something to be glorified. His lips curved. The caterpillar twitched.

Was this normal behavior? Had I somehow time warped back to college and fraternity rush week or something?

"We?" I asked, my voice weak. It was like a car crash I couldn't look away from.

"Everyone. The squadron. Fighter pilots. Pilots. The Air Force."

"Everyone grows a mustache," I repeated.

What the fuck?

He checked his watch. "Babe, I gotta brief soon." His voice became impatient now, and my annoyance grew. I got that in the grand scheme of life, it wasn't a big deal, but right now, it felt like a big deal.

I'd flown across the country to see him. Multiple times. My friends and family thought I was crazy. I was beginning to think I was crazy. He hadn't been able to pick me up, now he couldn't even stay, and then to top it off, he'd said he wanted me to meet his friends, and now he was going to miss out on most of that. I didn't know if it was the lack of sleep or what, but the mustache, stupid as it was, felt like the tipping point.

"Can we talk about this later?" he asked, his voice growing even more impatient.

Oh, yeah, I was getting pissed.

"No. No, we can't talk about this later. My sister's wedding is in eight days. Are you telling me that thing is going to be on your face in all of the family photos?"

He grinned, and I swore he almost puffed out his chest with pride. I couldn't.

"Yeah, it's awesome, right?"

Oh my God.

"No."

"Babe."

"No."

The smile slid off his face as my tone changed, my foot

tapping even faster. We hadn't been together long enough for him to see my temper, but I had a temper. A big one. And it was about to blow. I didn't like feeling like I was an afterthought or an inconvenience, and I definitely felt like both now.

"Everyone grows a mustache," he repeated.

"Even the women?"

"No."

"So not everyone grows a mustache."

Noah's eyes darkened, and I got the feeling *he* was getting pissed. If I'd been a little more together, I would have registered that he was probably not the kind of guy who handled being told what to do very well, but I was in the middle of losing my shit, so that *didn't* register.

"I don't have a pussy, so yeah, everyone in my world grows a fucking mustache in March." He glanced at his watch again, the gesture spiking my temper. "I don't have time for this. I need to go."

I glared at him. *Asshole.* "Well, you definitely won't have *my* pussy if you don't shave that thing off your fucking face."

I hated saying the P-word—did any girl actually like it?—but desperate times called for desperate measures. If I had to speak Fighter Pilot to get that shit off his face, I'd do it. Not to mention, I wasn't feeling too into him right now anyway.

Noah closed the distance between us, the expression in his eyes changing from slightly annoyed to supremely pissed off. Good, now we were even.

"You're saying you won't have sex with me for all of March if I have a mustache?"

I mean there was like a week left in the month, but I had to draw a line somewhere, flimsy though that line may be. It was my own *Lysistrata.* "That's what I'm saying."

Arrogance flashed in those beautiful dark eyes and I felt a fluttering in my lady parts. *Shit.*

Since he'd never seen my temper, and we'd never actually had a fight, we'd also never had angry sex. Which when done well, could be really freaking hot. And considering Noah did *everything* well, I didn't doubt he'd deliver there, too.

"Bullshit. You can't go the whole weekend without my cock, babe."

Possibly true, but right now this was the best play I had.

I leaned in closer, letting him get a whiff of my perfume and a chance to look down my shirt at the not-insubstantial cleavage there barely contained by the red lacy bra.

"Bet I can." I leaned back after a moment, after I knew he'd gotten enough of a show to want more, my gaze settling meaningfully on the area between his nose and upper lip. "Especially when you look like that."

His eyes narrowed. "Chicks dig the 'stache."

My hands fisted on my hips and a laugh escaped. "Newsflash, no one digs the 'stache. You look like Chester the Molester."

"Who the fuck is Chester the Molester?"

"Someone with a 'stache exactly like yours."

He groaned, the anger sliding off his face. "I'm not shaving no matter how cute you are."

Something fluttered in me as he said that, and a little bit of my anger slid away.

"Wanna bet?"

A gleam settled in his eyes as he leaned into my body, the thin fabric of his flight suit doing nothing to hide his growing arousal. Another flutter. *Shit.* I shifted slightly so his hips were pressed against mine and he was between my legs.

"I bet you can't make it through the weekend without my cock, babe."

Well, now my anger was completely gone.

"Can," I whispered, my voice shaky as he bent his head, his lips grazing my neck. My head fell back, my body clearly not getting the *Lysistrata* memo.

His lips curved against my neck and then his teeth nipped at the skin there and I felt myself getting wet. *Shit.*

Noah pulled back, a satisfied smirk on his face, and I knew he could read the arousal flushing my skin and the way my chest rose and fell.

"Sure, babe."

I should have realized that daring a fighter pilot to do anything would only encourage him.

"Tell you what. If you can make it without sex for the next *week*, I'll shave it off for your sister's wedding."

That seemed doable. I could make a week. Hell, I wasn't going to volunteer the information, but I'd gone months without sex when I was single—*vibrators didn't count, right?*

"Define sex."

His eyes narrowed. "What do you mean, 'Define sex'?"

"Like a week without sex, or a week without sex with you?"

The second the words left my mouth, I realized I'd chosen poorly. Really fucking poorly. I'd meant to clarify on the whole vibrator issue without getting *too* specific, but apparently I'd just inserted my stiletto into my mouth instead.

Arghhh.

"Are you thinking of fucking someone else?" Noah asked, his eyes wide, his tone incredulous. God, he was getting growly. This did serious things to my body. *Shit.*

"No."

"Then what does it matter if it's sex, or sex with me, it's all the same thing."

I made a face. "Hate to break it to you, but you are not my only supplier of orgasms."

His entire expression changed as I figured he got my meaning. "Babe. Gotta tell you the idea of you making yourself come is hot as fuck. Even hotter is the idea of me watching you do it."

Gah. He definitely got my meaning.

For a moment, I really had to wonder if the mustache fight was worth it.

He kissed me hard. "Gotta go fly, babe," he whispered against my mouth, tickling my lips. "You wanna bet? You're on. If you can make it a week, I'll shave. If you can't . . ." It lingered between us. "If you can't, you're mine the way I want it, when I want it. And the 'stache stays."

This was not necessarily a hardship. I was almost ready to throw it for sex on tap.

Focus on the 'stache.

I nodded. "Done."

He grinned, and I sank down on the edge of the bed, watching him swagger out of the room, my odds suddenly not looking so good.

$\mathscr{F}$OURTEEN

NOAH

I couldn't concentrate.

The sortie had gone well, the debrief fine. But my mind was back in my bedroom, back with Jordan. I couldn't help but wonder if I'd fucked up with how I'd handled things with her.

I felt like an asshole for not picking her up at the airport today. And I was even more pissed about the fact that I hadn't been able to spend the rest of the day with her. I'd been dying to see her, and when I'd gotten a call from Rush, who ran the scheduling shop, I'd known I was going to disappoint her. And maybe I should have mentioned the mustache, but honestly, it had never occurred to me. I'd been a fighter pilot for over a decade. The married guys did Mustache March. Their wives didn't seem to mind. Apparently, Jordan did.

I walked out of the vault where we stored all our classified materials and ran into Joker. As squadron commander, he worked even more intense hours than the rest of us and was always the first one in and the last one to leave, his office light on every weekend. I figured Dani was a little bit of a saint to put up with his continued absences.

He jerked his chin in greeting. "Did your girl get in okay?"

I nodded, my answer mostly true. I hesitated, feeling like an idiot, but also figuring I needed relationship advice, and considering my top choices were Easy, who fucked anything hot that moved, and Thor, who had a broken engagement behind him that he refused to talk about a decade later, Joker seemed like the best bet. Besides, there were a ton of married guys in the squadron, but few were as happily married as Dani and Joker appeared to be.

"Does Dani, uh, hate Mustache March?"

Joker let out a bark of laughter.

"Seriously?"

I guessed that answered my question.

"She fucking hates it."

"But you still do it."

"She deals."

In the years I'd known Joker and his wife, I'd never heard Dani raise her voice, never heard her curse. Somehow I didn't think she and Jordan would *deal* in the same way. Maybe I should have just shaved the thing. I'd gotten caught up in the moment and hadn't thought about how surprised I would have been if she'd radically changed her appearance or something.

"Let me guess, your girl isn't a fan?" Joker asked.

"That would be an understatement. She's pissed. I didn't handle it all that well, so now she's really pissed."

He shrugged. "She'll either get over it, or you'll cave. Just pick your battles. Is she coming tonight?"

I nodded.

I felt guilty about that, too. The party at the O-Club had started two hours ago. Maybe I shouldn't have suggested Jordan go with Easy. She'd definitely been nervous. *Fuck*. This was why I was shit at relationships. I was so used to just worrying about myself, my focus on my job and the mission, that I hadn't even thought about her feelings.

Joker grinned. "Good luck. See you at the club in a few?"

I nodded again, my mind back on Jordan. I'd been an asshole earlier. I needed to make it up to her. Somehow.

JORDAN

I ended up being spared from one-on-one time with Easy when he brought a date, a pretty, dark-haired girl named Sonya.

She talked the whole way to the base, her stories distracting me from the nerves rolling around in my stomach and making my heart race.

It turned out she was in vet school—*definitely* way too smart for Easy—and from the sound of things, their arrangement, or whatever it was, was really casual. Easy took a call from another girl to set up what sounded like a date while she was there, and Sonya legit didn't bat an eye. I would have kneed him in the balls, so I figured she was a better person than me. I didn't really get why he brought her. I mean, I liked her a lot. But Noah had definitely described this as more of a family thing. And neither Easy nor Sonya looked all that into each other besides the obvious physical intimacy between them.

Not my business.

Except she was young and nice, and sort of reminded me

of Meg, and I liked her. And I didn't trust Easy as far as I could throw him, which considering that body, wouldn't be far at all.

He took both of us to the visitor's center, repeating the process I'd gone through with Noah in Vegas.

Bryer was a smaller base than Nellis, but it had the same nondescript look. The buildings looked a little rundown, the architecture a hodgepodge that didn't quite match. Beige colors dominated. Function definitely reigned supreme. Easy pointed out the flight line, the rows of F-16s parked under giant metal hangars.

And then we were pulling into the parking lot of the club, and my nerves picked up.

Sonya flashed me a grin and I figured it was obvious I was freaking the fuck out.

"The guys'll be nice," she whispered as we followed Easy in. "Some of the wives are fun." She hesitated. "Some of the wives will ignore you 'cause you're not a wife." She shrugged. "You get used to it."

It was a little pathetic how important it was to me that this went well. Meeting the friends was so official, and I'd gotten the impression that because Noah's job kept him away from his family, his friends *were* his family. So I really wanted them to like me. Especially since I couldn't quite get my stride with his best friend.

Easy explained the history of the club as we walked in, and how the building was divided into an officers' side and an enlisted side, which seemed strange to me, but Easy just answered that it gave guys a place to relax and let their guard down among their peers. Still, weird. The whole rank thing and the way guys had saluted Easy going through the gate was just so different from what I was used to. Despite the manners my mother had attempted to drill into me, I was pretty laid back. The rules and customs overwhelmed me, creating way more opportunities for inadvertently insulting someone than I was comfortable with.

We hit the bar, and the nerves got worse as I surveyed the crowd.

The vast majority formed a sea of green flight suits. While not every guy was hot, there was an overabundance of fit guys dressed in uniform, so I figured anyone who had a man-in-uniform fantasy would be hard-pressed not to feel like they'd hit the mother lode. As long as they were willing to overlook the mustaches. Noah had not been kidding; all of the guys had mustaches, ranging from, *desperately trying to grow facial hair* to *attack of the giant hairy caterpillar.*

Interspersed between all of the green were the women who I guessed were the wives. By the look of things, Sonya and I had totally missed the mark on our outfits.

Fuck.

I glanced over at Sonya, who looked like she couldn't have cared less. I, on the other hand, wanted to sink into the ground. Most of the women were dressed in jeans, their bodies covered in sweaters or fleece. I'd toned it down a bit, minimized the cleavage, made the hair a little smaller, but in comparison I felt overdone and ridiculous.

I so did not belong here.

And then I caught sight of a woman walking toward us, and I figured if there were a poster child for being an Air Force wife, this was it.

She had long copper-colored hair, and pale skin that made her look like a porcelain doll. Her eyes were a startling green, her makeup flawless. She wore dark jeans that fit her like a glove and a black turtleneck. Gorgeous gray boots completed the ensemble.

She stopped in front of us, and her mouth spread into a

wide smile. She hugged Easy, who stiffened for a second, his usual swagger tempered. She pulled back and flashed that same smile at Sonya. And then she turned to me.

Her smile widened. Blinding. Genuine.

"You must be Jordan. I've been dying to meet you. I'm Dani."

She spoke with a soft Southern accent that called to mind sweet tea and porch swings.

So this was Joker's wife. The Dani that Noah had wanted me to meet.

"It's really nice to meet you," I replied. Something about her manner was instantly welcoming.

"I've heard so much about you since the guys got back from Vegas. I'm so glad you could make it to hang out with the squadron." She gestured toward the bar. "Do you want a drink?"

"I can get you ladies something," Easy interjected, his expression uncharacteristically serious.

You ladies?

I made a face, which I was pretty sure he caught by the snort that escaped his lips. Yeah, I was definitely not winning any points in the best friend department. Crap. Dani's lips twitched as she noticed both of our expressions. I figured we looked like a pair of bickering siblings.

Easy took our drink orders, and then Sonya decided to go with him to the bar, leaving Dani and me alone.

"Do you want to go sit?" she asked.

I nodded and followed her to a table, feeling like all eyes were on me.

"I'll let Noah introduce you around," she said as we sat across from each other. "He should be here soon. I just spoke with Joker and they're wrapping up work."

I was ready to have Noah beside me. I definitely kept

garnering a lot of stares, and while Dani was really nice, I wasn't sure I could say the same for the rest of the crowd.

"It has to be kind of awkward coming to one of these things on your own." She smiled. "The first time I went to a military function with Joker, I was scared out of my mind. We'd only been together for a few months and he invited me to the Air Force Ball. It was romantic, but not only was I obsessed with making sure I had the perfect dress, I was also petrified that I'd make a protocol faux pas or something."

I grinned. "Yeah, that about sums it up. I'm way out of my depth here. The military is definitely a bit of a foreign concept to me, although Noah's been awesome about giving me a little Air Force primer. How long have you and Joker been married?"

"Five years."

She looked to be about my age now.

We chatted for a few minutes until Easy came over with our drinks, minus Sonya. Noah was right. I liked Dani. A lot. She had a way of making people feel comfortable and we'd clicked. I really hoped we'd become friends.

I expected Easy to drop off our drinks and go in search of his date, but instead he filled the empty seat. Within seconds, it was obvious he and Dani were close. The smirk and attitude he so often displayed had disappeared, and instead he almost seemed like a nice guy. He made a few jokes, asked her some questions, listened when she spoke. It was like his asshole persona had disappeared completely behind a veil, leaving me wondering which one was the real Easy.

Eventually Dani excused herself to greet some of the new arrivals. I got the impression that her position as the squadron commander's wife made her the social hostess, a role she seemed well suited for considering how nice she was. Before she left, she turned to me and gave me her cell number. "If you ever need to talk, or just want to hang out while you're visiting Noah and the guys have to work or something, give me a call."

I grinned, feeling like I'd definitely made a new friend. "I will."

She walked off, leaving me at the table with Easy. I had no idea where Sonya had gone.

I gestured toward where a group of guys congregated around a pool table, shouting and elbowing one another, raucous laughter spilling out over the club.

"I'm okay if you want to go play with them. You don't have to sit with me all night."

Easy's smirk returned. "I'm fine. I told Noah I'd keep you company until he got here."

"So you're, what, my babysitter?"

He laughed, completely unfazed by the bit of bitch I threw his way. "Something like that."

"What are they playing?" I asked.

He didn't bother looking; clearly this was a common occurrence. "Crud."

"Crud?"

"Fighter pilot game."

My eyes narrowed as I watched the guys running around the pool table, arms and elbows out, a billiard ball pinging between them. It looked intense and more than a little violent. The odds of serious injury seemed high.

"So basically, it's fighter pilot Quidditch."

A strangled laugh escaped his lips. "Please tell Noah that."

I barely stifled my eye roll.

"You don't like me, do you?" Easy asked, using that same tone he always displayed when he talked to me, so different from the one he'd used with Dani. As though I amused him and more in a "laughing at me" than "with me" sort of way. He definitely felt like the annoying brother I'd never had or wanted.

"Not particularly."

At this point, it seemed ridiculous to deny it.

"Why?"

"You kind of seem like an asshole."

"That's because I am kind of an asshole."

God, he really was. I didn't get it.

"What's the deal with you and Noah?" I asked.

"What do you mean?"

"The bestie thing."

He looked even more amused. "The *bestie* thing?"

"You know, you're Robin to his Batman."

"Why do I have to be Robin? Noah's my wingman way more than I'm his."

I laughed. "Is that why you keep throwing me attitude, because I didn't fall all over myself when I saw you and instead chose Noah? Did I hurt your pride?"

He smirked. "He's going to have his hands full with you, isn't he?"

I ignored the implication that I was high maintenance because, really, tell me something I didn't already know.

"And that's a bad thing? Let me guess, you like your women to shut up and put out?"

"Honey, you have no idea how I like my women. And for the record, no, I don't think it's a bad thing that you challenge Noah. He's serious. All the time. Flying has been his life for as long as I've known him. He needs more. He smiles with you. And he's trying to make this work, even though relationships aren't exactly his forte."

I blinked.

"Really. Trust me, I've been through enough disastrous relationships with Noah to appreciate when he has a good thing going."

"So if you're so happy about me and Noah, why do you give me such a hard time?"

He shrugged. "I give everyone a hard time."

"You didn't give Dani a hard time. You actually seemed almost normal with her."

"Dani doesn't need me giving her a hard time." He was silent for a moment. "You should take her up on the offer to talk. Trust me, there are definitely going to be moments when you get frustrated with this lifestyle. You couldn't ask for a better person to have in your camp. And she could use a friend."

I studied him for a beat. "So are *we* friends now?"

"Something like that."

"More like annoying siblings?"

He let out a bark of laughter and a smile that shed some light on why women put up with his shit.

"Basically." His smile deepened as his gaze drifted over my shoulder. "Oh, this is fucking great."

I looked up and saw Noah standing over us, dressed in his flight suit. He dipped his head, pressing his mouth to mine. He pulled back and I blinked.

Ohmigod.

Easy snorted and said something under his breath that sounded a lot like "whipped," but I didn't care.

He'd shaved his mustache.

I rose, cupping his face in my hands, running my thumbs

over the warm skin around his mouth. He nipped at the pads of my fingers, and my nipples tightened.

"You shaved."

"Ran by the BX before I came here. I'm sorry I was a dick earlier. I'd be lying if I didn't admit that I'm pretty shit at relationships. And I've been on my own for so long that I'm kind of used to doing whatever I feel like without thinking about anyone else. I don't want to do that anymore, though. Your sister's wedding is important to you. So it's important to me."

I shook my head. "It was a stupid fight. I was overwhelmed and a little freaked, and I overreacted. I do that. A lot. You didn't have to shave." I looked around at the group—a veritable sea of 'staches—and back to Noah again.

"Are you going to get in trouble?"

He grinned. "No, babe. They'll give me shit about it for a while, but it's fine."

"Try longer than a while," Easy interjected.

Noah wrapped his arm around me, holding me snug against him.

"They're just jealous," he joked. "Ignore it."

Easy smirked, but there was more sarcasm than amusement in the gesture, and for a moment I saw a flash of something darker than anything I'd ever seen on Easy before.

"We aren't all lucky enough to get what we want."

I waited for Noah to throw back a jab, but instead his mouth just got tight, and a look of guilt flashed in his eyes, like if he could take his words back, he would.

Easy rose, his smirk back in place.

"I'll leave you to your girl." He patted Noah on the shoulder, and something I didn't quite understand passed between them, and then he was gone, and Noah was kissing me again, and I sort of forgot to think.

NOAH

"Did you have fun tonight?"

Jordan nodded. "Your friends seem nice. I really like Dani."

"Dani's awesome."

I pulled into the garage, putting the car in Park and turning off the engine. We'd ended up staying longer than I'd anticipated, but Jordan had looked like she was really enjoying talking to everyone. Unsurprisingly, she'd been a big hit with the guys. She'd seemed to enjoy talking to the wives and I was glad to see her hitting it off with the other women. We had a squadron TDY coming up to Alaska, and I liked the idea of her having a support network while we were gone if she wanted it. I knew she had her family and friends—and it wasn't like we weren't already used to being apart—but I figured having other people around you who were in the same situation and understood the weird nuances of military life could be helpful. Besides, I wanted her to see other couples that were able to make military relationships work to show her that it was possible.

We got out of the car and walked into the house together. Easy wasn't home yet, and since he'd left the O-Club before we did, I figured he'd gone to Sonya's.

Holding hands, we walked back to my bedroom. It had been a long day and I couldn't deny that I was exhausted, but at the same time, it had been two weeks, and I was dying to get inside her again. I figured the shaved mustache had to buy me some sex points.

We hit the bedroom and I began stripping off my flight suit, feeling disgusting after double turning today, the second flight even more intense than the first.

"I'm going to hop in the shower."

Jordan nodded, taking off her boots, which was really a shame because they were . . . inspiring, to say the least.

I took a faster shower than normal, praying Jordan wouldn't be too tired from traveling. The phone sex had been great and all, but it definitely wasn't a substitute for the real thing.

I stepped out and dried off, wrapping the towel around my waist. I walked back into the bedroom just as the soft strands of music hit me and I froze in my tracks.

Holy fuck.

Jordan lay on the bed, naked but for a tiny, lacy black thong, heels, and a smile.

This girl . . .

"I'm throwing the bet."

I blinked. "What?"

"You shaved. I'm throwing the bet. You get me, any way you want me."

I groaned, my cock immediately hard, my heart pounding. She was already kind of a freak in bed, and I meant that in the best possible how-the-hell-did-I-get-this-lucky sort of way. So to say I hadn't been holding back with her was kind of the understatement of the century. But this?

This was freaking unreal.

She rose up on her hands and knees—ass and tits exposed—and I died a little bit.

She summoned me to the edge of the bed without words, the image in front of me a freaking magnet.

Her lips curved into a naughty smile as she reached out, her fingers tracing my abs, stroking, dipping beneath the edge of the towel. My stomach contracted, balls aching, cock hard. I'd never wanted anyone as badly as I wanted her. Ever. Never found someone who fit like this.

For a moment we both froze, as though someone had pressed Pause on the whole night. I just stood there, staring at her, falling. She was so beautiful. So sexy. So vibrant. The kind of girl you couldn't get out of your mind once you'd had a taste.

She was incredible.

Our gazes locked, and I forgot everything but Jordan and the intense pleasure I found with her. Forgot everything but my own want and need.

I didn't know what it was—the absences that punctuated our relationship perhaps, or the passion that seemed to seep through her pores, or the chemistry between us that I couldn't even describe—but there was something here. Something different. Something more. Something that made me desperate for her. Something I swore I saw reflected in her eyes.

And then she moved, her hands gripping the side of the towel, stripping it from my body until I stood naked before her. Her eyes flared with heat, a sigh escaping those pouty lips, and then she was moving again, and I felt the tip of her tongue caress the tip of my cock.

Heaven.

I groaned, my hands fisting her hair, pulling her toward me, pushing against her until I felt her lips part, and I was thrusting inside.

I released her hair, cupping her tits, my fingers tweaking her nipples, the feel of her moaning against my cock the best thing ever. I wanted the whole night with her like this. Wanted to surround myself in her warmth and her moans.

Her hand circled the base of my cock, fisting me, the warm, wet suction of her mouth weakening my knees. She knew exactly how to touch me, knew what my body wanted before even I did. She took over, alternating between sucking me deep and running her tongue along me, teasing me, dragging my orgasm out until I was desperate to come.

And then my eyes slammed closed, the force of it building in the base of my spine, and I found my release.

$\mathcal{F}$IFTEEN

NOAH

I lay in bed, watching Jordan sleep, feeling like our relationship was just a series of repeats—seeing her, wanting more, the time slipping away from us, saying good-bye. Even when I saw her, some part of me was already mentally counting down to the time when she would leave again. We were always coming or going, never staying, and part of me wondered how we could continue like this.

Jordan stirred beneath the covers, rolling to her side, throwing an arm over my waist, her cheek coming to rest on my chest. I stroked her hair, wrapping the golden strands around my fingers while she settled into me even more.

Her flight left in five hours. I didn't want to let her go.

Yesterday had gone by in a blur. We'd spent the entire day in bed, watching TV and being lazy, taking breaks for food and fucking. It had been the perfect day and, at the same time, had gone by far too quickly. And now, like always, time was up.

I wanted to talk to her, to see if we were on the same

page, if this was going somewhere more permanent than these weekend trips, and yet I felt like I was coming to her with empty hands. This was the hard part. I didn't know what to say to her, didn't know what I had to offer. What could I say?

I really like you, think I might be falling in love with you, so do you want to give up the business you've built and your friends and family to follow me around the world?

It was fucking hard.

I couldn't meet her halfway, couldn't make a sacrifice of my own. I'd made a commitment to the military and there was no getting out of it, no other option. If she wanted to take this relationship to the next level, then it was all or nothing. And I wasn't sure I could ask that of her. Maybe it would be easier if we were younger. If she hadn't already built a future for herself, or if she had a career that was more portable, one that could move with the military lifestyle.

I wished we could have dated like normal people who just enjoyed each other's company without the added pressure of making big decisions early on. But I only had a year left in Oklahoma and I was a few months away from having to submit my "dream sheet" of where I wanted to go next. As long as I was flying the Viper, I didn't really care, but now there was the added pressure of Jordan to think about. I would have been cool with going overseas, but a long-distance relationship was tough enough without the added hassle of living in different countries.

I wasn't far off my lieutenant colonel promotion board, and my next assignment mattered. I couldn't afford to make a choice based off a relationship that was just casual. And at the same time, I'd spent my whole life choosing the Air Force. I couldn't give everything up for Jordan, but I could try my hardest to make it easier for us to be together. I just needed to know she was on board, too.

It was the kind of conversation that was serious enough to merit speaking in person, and at the same time, when we only got two days to spend together, it was difficult to want to use that time talking about a future that was daunting to say the least. And part of me resented even having this conversation so early into dating. I felt boxed into a corner of my own making, paying the price for a decision I'd made at eighteen. I didn't regret my choice. I loved flying; there wasn't any other job I could see myself doing. But at the same time, it made things harder than they probably needed to be.

Jordan stirred in my arms again, her face tipping up to stare into mine. Her lashes fluttered and she gave me a sleepy smile.

"Morning."

I loved waking up to her. What would it be like if I could always have this? If every day of my life included seeing her face in the morning?

"Good morning."

She kissed the skin over my heart.

"Did you sleep okay?" she murmured.

"Yeah."

She was seriously adorable in the mornings. She clearly wasn't a morning person, and most of the time I woke up before she did, watching her sleep, enjoying the feel of her in my arms.

I groaned, burying my face in her hair. "I'm going to miss you."

"Me, too. I wish we lived closer."

"Me, too."

Silence descended between us, the impending good-bye already taking over.

"I'm sorry," I whispered, not even sure what I was apologizing for.

I'm sorry my hands are tied. I'm sorry being with me means giving up everything. I'm sorry I'm in the military. I'm sorry I can't put you first. I'm sorry you deserve better than what I can give you. I'm sorry I'm too selfish to let you go.

Jordan reached out, grasping my face in her hands, her gaze knowing, as though she could read the confusion in my eyes.

"You don't need to apologize. You told me what it would be like from the beginning. It sucks, but I knew that going into it. It was my choice. I could have left what we had in Vegas. I wanted to see where this would go. Wanted to give us a chance. That's not on you."

The rational part of me knew she was right, and yet the part of me that hated to see her upset or suffering couldn't ignore the pang I felt when I saw the sadness in her eyes. And I also couldn't ignore the voice in the back of my mind that wondered if it should be this hard; if maybe love wasn't supposed to be easier than this.

"Yeah, but did you know how hard it would be?" I asked her, a knot in my throat.

'Cause I hadn't.

I'd done long distance with girls before. It had never been particularly successful, but it hadn't been this. It hadn't been an ache in my chest like someone had ripped my heart out and used it as a stress ball.

"No, I didn't."

That was the tough thing about it. If I liked her less, it

would have been easier. And at the same time, if I liked her less, I wasn't sure I'd put myself in this position.

"Do you regret it?" I found myself asking, not even sure I was ready to hear the answer she might give.

Her gaze met mine, her expression solemn. "Not for a minute."

The amount of relief I felt staggered me.

"Me, either."

Jordan hooked her leg over mine, burrowing deeper into the crook of my arm, soft and warm against my bare skin, the sensation of having her close doing nothing to lessen the need humming through my body. Her hand drifted lower and my breath caught.

"I could stay like this forever," she murmured, her fingers lazy, stroking and gliding over me with enough pressure to bring me to the precipice without giving me what I craved.

I grinned. "Same." My hands drifted down her skin, tracing the curves there. I'd had her hours ago and I was already hungry for her again. "Have I mentioned how much I love your body?"

Her expression turned playful instantly, her voice taking on the husky purr my body instantly gravitated toward.

"Not in the last five hours."

"I love your curves," I murmured, rolling over and taking her with me until my hips rocked against hers, pressing her into the mattress. "So soft and sweet."

I tilted her chin, touching my lips to hers, my tongue thrusting in as she made a little hum of pleasure.

"I love your mouth," I murmured, my hands moving down and arching her forward as she wrapped her legs around my waist.

Jordan's hands twined in my hair, pulling us even closer

together, the kiss turning urgent and hungry as we made the most of the time we had left.

JORDAN

The Oklahoma City airport was quickly becoming both my most favorite and my least favorite place. When my plane landed and I walked toward the gate, my legs carrying me toward Noah, it felt like the best place on earth. But when he dropped me off there, when I waited by the security line, waited for the hug and release, for my legs to carry me *away* from him? Well, then it sucked. Big time.

It had been a good weekend. A great weekend. But I was sick of just having a couple days together. It wasn't exactly a sustainable relationship. And I wasn't sure how we were supposed to take things further if we could never spend time together. Maybe we should take a trip somewhere; I could suggest it after Meg's wedding. I figured meeting the parents was probably enough to spring on him without adding the pressure of a couple's trip. It felt like we were headed there, and at the same time, I couldn't get my bearings on whether things were happening too quickly for us or not quickly enough.

Noah stood next to me while I checked in for my flight and gave the attendant my bag. Whatever weird mood had settled over me like a miasma seemed to have affected him, too, and we wore matching grim expressions as though steeling ourselves for an unpleasant and arduous task.

I'd been lucky in my life. Sure, I'd gone off to college, but I'd only been a few hours away from my parents, and I'd gone with my best friends, so it hadn't been a big thing.

I hadn't had to say good-bye to a lot of people in my life, had always been fortunate enough to have the people I loved close.

I loved Noah.

I'd suspected I was falling in love with him since the beginning, had been able to recognize that this feeling inside me was something else entirely from the way I'd felt with other guys before. But now I knew. And given how complicated things were between us—the chasm created by his job and my difficulty coming to terms with how I fit into his lifestyle—I couldn't say I was entirely happy about it.

And I didn't know how he felt, or if we were even on the same page. We needed to talk about it, but I wasn't sure how to broach that conversation. It seemed counterintuitive to push for a future I wasn't sure I wanted.

God, I really was terrible at this.

We walked toward the security line, our hands linked, my chest tight.

I offered a lame attempt at a smile, not quite meeting his gaze.

"I'll see you in a week."

Noah squeezed my hand, the same conflicted expression on his face that I figured was mirrored on mine.

I waited for him to say something, hoping I'd somehow find the answers there. But he didn't speak. He moved forward with a jerk, cupping my face, lifting my head to meet him halfway as his lips came down to claim mine.

Whatever the question, this was the answer. It wasn't just a kiss—I'd had good kisses before him. It was the *rightness* of it. The inaudible click that I felt between us. It was something I hadn't found before and it was the thing that kept me holding on, even as I wondered if I was nuts for doing so.

I clung to him, my nails digging into his biceps as his

mouth laid waste to mine. It wasn't as much of a good-bye kiss as it was both promise and claiming, a memory I'd take with me as I got on the plane and left him behind.

He pulled away, his gaze brimming with purpose, his want and need blasting me.

I didn't speak. It was the kind of kiss that was a tough act to follow.

I walked through security, my heart heavy, lips swollen, throat thick with unshed tears. Each step took me farther and farther away; each step extended the invisible thread that connected us, the one I clung to now.

One week.

$\mathcal{S}$IXTEEN

JORDAN

"What do you think?"

I looked up from my phone as Meg walked out into the salon wearing her wedding gown.

She looked stunning. The dress was a princess ball gown with lots of tulle and lace. It showed off her tiny waist, and even though she'd worried that it would be too much dress for her since she wasn't tall, somehow it fit her perfectly. She looked like a delicate fairy.

"You look amazing."

Our mother pulled out a tissue, dabbing at her eyes. "My little girl—all grown up."

Meg grinned. "It's perfect, right?"

"Mike is going to love it. You look like a princess."

It was three days before the wedding, and Meg was having her final fitting to make sure nothing had changed and the dress still fit like a glove. I'd taken the week off to help Meg with last-minute wedding plans and to entertain all the out-of-town wedding guests who were beginning to trickle in. I'd already made four trips to the airport to pick up relatives and I still had to go back tomorrow to pick up Noah.

My mother and the bridal shop attendant fussed over Meg's gown and veil, and I felt tears welling up. Images of us growing up together flashed before my eyes. I was so going to cry at the ceremony.

My phone rang, the screen lighting up with the picture of Noah in his flight suit that I'd snapped last time we were together.

"It's Noah. I'll be right back."

I hit Accept and walked out of the shop.

"Hey," I answered.

"Hey, babe."

His voice sounded different; not the usual happy-to-talk-to-me that I normally heard when he called.

"What's wrong?"

He sighed. "I have bad news. I'm really, really sorry, but I'm not going to be able to make your sister's wedding. I got stuck with an ONE that I can't get out of. I'm so sorry."

"An ONE?"

"Operation Noble Eagle. Flying air support for high-profile targets. I can't say what it is, but the squadron got tasked with one for this weekend and manning is a bitch. They need an instructor to lead it and Joker wants me since it's high vis. I tried to get out of it, but there's no way."

Disappointment clogged my throat as silence filled the line. It was his job; I knew he couldn't do anything about it. I wasn't angry, just frustrated. And embarrassed. I didn't know how to explain to my family that he was canceling at the last minute. The military was such a foreign concept to them that I doubted they'd understand. And ugh, now I was dateless again. Not to mention the fact that I'd been looking forward to seeing him again. Really looking forward to seeing him. I felt petty for caring, but my family was important to me. I wanted them to meet Noah. Wanted him to see this side of my life. And I wanted to make memories together. To start building a life. It wasn't just him missing a weekend together; it was him missing a huge family event. Maybe it was stupid to let it bother me, but it did.

"Jordan?"

"It's okay. I understand."

"I know it's not okay. I feel terrible."

I forced myself to sound as cheery as possible. "You shouldn't feel terrible. It's your job. You told me it would be like this. I'm not going to lie and say I'm not disappointed, but I do understand. I know you would be here if you could."

I hoped I wasn't wrong about him, that he really was the guy I thought he was. It wouldn't be the first time I'd trusted what a guy told me only to find out it had all been one big lie. I really hoped I wasn't going to get burned on this one.

"I hate letting you down. Hate disappointing you."

"I know."

"I'm sorry I'm going to miss meeting your family. Maybe I can try to plan a trip to Florida after I get back from the TDY to Alaska."

He was going to be gone most of April and all of May, and it was officially the longest separation we'd had.

"Yeah. That would be good."

We said bye, and then he was gone, and I was standing outside the bridal shop, facing the unpleasant task of having to go explain to my mother and sister that Noah couldn't make it to the wedding. Considering the hard time my mother had given me about dating him, period, I figured this news would only bolster her argument that this wasn't a stable relationship for me. Maybe she was right. Maybe I was setting myself up for a lot of heartache. But either way, I didn't know how to turn off my feelings for him. Love wasn't always logical.

I sat at the reception with the bridal party, dressed in my pink satin bridesmaids' dress, the odd one out in what was now a table of nine.

The wedding had been beautiful. Meg had beamed walking down the aisle with our father, and the look on Mike's face when he first saw her had been so incredibly sweet. I'd cried while they said their vows, still not quite believing my baby sister was now a wife.

I'd spent the reception talking to family members, fending off questions of why I didn't have a date, and the ultimate, *When are you going to meet a nice boy and settle down?*

They asked it as though my single status were completely my choice, as though I was too "wild" for a relationship, an animal unsuited for domestication. Some part of me wanted to give a little overview of my last four failed relationships—the guy who had wanted me to wear flats whenever we went on dates because he didn't like how tall I was, the one who lived at home with his parents at thirty-two, the one who'd cheated on me with one of his co-workers, or the guy who'd insisted on splitting the bill on every single date we went on with alarming precision. Not exactly the stuff of great romance.

I didn't mention Noah. I wasn't up for hearing the questions of why he wasn't here or any repetition of my mother's concerns about how he wasn't a good bet for me. She'd pretty much freaked when I'd told her he wasn't coming after all—

not to mention how pissed they'd been about having to re-arrange the table setting and seating chart. My father had been better about it, but I could tell he was disappointed about not getting to meet Noah.

I missed him tonight. There was something about a wedding—the romance in the air perhaps—that made it suck to feel single. I wanted him to whirl me around the dance floor. To hold my hand. I wanted to share it with him.

"It's time for the bride to toss the bouquet," the DJ an-nounced. "We need all of the single ladies out onto the dance floor."

Ugh.

In my twenties, bouquet tosses had been fun and exciting. There was still that optimism and the romantic possibility that maybe there was some good-luck-slash-magic in those bundled-up flowers. Now it was just a scarlet fucking "S" for single, as the smattering of loners were herded onto the dance floor like cattle to be pointed at by all the happily married couples watching us with varying stages of pity.

I stayed in my fucking seat.

"Jordan! Aren't you going to get up there?" my mother called out from the table next to ours.

I gritted my teeth at the sound of her overly cheerful voice. It didn't matter if it was my third grade dance recital or my sister's wedding, my mother never shied away from embarrassing me.

I looked at the dance floor—four singles. Awesome.

"I'm okay."

"Don't be ridiculous. Go out there." She turned to her sister, my aunt Shirley, lowering her voice slightly, but still loud enough that I couldn't miss her next comment. "She's thirty this year. No boyfriend."

I bit my cheek trying to keep from offering up a retort. I did have a boyfriend. He just unfortunately had a wife in the United States Air Force.

"Are we ready?" the DJ asked, scanning the crowd.

Meg walked up to the front of the room, bouquet in hand. Our gazes locked across the room.

"Come on," she mouthed, gesturing toward me with her free hand.

I loved my sister, and it was her wedding. I stood, feeling like everyone's gaze was on me as I made my way to the group of girls eagerly awaiting the toss.

Oh God, my seventeen-year-old cousin was here.

So freaking embarrassing.

Meg turned her back to us, and then she heaved the bouquet over her head, the flowers sailing through the air.

I didn't know if she did it intentionally, or if the bouquet gods had just decided to add to my embarrassment, but either way, the thing practically fell into my waiting hands as though pulled there by a magnetic field.

Meg grinned, coming over and giving me a big hug, while all the people cheered.

Whatever.

NOAH

I was exhausted after the ONE, my day spent essentially flying circles in the sky. I was in a shit mood, knowing I'd let Jordan down again, my mind with her the entire time. I didn't want her family to think I'd flaked out, didn't want her to think that, either.

I checked the time in Florida and pulled out my cell and

called her, wondering if she would be back from the reception yet. She answered immediately.

"Hey. How was the wedding?"

I could hear the excitement in her voice, and the telltale sign that she'd been partying a bit. "Really beautiful. Meg was so happy."

"I'm sorry I couldn't be there." I stared at the picture she'd sent me earlier of her dressed in pink, flowers in her hand; I'd made it my backdrop. "You looked gorgeous. Did you have a good time?"

"Yeah, I did. I caught the bouquet."

I grinned. "Really?"

"Yeah."

"I'm sorry I missed that."

"Me, too."

Silence filled the line.

Worry hit me.

"Are we okay?"

She took a deep breath. "Yes. Maybe a little no."

A pang hit my chest. "That's fair."

"I know this is fast, and believe me, I kind of feel like an idiot for even bringing it up, but I'm thirty and I just caught the bouquet at my little sister's wedding and endured days of relatives asking me why I hadn't met a nice guy, and I've drunk like a freaking bottle of champagne, so I'm just going to ask—this is going somewhere, right?" She took another deep breath. "I'm not crazy here, thinking we're on the same page when we're not."

I'd had the talk before with girlfriends, and honestly, it had never been something I enjoyed, but with Jordan, it felt different. I didn't blame her for asking, and maybe it was too soon in the sense that we'd only known each other over a month, but in a way, it didn't feel too soon. I'd been with girls for six months and felt less for them than I did for Jordan after just six weeks—a lot less.

"Yes. This is definitely going somewhere."

"I don't mind having fun, and I'm not asking for a proposal or anything," she added, "but I really care about you, and even though I have no clue how it would work with our lifestyles, I could see myself having a future with you. I want to work toward that."

God. Me, too. I was falling in love with her. I wanted to be able to tell her that we had a future together, wanted to give her the possibility of forever, even when my forever came with a host of military-provided caveats and asterisks.

"I don't know what our future holds, and given the way everything has gone with my life in the military, I can definitely promise that it will be bumpy, but I'm with you—I want to work toward building a future together. I know it's early, and I know it's fast, but I've never felt this way about anyone before. You have me for as long as you want me."

"Promise?"

"Promise."

Silence filled the line again and then I could hear the smile in her voice. "How was your flying thing?"

I grinned. "It was good. Wish I were in Florida with you, though."

"Can I come see you soon?" she asked.

"I was hoping you would. I miss you."

"How about next weekend?"

"Next weekend is perfect."

Relief filled me. I'd been so worried that this would screw things up between us, but now I clung to the hope that there was still a chance.

"So what are you wearing?" Jordan asked, breaking the silence, a teasing note in her voice.

I grinned. "Are you propositioning me?"

"Maybe. I don't know if it was being a bridesmaid, or the wedding, or the champagne, but I sort of feel like I owe the dress some sex. Think you could help me out with that?"

That I could definitely do.

$\mathcal{S}$EVENTEEN

JORDAN

I took a sip of my beer, burrowing deeper into the curve of Noah's arm. I was spending the weekend with him in Oklahoma and we'd gone out to dinner with Joker, Dani, Easy, and Thor.

I was slowly eating my way through the Oklahoma barbecue scene and this place might have been my favorite of all the restaurants we'd gone to. The brisket was one of the best things I'd ever eaten and the baked beans were to die for. I could have written poems about the coleslaw.

I was surprised at how much fun I was having, at how seamlessly the group fit together. Dani and Joker were adorable as a couple, and I'd pretty much decided I wanted to be them when I grew up. Even though they'd been married for a while, they still looked like they were newlyweds in love. They held hands and finished each other's sentences in a way that was cute rather than annoying.

The guys talked about flying for the most part, and I'd gotten used to the fact that most of our conversations revolved around jets. When it was just the two of us, Noah kept the fighter pilot talk to a minimum, but when he was around his bros, they all basically geeked out on it. I didn't always understand what they were talking about, but I was slowly picking up some of the lingo.

"Do you mind if we go play pool?" Noah asked. "Do you want to play?"

I grinned. "Thanks, but I'm horrible at pool." I met Dani's gaze across the table. "Do you want to just hang out here?"

She nodded. "Sounds like a plan to me. We can have a break from talking about F-16s."

Easy shot her a sheepish grin. "Sorry about that."

The guys got up from the table and I watched them walk away, not bothering to hide how much I enjoyed the view. As much as I teased Easy and Noah about their bromance, there was something cute about seeing them all together. Plus, the fact that they were fine as fuck didn't hurt.

My gaze met Dani's and her lips twitched. "The flying conversations ad nauseam can get a little old, but there are definitely perks to this."

I laughed. "So true."

We'd started chatting and texting in the weeks since we'd met, and she kept me in the loop on all the squadron functions. I was kind of surprised by how active the wives were—they had monthly coffees and what seemed like social functions nearly every week. I hadn't been able to make any of them yet, but I really appreciated Dani including me. Not all of the wives had been as welcoming as she was, and she was definitely the only one I felt close to.

I was feeling a little lost in this whole military girlfriend thing, and it was nice to hang out with someone who understood the ups and downs better than anyone. I'd tried talking to Sophia about Noah after Meg's wedding, and she'd listened, but it wasn't quite the same. My family and friends kept asking me if I wanted to be with a guy who didn't seem as invested in the relationship as I was—how I was okay with the fact that I was always the one visiting him—and as much as I tried to explain that his job complicated everything, they just didn't seem to understand. I knew they loved me and wanted me to be happy, but right now I needed to talk to someone who got it.

"You guys are adorable together," Dani commented, a smile on her face. "I've known Noah for years now and I've never seen him as happy as he is with you."

I really needed to hear that right now.

"How's the adjustment to military life?" she asked.

"It's going, I guess. Sometimes it doesn't feel like that big of a deal, and other times . . ."

Sometimes I forgot he didn't have a normal job, then inevitably, something happened and I was right back to being terrified every time he told me he was about to fly, my stomach in knots until he texted to tell me he'd landed.

"Yep. That pretty much sums it up." She took a sip of her drink. "I heard about your sister's wedding. That had to have been rough."

"Yeah, it was. I understood, but that didn't make it any less disappointing, or easier to tell my parents. Does that kind of stuff happen a lot?" I asked, not entirely sure I wanted the answer. Although in this case I was beginning to learn that it was better to prepare for the worst and be pleasantly surprised than to set myself up for disappointment.

"More times than I can count. Sometimes it's not so last minute, but often it is. Trust me, you don't know how many times I've had to cancel travel plans. It's gotten to the point where I just avoid making plans or booking trips until the last minute. And if something does come up that requires a lot of lead time, like a wedding or something, I just assume Joker won't be able to make it."

"That has to be hard."

"It is. As hard as it is with the two of us, I'm worried about when we have kids. I know a lot of the wives do it, but at the same time, I've seen so many of my friends celebrate their kids' milestones while their husbands are gone. I worry that Joker's going to miss out on the important stuff. And honestly, given how much he works, the day-to-day stuff, too.

"As much as I know that I can handle basically being a single parent on my own, there's this part of me that wishes things could be different. That he could have a normal job that would let him be around for birthdays and holidays, and not gone more than he's home."

I hadn't even thought about what it would be like to raise kids in this lifestyle. She was right; I struggled to imagine a family like that. Not when mine was so close.

"Sorry, I didn't mean to pile on you. The kid thing has been on my mind lately." Sadness flickered in her eyes. "We've been trying to get pregnant for a while now."

On the one hand, I was surprised she'd share something so personal with me, but at the same time it felt like there was a connection forming between us. Maybe it was part of being in this sisterhood of sorts. There was something about this lifestyle—the common experience that so few people shared—that had you forming bonds more quickly than you otherwise would.

"We've been trying for the last couple of years and it isn't happening," she continued. "I keep telling myself I just need to be calm about it, but it's hard when I've been wanting it so badly for so long." Her eyes welled up. "I had a miscarriage six months ago, and it's just been really tough since then."

"I'm so sorry." I reached out and squeezed her hand.

"Thanks. It's just been tough for us. Joker was TDY when I miscarried, and he came home for a bit, but then he had to go to Vegas for Red Flag, and now this TDY to Alaska. Normally I'm fine with him being gone, but I don't know . . . I think I'm just a mess after losing the baby. And it's hard to get pregnant when your husband isn't home."

"I can't imagine what it must have been like to go through something like that by yourself."

"Joker was able to get home the next day, but it was really difficult not having him with me. Thank God for the squadron, though. The wives pitched in until he came home. And Easy took me to the hospital and stayed with me the whole time."

That surprised me. I must have made a face because her lips twitched.

"You don't like Easy very much, do you?"

I hesitated. "I don't dislike him. He's just not my favorite person. Something about him rubs me the wrong way."

"I can see that. He comes off like a bit of an asshole, but I promise, he's a good guy. He and Joker have been close for a while now and I've gotten to know him. He was really amazing to me when I needed him, and he's been a good friend to Joker. And he does really care about Noah. He's the kind of guy who you want to have your back.

"This life can be hard, but you'll learn to make friends who will become like family to you. A lot of times you won't have a family support network near you, so you'll find people around you who can be that for you. It isn't always easy, but it helps. It can be difficult for your family and friends to understand what it's like, and you'll need people you can talk to. And seriously, if you ever need a friend to listen or a shoulder to cry on, call me. Noah's like family and I'm so happy he's found someone he cares about and who's good for him. Anything you need, I'm here."

"I'll definitely take you up on that."

She grinned. "Good. We're having a party at our house tomorrow night. You guys should come over; you can meet more of the wives."

"I'd like that. A lot."

We chatted for the rest of the night, watching our men play pool, and as chaotic as everything felt swirling around me, I couldn't deny the fact that I felt like I was putting down some roots here and finding a place for myself in Noah's life.

EIGHTEEN

JORDAN

We spent Saturday night at Joker and Dani's house, hanging out at the barbecue they hosted for the squadron. Judging by the number of people filling their home and spilling out onto the deck and lawn, it looked like all the Wild Aces had come out to party. Kids ran around, playing with toys and shouting. It was a big, chaotic, messy family of people.

I hung out with Dani for the most part, helping her get the food together. Noah got into a discussion about sports and I left him talking with Joker. As the night progressed, the families began to leave and the crowd thinned out a bit, until we were one of the few couples left. I hung off to the side, taking a minute to breathe. It had been an awesome party, but it was one of those nights when I felt like I needed to be "on," wanting to make a good impression on Noah's friends.

I watched him talking to Dani and Joker, happy to see he was having a good time. My gaze swept over the crowd, stopping on Easy.

Easy stood at the edge of the group, his arms crossed over his chest, highlighting his impressive torso, a bottle of beer dangling from his fingers. I was surprised to see him on the fringes; he wasn't the kind of guy you expected to be alone at a party like this. I figured he'd be in the thick of it, entertaining everyone with a joke, his arm around a hot girl.

He lifted the bottle to his lips, taking a long pull, his gaze on something across the room. I turned, my attention already drifting back to Noah, when all of a sudden I saw Easy's entire body go stiff as though he were bracing for a blow. A flash of pain drifted across his face—a kind of loneliness, longing, sadness, melancholy, all rolled up into one ball of horrible that I couldn't look away from.

My gaze followed his across the room, trying to figure out what the hell would make a look like that come into his eyes.

Dani stood across the room, her body tucked against Joker's side, a blinding smile on her face. She pressed her lips to her husband's, and my attention jerked back to Easy.

He looked like someone had punched him in the face. No, worse. Physical pain would be tame compared to the look in Easy's eyes now. No, he looked like a man who'd had his insides scraped out with a grapefruit spoon, leaving a mess of entrails and emotions. And then as quickly as it had come, it was gone, his usual mask in place.

It hit me—how he acted differently around Dani, the change in his voice when he spoke to her, the look in his eyes. It had been there all along.

Easy turned away, setting his beer bottle on the table, and headed toward the door, leaving me staring after him, the desire to do something to make it better, even when I didn't know what, an urge I nearly couldn't resist. I'd never imagined that I'd feel sorry for Easy, and yet I did.

There wasn't anything much worse than wanting someone you couldn't have.

NOAH

I walked away from the group, not in the fucking mood to discuss flying right now. I'd seen the look on Easy's face, like someone had put his dick in a vise at the sight of Dani and Joker together. And I'd seen Jordan see it. And if Easy wasn't fucking careful, everyone would see it.

I knew Easy. He wasn't the kind of guy who would ever make a move on Dani. For all that he could be a player, he was loyal to his friends. And even if he were the kind of guy who would make a move on a bro's wife, Dani wasn't like that at all. Still, this was not good for the squadron. Not to mention, my best friend looked more torn up with each day that passed. I kept thinking that this would go away; it wasn't like he was known for sticking with a girl for longer than a few days anyway. But it wasn't going away. And that made it so much worse.

Jordan walked over to me. I reached out and gripped her hand, linking our fingers. We didn't speak; we just stood there, holding on to each other, as though we both realized how lucky we were to be together. Seeing the naked pain on Easy's face made me hope that I never had to go through the experience of loving someone I couldn't have.

Jordan squeezed my hand. "You should go talk to him."

She was right, of course, but the truth was, I had no idea how to talk to him.

"I don't know what to say," I muttered, more than a little embarrassed to admit that I was helpless when it came to my best friend.

"You'll figure it out."

"I'm a guy. Relationship advice isn't exactly my forte."

Her lips twitched. "That has not escaped my notice. But it also hasn't escaped my notice that you guys have a bit of a bromance going on. If he's going to talk to anyone about this, it'll be you."

She was right, and still, I had no clue how to broach a conversation that would basically go along the lines of, *You need to stop fantasizing about our boss's wife.*

"I'll go talk to him."

Jordan's lips pressed to my cheek, her soft curves colliding with my body.

The words hovered between us, unspoken.

I love you.

It was fast. Really, really fast. And despite numerous relationships and the fact that I was thirty-three, I'd never actually said the words before. Never told a woman I wasn't related to that I loved her.

I loved Jordan.

I loved her kindness, her enormous heart. Loved her smile, and her sexiness, and the attitude that perfectly complemented the over-the-top body. She was fun. She made me smile, made me feel things I'd never felt before. And more than anything, I wanted to make this work.

My arms tightened around her as I pulled the words back inside me. A squadron barbecue wasn't exactly the best time or place to tell her how I felt.

She nudged my hip. "Go."

I grabbed my beer and headed off in search of Easy, slipping out of the party and into Joker's enormous backyard.

Easy leaned against the deck railing, beer in hand, looking up at the stars. He didn't turn as I walked toward him, but we'd had enough nights like this that we both slid into the roles of over a decade of friendship with ease.

I stood next to him, following his gaze up to the sky. It would be a gorgeous night to fly. We drank our beers in silence, the unspoken words between us an elephant in the room.

"I'll get it under control."

My hand froze in midair, the bottle partway to my mouth. He sounded bad. Really bad.

I turned to face him. "Are you sure you can do that?"

His jaw clenched as he threw back the beer again.

"I don't know."

I lifted my beer to my lips.

"I'm not going to do anything."

"I know."

"It's obvious, isn't it?"

I didn't know what to tell him. It kind of was; I'd figured it out months ago. Of course, I knew Easy better than anyone. And Dani was so far from the girl you expected Easy to be attracted to, that I figured most people hadn't picked up on it. But it was only a matter of time. Especially if he kept looking at her the way he did.

I didn't say anything, but I figured my nonanswer was answer enough.

He emptied the bottle of beer, setting it down on the wooden railing.

"Go back to your girl. I'll come inside in a second."

"You sure?"

He nodded.

I turned to walk back into the party and Easy's voice stopped me in my tracks.

"Don't fuck it up with her. She's the kind of girl you work your ass off to keep. You're not going to find another one like her. Take it from me, nothing sucks more than watching the girl you want be just out of your grasp."

JORDAN

We got home from the barbecue late, a weird tension descending on the group. Noah was quiet and left to take a shower. Easy went to the living room and turned on the television. And I hovered in the hallway, wondering if I should say something to him because the look of utter defeat on his face suggested he desperately needed someone to talk to.

Finally, Easy broke the silence for me.

"You can just say it. I know you saw."

I swallowed. "You love her."

The look he sent me was an awful mix of pain and panic.

"No."

My gaze didn't waver.

"Yeah," he admitted, his voice low.

That word. He said it as though it clawed its way through his throat. I'd always thought of Easy as shallow. And I'd never really understood Noah's friendship with him. But the look in Easy's eyes, the sound of his voice—there was a depth there I'd never imagined. And even more surprising, it had been Dani who brought it out in him.

"Do you want to talk about it?"

He rubbed his jaw, that same haunted stare in his gaze.

"No."

"Do you need to talk about it?"

He nodded.

An idea hit. Maybe it was stupid, but I felt the need to do *something*.

"Wait here."

I walked to the kitchen, rummaging around in the freezer until I found the carton I was looking for. I grabbed two spoons from the drawer and headed back to the living room.

I bit back a laugh at the look of curiosity on Easy's face. Given the state of their kitchen before I'd gone grocery shopping, I figured there wasn't a lot of mint chocolate chip in his life. It was a travesty I was determined to rectify as soon as possible.

I handed him a spoon and the carton of ice cream.

"Eat."

The side of his mouth twitched. "Is this supposed to make it all okay?"

"Not even close. But it's good. Really good. And perfect body aside, you need a little splurge."

The twitch grew. "Do you force-feed Noah ice cream?"

"I have other means of making Noah happy."

He grinned. "I've heard."

I made a face.

"No, literally, you guys are loud as shit. Noah hasn't said a word, though."

My cheeks flamed at the idea of Easy hearing us have sex. It wasn't lost on me that I was, indeed, loud.

"Do you and Noah usually talk about your sex lives?"

"Usually?" Easy shrugged, opening the carton. "Sometimes. Not about you."

That was a relief, at least.

"This is good," he commented, polishing off a spoonful of ice cream. "Did you get Noah to buy this?"

I nodded. "The rabbit food got old."

Another smile. He really was beautiful. "Rabbit food?"

"Almonds, celery, carrots."

He laughed. "Fair enough."

We sat there in silence while he ate the ice cream, occasionally holding the carton out to me so that I could dig out a spoonful. And with the magic of mint chocolate chip, he started talking.

"I keep thinking—hoping—it'll go away. That I'll look at her and this feeling in my chest won't be there anymore. I keep waiting for it to die."

I winced. "When did it start?"

"First time I saw her. We had a Hail and Farewell. It's a squadron function where we welcome new pilots that come in and say good-bye to ones who are leaving. I'd been TDY so I'd missed the change of command, didn't even know who she was. I just walked into the squadron bar and saw this girl standing there, playing with one of the kids, this smile on her face . . ."

His voice broke off, that look back in his eyes.

"I've never felt that way. Ever. I wanted to know who she was, hell, I think part of me stopped thinking and I just went over there, determined to make her mine, my brain not even considering the idea that she would already be with someone else. It seemed wrong that she should be with someone else, that she wasn't meant for me."

Oh my God.

Oh.

My.

God.

I'd never heard a guy say stuff like this. And given the time I'd spent in the fighter squadron, I'd *really* never heard a guy like Easy say stuff like this. There didn't appear to be a lot of sensitive and deep feelings within the Wild Aces, but now I realized I was wrong.

"Then Joker came up and wrapped his arms around her and I realized who she was."

I could only imagine how he'd felt. The pain. The epic disaster of it all. And I had to imagine that the thing that made it worse was that Joker was a good guy. This wasn't a situation where Dani was unhappy in a loveless marriage. She adored her husband, and it was pretty clear that he adored her, too.

"How long has it been?"

"A year."

I didn't even know what to say. It was a crappy situation. A really, really crappy situation.

"That sucks."

"No shit."

"Maybe you'll meet someone else," I offered.

Easy gave me a look of amusement. "I meet a lot of girls."

True.

"You've met her. Do you think I'm going to meet anyone else like her?"

I got his point. Dani seemed pretty special.

"Maybe you'll meet someone who isn't like her, but who you like even more."

He didn't respond, just kept digging at the ice cream. I didn't know if there was anything I could say to make this better; I was beginning to suspect there wasn't. Maybe Noah had been right about all of it and I should have just left it alone.

Fuck.

I sucked in a deep breath. "You know Dani told me about what you did for her. About the miscarriage."

His jaw clenched.

"And she told me that you were a good guy. A really good

guy. She cares about you. A lot. I know it's not the same way you feel about her, and believe me, I know it hurts to want her and not be able to have her, but you are special to her. She sees the deep in you, and even though I didn't see it before, I see it now."

I reached out and squeezed his hand.

"It's not my business, but you're important to two people I care about, so you're important to me. You deserve more than girls who are trying to bag a status symbol. And the girls who care, who want more, deserve better than a guy who's just fucking his way through heartbreak. So be the guy everyone thinks you can be. Maybe you can't have Dani, but I promise you, there's someone out there for you. You just have to find her."

A moment passed, and then Easy pulled me into a side hug, the carton of ice cream between us.

"Thanks." He released me, picking the spoon up. "Go back to Noah. I'm going to drown my sorrows a bit longer."

"Are you going to be okay?"

He nodded.

I squeezed his hand again and got up from the couch, heading down the dark hall to the bedroom. I stopped short as my body nearly collided with Noah's. I stifled a shriek.

He leaned against the wall, pajama pants slung low on his hips, cotton T-shirt rumpled. Pieces of his hair stuck up at weird angles from just getting out of the shower. Clearly he'd been listening to my conversation with Easy. He tucked me against his body, his arms at my waist. His lips brushed my hair, and then he whispered in my ear, his voice achingly soft.

"I love you."

I froze, those three little words suddenly life changing.

I pulled back, my face tipping up to stare into his, my hand reaching up to trace the stubble at his jaw. His eyes closed as he leaned into my touch, and a whole other part of me melted.

"I love you, too."

It just came out without thought or design. It just was.

"I don't ever want to lose you," he whispered.

"Me, either."

"Promise me we'll find a way to make this work."

"I promise."

We stood still, our limbs wrapped around each other, our heads bent, foreheads pressed together.

His grasp on me tightened. "Thanks for being nice to Easy," he whispered.

"I was wrong about him. I didn't understand you guys before, but I get it now. He's a good guy."

"Yeah, he is."

Noah jerked his head toward the bedroom. "It's late. Come to bed."

He clasped hands with mine and we walked down the hall to the room that was beginning to feel like *our* room, to the life that was beginning to feel like *our* life.

It was funny how three little words could change so much, and yet, somehow they did.

NOAH

The weekend went by quickly, and then I was back at work on Monday, four flights scheduled for the week.

"You got a second?"

I looked up at Joker standing in the doorway of my office.

"Yeah. What's up?"

"I just got a call from the guy who runs the Fighter Porch."

"About me?"

One guy at the Fighter Porch handled all of the Air Force fighter assignments. We were put in groups known as VMLs based on the months when we arrived at our current assignment and then we received our new assignment based on our VML. Mine was still two VMLs away so it was weird that they'd call my squadron commander.

"Yeah. They're still fighting manning issues in Korea. Osan and Kunsan. They're nonvolling guys who have been on station for at least two years in their current assignment."

Oh, fuck.

Joker saw my face. "Sorry, man. I know the timing sucks."

"Sucks" didn't begin to cover it.

"When?"

He winced.

"Three months. Your Report No Later Than Date is July thirty-first."

Motherfucker.

"Which base?"

"Osan." Joker sighed. "I know this is a kick in the nuts personally, but he did tell me that they want you up at the Wing. Wing Weapons Officer."

It was a good opportunity for me. I'd been stationed in Korea before, and as assignments went, it wasn't high on my list, but working at the Wing level was the kind of career advancement that would look great when my promotion board came around. But fuck, the timing couldn't have been worse.

"We're going to be sorry to lose you, man."

I nodded, still processing this. A year ago, it wouldn't have fazed me. If my Air Force career had been defined by anything, it was that the one thing you could expect was the unexpected. But now?

Joker left and I sat there, staring at the phone, wondering how the hell I was going to explain this to Jordan. I'd always told her I had a year left in Oklahoma. We'd never even broached the possibility of my next assignment taking me outside of the United States. Or that it would spring up on me like this.

Fuck.

It was a two-year assignment. And I'd only get thirty days of leave a year. So even if I could take leave, which with the high ops tempo would be difficult to say the least, that meant we'd only have thirty days a year to spend together. How did you sustain a relationship like that? Especially a new relationship?

Sure, we loved each other, but it wasn't like we were married. How could I ask her to wait two years for me? Two years of having a boyfriend and spending holidays, birthdays, anniversaries alone. Two years of me not being there for all the things that mattered in her life. How long would it be before she met a doctor or lawyer who worked normal hours and had some semblance of control over his life? How long before she got tired of waiting around for me and found someone who could make her happy and give her the things she wanted? She was thirty. She wanted kids, wanted to settle down.

When would I be able to give that to anyone?

Panic clawed at me. I loved her. I loved her and I was terrified that this would be the tipping point and I'd lose her. I'd screwed up when I'd missed her sister's wedding, was getting ready to go to Alaska for a fucking month and a half. And then when I returned, we'd have less than two months together before my ass would have to be on a plane to Korea.

Fuck.

JORDAN

I curled up on the couch, Lulu sitting on my feet, showing me her sad eyes, begging to be petted. I scratched her ears as she head-butted me, giving me soft little kisses.

Today had been a shit day. A really shit day.

Work had been hectic and I was exhausted by the time I got to my parents'. Only to be blindsided by another attempt to "fix" my love life. I'd sat there for a fucking hour, listening to my mother throw some major shade about Noah missing Meg's wedding and all the ways he was wrong for me. Not to mention her not-so-subtle attempts to fix me up with pretty much every single guy left in town. At this point, I wouldn't have been surprised to learn that she'd set up an online dating profile for me and started vetting the future father of my children.

Ugh.

I definitely shouldn't give her any ideas. She'd jump on that one.

I would never have admitted it, but the truth was, her barbs were unbearable because I felt them. I knew I loved Noah, and he said he loved me, and yet I'd been burned enough times to question it. And I missed him. I hated that he was never here. Hated the distance between us. And now with this trip to Alaska coming up . . .

It just felt like I would always come second to the Air Force. And while part of me—the rational, adult part— understood that he couldn't help it, another part of me wondered what I was getting myself into.

In a way, my mother was right. Ugh. That never got easier to say. There was an element of this that screamed, *Danger: Heartbreak Ahead*. I didn't know how to love him and not want to be with him. And at the same time, I loved my job, had worked hard to get where I was. I loved my family, loved my life in Florida. Giving that up to follow Noah seemed foolish. Or at the very least, terrifying.

Love was scary enough. Loving a military man was something else entirely. Because it wasn't just a matter of did he love me, or could he make me happy? It was did he love me *enough* to make me giving up everything else worthwhile? Could he make me happy *enough* to make it worth me giving up a career that fulfilled me? It was a lot of pressure to put on anyone, especially on a new relationship, and it seemed like the questions I needed answers to were the ones that required a giant leap of faith.

Why did adulting have to be so freaking hard?

I grabbed my cell, ignoring Lulu's soft growl of protest when I stopped scratching her. I needed to hear Noah's voice to erase the sound of my mother saying things like, *What are you doing with your life?*

It was still kind of early in Oklahoma, and considering how late Noah usually worked, I figured the odds of reaching him were iffy, but I didn't care.

When he answered, I felt the first surge of relief.

"I wasn't sure if you'd be still at work."

"I cut out a little early. I needed to come home and deal with some stuff."

His voice sounded funny again.

"Are you okay? Did you have a bad day at work?"

Silence.

"Noah?"

A sinking feeling spread through my stomach. Something wasn't right.

"Are you okay?" I asked again, worry filling my voice.

"We need to talk."

Those four words knocked the wind right out of me. This was it. Maybe I should have realized sooner that if it sounded too good to be true, it probably was. Hell, fifteen years of dating had taught me that if nothing else. Chupacabra, my ass.

My voice got tight.

"What's up?"

Did he meet someone else? Was he tired of long distance? Was he just not into me anymore? What the ever-loving fuck?

"I'm PCS-ing to Korea."

That was one I hadn't heard before.

"PCS-ing?" I squeaked the word out, my mind racing, everything off.

Noah cursed. "Moving. It's my next assignment."

I couldn't.

"For how long?" My voice sounded like it was far away, like part of me was drowning.

"Two years."

I was going to be sick.

"I don't understand. You told me you weren't going to move for another year."

"I wasn't supposed to. But they need guys to go to Korea and it's not necessarily a popular assignment right now. Especially for guys with families. So they've started non-volling guys, which basically means in my case, that because I've been in Oklahoma for two years, they're able to move me to Korea even though I wasn't in the cycle to move and I didn't volunteer for the assignment."

I couldn't get my bearings, couldn't even come up with anything to say in response. It all just sounded so bizarre. I mean, yeah, I'd accepted that he lived in a world that was unlike any I'd ever known, and one I'd probably never understand, but this was just so unexpected, so fucked up. I couldn't process it. It felt like he was delivering this news to someone else. I heard the words, but I couldn't wrap my head around how they related to me.

"When?"

How much longer did I have with him?

He was silent for another beat, which I'd already figured out was his precursor for bad news.

"At the end of July."

My stomach sank.

"That's in three months."

More silence.

Another thought occurred to me. "You're going to Alaska for a month and a half."

"Yeah."

His voice sounded as bad as I felt.

"I—"

I struggled to calm down, to organize my thoughts, struggled to get my shit together.

"I don't know what to do with this."

"I know."

Maybe it was a good thing for him. Maybe it was good for his career. I should have been happy for him. Shouldn't have been as freaked out as I was. But we'd just said, *I love you.* We'd gotten to the point where this no longer felt like a casual fling, or a relationship in that awkward phase of where-do-we-stand, and instead felt like *something.* Something that was us trying to build a life together. And now he was leaving.

And it felt like my heart was breaking. And, oh God, I was going to start crying.

"Listen, I, uh, need to go, but I'll call you later, okay?" I pushed the words out, my voice cracking, heart hammering.

"Jordan."

God, this sucked. So freaking much. Why couldn't I have fallen in love with a dentist? Someone with a nice, normal job. My mother was right. I was a romantic shitshow.

"Jordan," he repeated.

"I can't talk about this," I whispered, the first tear trickling down my face. I didn't want to put my own shit on him. Didn't want him to hear me completely fall apart. And I was like a minute away from completely losing it.

"We need to talk about it."

I wiped the tear off my cheek. "I'm not sure what there is to talk about."

He sucked in a deep breath. "Us."

"What us?"

He was silent again. When he finally did speak, his words brought more tears.

"I don't want to lose you."

God.

I closed my eyes, unable to stave off the onslaught of tears any longer.

"I don't want to lose you, either."

He groaned. "I can't stand the thought of you crying."

I sniffled, the sound nothing like the cute, birdlike sniffles you heard when girls cried on TV or in movies. I was an ugly crier in the extreme.

"I'm sorry. I don't want to make this worse." I wiped at my face again. "I just wasn't prepared for this."

"I know. I wasn't, either."

I closed my eyes. "Is this good for you? Professionally, I mean? Are you excited about it?"

I remembered that he'd been stationed in Korea before. Maybe this wasn't as weird for him as it was for me. He was probably used to the moving and everything that came with it.

"A year ago, it would have been fine. Now . . ." He sighed. "I love you."

That was the part that made it even worse. I could see myself being with him. Really being with him. If you stripped away the military stuff, I had no doubt that I would want to marry him. That he would be it for me. Even with the military stuff . . .

"I need to know what this means for us," he continued, his voice thick with emotion.

"I—"

I didn't know what it could mean for us. Long distance was hard, but doable, when we were a somewhat short plane ride away. But flying to Korea? Maybe we could do it a couple times, but nowhere near as often as we saw each other now, and even that didn't feel like enough.

How did you make a relationship work if you never saw each other?

"I don't know," I answered.

"Okay."

The sadness in his voice pulled at my heart.

"Do you want to break up?"

And that pierced me.

"No." I didn't even have to think about it, the word just escaped, partly in a panic. I had no idea how this would play out between us, but I did know that I wasn't ready to give up on us.

"Do you want to break up?" I asked, fear clogging my throat.

"No."

"So what then?"

"I don't know. I know it's a lot to ask of you. It's two years. I'll get maybe a month off each year. It sucks, I know. But I promise I'll come see you every chance I get. And maybe you could come out there for a few visits."

It wasn't much, but I knew he was trying. Seeing each other a little bit was at least better than not seeing each other at all.

So why did I feel like crying? Why did I feel like the writing was already on the wall?

"I'm so sorry."

I knew he was. I could hear it in his voice. But it didn't make it easier, or better. And it wouldn't make up for the fact that I felt like I was in a relationship, but not really in a relationship. Like we were playing at being a couple without the intimacy I craved. I'd been single most of my life. I wanted someone to spend holidays and special events with. As corny as it sounded, I wanted someone to make memories with. To come home to after a long day. And now Noah would be even farther away and I wondered at what point the phone calls would cease to be enough. For both of us. Hell, we had a tough enough time talking now—what would it be like with the time difference?

"What are you thinking?" he asked.

I couldn't lie.

"I don't know how we can make this work."

He sighed. "Me, either."

"I just keep wondering if it should be this hard."

"I know. I'm worried that I'm asking too much. That you aren't going to be happy if we're always apart, if I can't ever be there when you need me." His voice was strained. "I'm worried you're going to meet a guy who can give you all the things that I can't. And part of me wants you to meet that guy. You deserve to meet him." He groaned. "And part of me hates the idea of you with someone else and is terrified to lose you."

I knew exactly how he felt.

"Maybe we just give this a shot and see where we end up. Take it one day at a time," I suggested. "Neither one of us was expecting to be here now. Maybe we just need to come to terms with this a bit more before we make any drastic decisions."

"Okay. That sounds like a good plan." He paused. "Are you still coming out here before we go to Alaska?"

"Yeah."

He was quiet for a long beat. "I miss you. And I love you."

He'd never felt farther away than he did now.

"I love you, too."

I didn't tell him I missed him, couldn't put words to the ache inside me. We hung up the phone and I cried myself to sleep.

$\mathcal{T}$WENTY

NOAH

I went through the motions of preparing for the squadron's TDY to Alaska and trying to get my orders for my PCS to Korea, the whole time my mind on Jordan rather than the mission. I'd never really cared all that much where the Air Force sent me. As long as I remained in the cockpit, flying the Viper, the rest was just window dressing. But I cared now. A lot. And I was fucking pissed that out of all my assignments, *this* was the one when I got nonvolled to Korea.

I drove onto the base, pulling into the squadron parking lot, my hand linked with Jordan's, the sound of music the only noise in the car. She'd decided to come out and visit before I left for Alaska, and then we'd had some of the tankers who were supposed to refuel us midair fall out due to scheduling conflicts, and our dates had gotten moved up. So basically, Jordan had arrived in time to see me off, and the days we'd planned to spend together had fallen away.

She hadn't said much when she'd landed and I'd broken the news to her, so I couldn't figure out what she was feeling, although pissed seemed likely. I figured she'd add it to her tally of things I'd done to disappoint her. Hell, I'd break up with me at this point.

I'd spent the past two weeks going over everything in my mind, trying to figure out how to make our relationship work. We still talked, but I felt like she was pulling away from me, like the stress of things was an albatross weighing us down. Or maybe it was just my own paranoia, my own fear that overshadowed everything else. The more I thought about it, worried about it, the more I realized that I loved her. I didn't want to lose her. I *couldn't* lose her.

I put the car in Park, my limbs reluctant to get out and leave her once again.

And then the idea that had been rolling around my mind for two weeks now came out of my mouth.

JORDAN

"What if we got married?" Noah asked, his voice, and the question, jerking me out of my mental freak-out.

I froze, my hand suspended over the car radio knob itching to change the channel, the word "married" sending my world to a crashing stop. I blinked, wondering if I was dreaming, if this was really happening. As far as proposals went, it wasn't exactly romantic and it had the same feel as, *Do you want pizza or burgers for dinner?*

I wasn't sure if I was pissed, or excited, or just plain shocked. Or some combination of all three.

"Jordan?"

I blinked again, waiting for him to tell me he was just kidding or to take it back.

He didn't.

Noah stared at me, his gaze unblinking, strangely serious.

Was I supposed to treat that like a proposal? Had he lost his mind?

We were sitting in the squadron parking lot, he was getting ready to leave for Alaska, hip-hop music playing in the background, it was ten in the morning, and I'd thought we'd decided not to make any drastic decisions. There was nothing romantic about this.

"Are you joking?"

"It was a stupid idea," he muttered, turning the car off with a flick of his wrist. He unbuckled his seat belt.

"Wait."

"What?"

God, I needed a minute. I hadn't been prepared for this, didn't know how I was supposed to handle a question like that. Was it even a question? Or was he just throwing ideas out there? And why did he seem pissed now?

"Are you serious?"

He let out an oath. "Yes. No. I don't know." His mouth set in a grim line. "I don't know what we're doing here. Every time I have to say good-bye to you, it feels like I'm being sliced in half." His expression darkened. "Loving you fucking hurts."

I closed my eyes, the pain in his voice piercing me. He wasn't wrong. I just didn't know what the answer was. I wasn't going to marry him on a whim, on some half-assed attempt to bring us together when circumstances threatened to pull us apart. But if he was serious?

I reached out, grabbing his hand, linking my fingers with his, holding on, afraid that the effort of us was eventually going to be too much, that he'd meet an easier girl who would jump at the chance to spend her life with him, who would view all of this as an adventure rather than the sacrifice I feared.

"I love you," I answered, trying to give him as much as I could.

"I know."

He didn't say the rest, but it lingered between us . . . *but is it enough?*

And I didn't know. I didn't want to throw away my chance at happiness, and at the same time, I was scared to reach out and take it. Afraid of the sacrifice it required.

"What would happen if we got married?" I asked, trying to picture it, struggling to figure out a way to make him fit in my life.

"You could come to Korea with me."

That sentence both thrilled and terrified me.

"You would be a dependent. You'd have healthcare and access to the military facilities. We could get an apartment on base and live together."

"You're asking me to move to Korea?" I sputtered.

He sighed. "I don't know. If you wanted to, I guess."

"What would I do for work? I don't speak Korean. What would I do all day?"

He ran a hand through his hair. "I don't know."

I didn't know what to say. Didn't know what I wanted. It was fast. Everything about this was fast. And it was too much. I loved him. So much. But why did love mean I had to give up everything? Why did love require this giant fucking leap?

And even though I knew I shouldn't even entertain the thought, a part of me resented that he didn't have to make any sacrifices in this scenario. I knew it wasn't his fault or even his choice anymore, but still it bothered me.

It wasn't just going to a foreign country, or how far away I'd be from my friends and family, or even not speaking the language—it felt like I was putting my life on hold. What would happen to the store if I just took off to Korea for two years? On the one hand, it was just a store. On the other, it was years of hard work and sacrifice. It was everything I'd wanted it to be. Business was better than ever and the idea of abandoning all of that was ridiculous. Especially to a giant unknown. Not to mention how much I'd miss my family. My friends. My dog. Could I take Lulu to Korea?

It was way too much. Like it wasn't enough that he was getting ready to leave for six weeks; now he was dumping this on me, too.

And just like that I went from confused to more than a little pissed off with Noah.

"Do you even want to marry me?" I asked.

"What's that supposed to mean?"

I could feel my temper building, the explosion lurking just beneath the surface.

"That's your proposal? You just throw out there the mention that, hey, maybe we could get married? We've never talked about it, you're about to leave for Alaska, and now you think it's a good idea to dump more on me?"

His gaze narrowed. "Sorry. I didn't realize the idea of marrying me would be so stressful for you."

"We've never talked about it," I shouted. "You just told me you loved me weeks ago. I'm not even a little prepared for this."

"And I am?"

"You're the one who mentioned it," I snapped.

"Because I'm trying to figure this out, too. I'm just as

confused as you are. I'm trying to figure out a way to make this work."

"And I'm not?" Was he joking? "You do realize, that for you, getting married isn't that big of a change. But for me, it isn't just adding a husband and making a commitment to spend the rest of my life with someone. It's also moving to another country, away from everything I know and love. It's giving up the business I've worked my ass off to build. Would you give up flying for me?"

I threw it out there, not sure I wanted to know the answer.

His jaw clenched. "You know I don't have an option."

I knew. And I knew it was unfair of me to care, to weigh our love as though it could be measured by a set of scales. But I did. Because I didn't want to be second in his life when he was always first in mine.

As far as good-byes went, ours pretty much sucked. We stood outside the squadron, the same awkward tension that had descended since Noah's faux proposal lingering like a bad smell.

We were both clearly pissed, and now was definitely not the time to discuss it, so we just stood there, trying to hold back the floodgates that nearly burst at the seams with the desire to air our personal laundry in the squadron parking lot.

"Look, maybe we shouldn't talk for a while," Noah suggested, his gaze trained on a point over my shoulder.

"Are you serious?"

I knew he was upset, but not talking seemed like the worst thing we could do.

"Maybe we need some time apart to figure out what we want."

"Are you breaking up with me? Minutes after you proposed to me?"

"No. God, no. I just think we might need some time to think about things."

"About what? Whether we should be together? Because that kind of sounds like a breakup."

"It's not a breakup. It's me trying to give us some space to figure out what we want."

"Still sounds like a breakup."

"It's not," he muttered through clenched teeth. "You aren't the only one who's confused here, Jordan."

I looked up at his face, his eyes shielded by aviators, a knot tightening around my heart.

"I don't want to leave things like this."

"I think we need time to figure out if this is what we really want," Noah replied. "I love you. But I think we need to decide if love is enough for us to make this work. And I think space will help us get there."

I didn't agree with him, but I also didn't know what to do anymore.

He moved, opening the trunk, pulling his bags out.

A lump formed in my throat.

His head jerked toward the building. "I gotta go."

I couldn't believe this was how we were leaving things, but I didn't want him distracted and upset before he had to fly. And the problems between us seemed bigger than the five minutes we had left. I swallowed the hurt and fear pummeling me.

I stood on my tiptoes, pressing my lips to his, trying to keep my emotions together when they threatened to spill over and rip me to shreds.

"I love you," I whispered. "Be safe."

"I love you, too."

I stood in the parking lot, watching him walk away, wondering where we could go from here, and how I was going to get through the next month and a half without him, leaving our relationship hanging by a thread.

$\mathcal{T}$WENTY-ONE

JORDAN

It was the longest six weeks of my life. We spoke every few days, our conversations short and stilted. He didn't bring up Korea or marriage again, and neither did I. For the most part, I threw myself into work, spending time at the store and with Sophia, hanging out with Lulu. I tried to picture giving it all up, living a different life, wondering if I should have said "yes" to his proposal or whatever it was in the car. Wondering if he regretted asking me.

I flew to Oklahoma a few days before Noah was scheduled to come back from Alaska, no closer to knowing what I wanted to do. It felt weird going to his house when he was still away on his TDY and things were tense between us, but I'd had the flight booked for a few weeks now and his return date had changed so many times, I'd given up trying to predict when he'd arrive. I used the key he'd given me and tried to make myself comfortable. And I called Dani.

She came over to have a glass of wine and to give me some much needed military life advice.

We sat on Noah's couch, his place the cleanest I'd ever seen it. I hadn't been able to resist the urge to straighten up, rationalizing it by telling myself that no one wanted to come home to a messy house after a few weeks away. Also, cleaning kind of calmed me and right now my life felt like such a chaotic disaster that I craved the normalcy of a routine.

I missed him so much.

"How are you doing?" Dani asked, a knowing look in her eyes.

I figured it was pretty obvious that I was kind of a mess.

"I'm not sure."

"Noah's assignment had to have been a blow."

"Yeah, it was."

"Have you guys talked about what you'll do when he goes to Korea?"

I took a sip of my wine, gathering the courage to talk about it. I hadn't told anyone about Noah's proposal, had been a little too freaked about what my friends and family would think if I confessed that I was considering marrying a guy I'd only known a few months. And the scariest thing was that I was considering it. A lot. Even as it utterly terrified me.

"He asked me to marry him."

I figured her lack of a response was a testament to Dani's familiarity with military relationships. Maybe this was normal when your life was unstructured. It just didn't feel normal to me.

"What did you say?"

I winced.

"I kind of freaked out. It wasn't exactly my finest moment."

"Understandable."

"I don't think he understood. We're sort of taking a break right now to figure out what we want."

"He's a guy and a fighter pilot. Sometimes it's hard for them to see beyond the target," Dani answered, her tone sympathetic.

"So you don't think I'm crazy?"

"I'd think you were crazy if you weren't a little scared. Marriage is a big step. Military marriage is a leap without a net to catch you. It's all or nothing, and that's a lot to ask. Especially when you guys haven't known each other that long. I don't blame you for being scared. We all are." She made a face. "I'm still scared."

It was strange to hear Dani confessing to being anything other than completely comfortable with this lifestyle. To the outside eye, she thrived here. I envied her ability to manage everything with the kind of aplomb I could never adopt. I needed some kind of military wives handbook, or at the very least, advice from a really good friend who'd run the gauntlet and come out the other end unscathed.

"So how do you do it?"

"Do what?"

"Any of it. All of it. How do you stay sane?"

"The truth?"

I nodded.

"I don't know. I just do. I'm scared every second of every day. Always. That fear is a knot that lives inside me. It never goes away. It never shuts off. It just is. When he's gone, when's he up in the air, it's like I'm underwater holding my breath. The world around me ceases to exist. Everything hinges on the moment when I know he's safe. And when he's back, I can breathe again."

"Do you ever . . ."

"Wish I'd fallen in love with someone else? An accountant? Someone who doesn't take his life into his hands every single time he goes to work?"

I nodded, a lump settling in the pit of my stomach.

"Yeah. I do. It's hard to explain, but there's a part of me that thinks this would be so much easier if I didn't love him so much. If I loved him a little less, maybe the absences and the constant fear that I'm going to lose him wouldn't hurt so much. But then again, if I loved him any less, I'm not sure I could do this. Not sure the life would be worth it. I love him just the right amount to make it hurt so much that I can't walk away."

"I'm scared." I whispered the words I hadn't been able to tell Noah, the feeling inside me that I was afraid to give a voice to.

She squeezed my hand. "I know. I wish I could tell you that it's going to be easy, or that you have nothing to fear. Wish I could tell you that this life won't take a chunk out of you; but as hard as it is to be in a relationship, it'll be that much harder to be in a military relationship. I know it sounds tough to believe, and it isn't easy to comprehend until you're in it, but in a lot of ways this is the most difficult thing you'll ever do. Still, there are two kinds of military wives. The ones who lean on their men, and the ones who are strong enough to give their men somewhere to lean when they come home after a six-month deployment that has beaten them down or a week of working twelve-hour days.

"If you love him, really love him, and you can't be the second kind of wife, then you really need to think about whether or not you guys can make this work. I'm not saying it'll be easy, or that you won't have days when you'll just sit and cry for a few minutes, but you'll have to be strong for him. Stronger than you think you can be. Because at the end of the day, his mind can't be on a fight you had that morning or on whatever problems you might be dealing with at home. It has to be on the mission. On coming home safely. Because in their line of work, the smallest mistake can be the difference between life and death."

"I'll always be second to the Air Force."

She nodded. "Some wives resent that. It's a hard pill to swallow, and believe me, I've struggled with it. But if you find a good man, one who loves you—and Noah loves you—he'll put you first every time he can. And the other times when he can't, when he doesn't have a choice, those moments when he does choose, when he chooses you, will have to be enough to get you through the times when you feel like your entire life revolves around something you didn't sign up for, when you start to lose parts of yourself and the only thing you have to hold on to is him.

"It's corny, but true—military marriages make a good marriage stronger and a bad marriage worse."

"How do you know? How do you know if your marriage is going to be one of the ones that makes it?"

I was so over my head. I'd always had a messy approach to dating. Romantic guru, I was not. I'd screwed up my fair share of relationships, but this one—the stakes were so much higher this time. I didn't want to hurt him. And I really didn't want to get hurt. And I had no clue what the fuck I was doing.

"When I decided I wanted to marry Joker, I thought about the life we'd lead together. I tried to envision what military life would be like, but to be honest, I had no clue. No one does. Being a military wife is a lot like getting thrown into the deep end to learn how to swim. You just have to deal with things as they come and adapt. But I did make myself a promise.

"I knew I couldn't live my life the way I had when I was single. I knew there would be times—way more times than I'd like to count—when it wouldn't be about me. When I would spend holidays by myself, when I'd have to give up my career because his job meant we moved so much that steady employment was pretty much impossible. I knew there would be times that I would want to give up. But I told myself that no matter what, every decision I would make after I married him would be the best decision for the family we built. For our marriage. Even if sometimes it meant sacrificing what I wanted."

"And that's what you do?"

She nodded.

"And you don't resent him for it?"

"For moments? Sure. But that's where the part of finding a good man comes in. He loves me. I am the love of his life. And he has given me an amazing life. So for every moment when I'm pissed off that I'm spending another Christmas by myself, for every time I've binge eaten chocolate on the couch on my birthday because I'm alone, there is always a moment, every single day, when I feel like I'm the luckiest girl in the entire world, because I am loved by a man who looks at me the way he does. Who fights for me every day of his life. He would die for me. Without question. So yeah. That's enough for me."

I batted at the tear that trickled down my face.

"Noah loves you like that. He would be that for you if you let him. You just have to decide if you feel the same way."

"It's fucking scary."

Dani grinned. "Yeah, it is. It's all or nothing, which makes it a leap-before-you-look sort of situation. And no matter how much you plan or try to imagine what it'll be like, there's no way you can know until you're in it. It's jumping into the deep end and hoping you don't sink to the bottom."

"And it's a whole other country. I mean, it's not just me

becoming a military wife; it's me becoming a military wife and moving to South Korea. I don't speak the language. I've never even been outside of the U.S."

"For what it's worth, our overseas assignments were some of my favorite times in the Air Force."

"Where have you guys been?"

"Italy and Germany."

I'd never really been one of those people who craved adventure. My idea of a perfect night included curling up on the couch with take-out Chinese and a *Friends* marathon. I wasn't Noah. I wasn't looking to take on the world. But the problem was that now, when I looked at my idea of the perfect night, he was right there next to me.

"You could try long distance," Dani offered, the tone of her voice conveying her true feelings on the subject.

"Noah hates the idea."

"When they make their mind up, they tend to stick with it."

I grimaced. "I've noticed. It's super fucking annoying."

She grinned. "Trust me. Five years of marriage. I get it. And for what it's worth, Joker's even older and even *more* set in his ways. I've given up at this point."

"How do you handle it? The bossy factor?"

"I let him run the things that are important to him, and sort of do what I want with the rest of it."

"And that works?"

She shrugged. "Sometimes. It's not easy. Sometimes it feels like there's something about being a fighter pilot that takes normal annoying masculine traits and magnifies them by a thousand. But it also has its perks."

She had a point there.

Dani reached out and squeezed my hand. "It'll be okay. Promise. The answer will come to you."

My voice cracked. "He doesn't understand. He's pissed and he doesn't understand, and I'm worried that if I don't decide soon, he's going to just get fed up and give up on me."

"He won't. He's scared. He doesn't want to lose you and right now he's worried that he's asking too much of you. And I can promise you, he knows how much he's asking you to give up."

I hoped she was right. I hoped I hadn't fucked everything up.

$\mathcal{T}$WENTY-TWO

JORDAN

The sound of my cell going off jarred me awake.

I reached for Noah and came up empty. Then it hit me—he was gone. Alaska. I was in his bed in Oklahoma by myself.

I flicked on the light, rubbing my eyes as I answered the call. The clock on the nightstand said it was six in the morning. Was it Noah? What time was it in Alaska? I tried to do the calculation, but I was too tired. At least he was calling.

"Noah?"

"Are you okay?"

Confusion filled me as Meg's panicked voice came through the line.

"Meg? Yeah. What's going on?"

She sucked in a deep breath. "Jord."

There was something in the way she said my name, something that combined with the early morning phone call, filled my stomach with dread.

"What's wrong?"

I sat up in bed now, pulling the sheets up around my chest, heart pounding.

"Are Mom and Dad okay?"

"Yeah. Mom and Dad are okay." Her voice shook and I could hear the effort it took for her to pull herself together. "You need to turn on the news. There's been a crash."

Four words. With four words, she brought my entire world crumbling down.

I grabbed the TV remote off the nightstand, my cell phone sliding out of my other hand.

Noah.

His name thundered through my head like a prayer, terror flooding my body. I flicked through the channels, panic filling me until I hit the news station and the panic became something else entirely. Something I'd never felt before.

F-16 Crashes in Alaska.

Four words. Four words that before Noah wouldn't have meant much to me, but were now everything.

I turned the volume up, heart pounding, scanning the headline, waiting for them to say something about the pilot. I should know, shouldn't I? If something happened to him, I would know. Someone would have called me. This couldn't be Noah. This couldn't be happening.

F-16 Crashes in Alaska.

I heard my sister's voice yelling at me through the speaker and I picked up the phone.

"Jord."

"I have to go." I struggled to get the words out, fought to push them past the panic clawing at my throat. "I need to call Noah."

"Call me as soon as you hear anything. If you need anything, Jord—"

"I have to go."

I hung up on my sister, my fingers shaking as I called Noah.

"Please answer. Please."

I just needed to hear his voice, just needed to know he was okay. It couldn't be Noah.

His voice mail picked up immediately and the first tears began to fall.

"Babe, if you get this, please call me." Tears ran down my cheeks. "Please. I need to know you're okay." I choked on a sob. "I love you, Noah. Please call me."

My body curled into a ball, numbness spreading through my limbs. I pulled up the Internet on my phone searching for news, something, anything.

F-16 Crashes in Alaska.

Each news article said the same variation of that one line. They told me nothing. Absolutely nothing. A feeling of help-lessness hit me, followed by frustration and rage.

I wanted to scream. I couldn't stop crying, couldn't stop the tremors wracking my body.

It was surreal, sitting here, seeing my life—my entire fucking world—on television like that. How many times had I seen a similar headline and not thought twice about it? How many times had I heard a story about a soldier who died serving his country? And each time I'm sure I'd thought it was sad. But I hadn't ever thought about it like this. Hadn't ever thought about the fact that at that very moment there was someone waiting to hear if their loved one would come home.

It had never seemed real before. And now those four words were a knife in my chest.

I needed someone to call me. Someone to tell me Noah was okay. I needed to hear his voice. I needed to know if the pilot had made it. They could eject. Noah had told me about that. What if the pilot had ejected?

Why didn't they say something?

If it wasn't Noah, if *God, please*, if Noah was okay, then it hit me that those four words still meant that someone else was sitting at home with the same terror and panic I felt. I thought of all the families I'd come to know, of guys like Easy, of the kids I saw at the barbecues and parties. And it hit me like another knife to my chest that even if Noah was okay, we'd lost someone tonight. Or almost lost someone.

Oh my God.

Dani.

If anyone would have news, it would be Dani. It was early, but maybe she was up. Or maybe someone had called her. Surely, she would have heard something. I needed to call Dani.

I dialed her number, taking deep breaths, struggling to keep my tears under control, to keep my voice from cracking. She answered on the first ring.

"Jordan?"

"Did you hear?" The words were a whisper that sounded like they came from someone else.

"Yeah." Her voice was calmer than mine, but I could hear the fear there. "I haven't heard anything beyond what's on the news, though."

"What do we do?"

Her voice was grim. "We wait. Notification can take a while. They have our contact information from the emergency forms the guys filled out. They'll notify the family when they have information. Until then, none of the guys will be able to call out or contact anyone. It's standard procedure to make sure the family is notified through official channels. The news won't release a name until twenty-four hours after the family has been notified."

"Will the news tell us—" My voice cracked. "Will the news tell us if the pilot's okay?"

"The Air Force is usually faster when it comes to that."

"So we wait."

"Yeah." Dani's voice shook. "Do you want to come over? If you have your cell, that should be enough. You can leave a note on your door or something to let people"—we both knew what she meant—"know where you are. Just make sure you bring your cell in case Noah or someone needs to get ahold of you. I don't want to be alone. I need to handle some squadron notification stuff to explain that there's been an incident and we're waiting for information."

The last thing I wanted was to be by myself tonight. And I figured if I was going to be with anyone, at least it would be with someone who understood this feeling pummeling me.

"Okay."

We sat next to each other on Dani's couch, our bodies huddled together, our cells clutched in our hands, a blanket wrapped around both of us. Our eyes were glued to the TV.

It had been five hours. Nothing.

Dani had been investigating on her own, but we still didn't have any information. All we knew was that a jet had gone down. We didn't know if it was one of ours or what was happening with the pilot.

It was the scariest five hours of my life.

I called Noah over and over again. And still we waited.

We didn't even speak, didn't give a voice to the fears filling our heads. At some point, I reached out and grabbed Dani's hand. She didn't let go.

Part of me felt like I was dreaming, like this couldn't be reality. I kept thinking it was all a nightmare. He had to be okay. And yet no matter how many times I tried to convince myself it was true, I couldn't quite remove the knot of fear from my chest.

The doorbell rang.

For a moment we both froze, the sound intruding on the haze we'd wrapped around ourselves. For a moment, that sound could be anything. And then it was everything.

We both rose from the couch as if in slow motion. We didn't speak, didn't even make eye contact. But we stayed together, our hands locked, as we walked toward Dani's front door.

Ice filled me. Our hands squeezed tighter. I was too overwhelmed to cry, too scared to think beyond what was on the other side of that door.

Dani stopped in front of her front door and took a deep breath, her body bracing as she reached for the doorknob.

And then the door opened and I felt all the tension in her body pass through to mine.

Three service members in uniform stood in the doorway.
No.

For a moment, I didn't hear anything. I could see their lips moving, but the sound was gone. It had been swallowed up. I knew Dani was speaking, and yet nothing made sense.
No.

I kept repeating his name like a chant through my head—*Noah, Noah, Noah.*
No.

And then I heard it, their words finally breaking through the haze.

"Mrs. Peterson, we regret to inform you . . ."
No.

No.

I felt Dani's weight give out through our locked hands, her body hitting the floor, taking me down with her. The casualty officers rushed forward, but I moved, wrapping my arms around Dani as she screamed.

No.

Not Joker.

No.

$\mathcal{T}$WENTY-THREE

JORDAN

Part of me stayed with Dani in the home she and Joker had built together. Part of me was in Alaska with Noah, desperate to hear his voice.

We didn't have any information besides the fact that Joker had crashed and didn't survive. They were going through the recovery process now, searching for his remains, but the communication blackout had yet to be lifted. We couldn't call the guys and they couldn't call out. I clung to the knowledge that Noah was okay, even as Dani clung to me in her grief.

I held her hand while she called Joker's parents, knowing I'd never forget the pain in her voice and on the other end of the line. I'd never experienced anything like this in my entire life. Never known a loss this great. There were simply no words. There was just an unspeakable pain. I focused on the little things, on helping Dani, focused on anything but the fear, and panic, and sheer devastation that filled my body.

I operated on adrenaline and little else, determined to keep it together, determined to give Dani someone to lean on.

The squadron's Director of Operations' wife had been mobilized already and was taking over the military protocol stuff. Things I had no clue how to handle and arrangements Dani didn't need to worry about. I tried to do what I could to just be there for her—fussing over her until she ate, until one of the flight docs came and sent her to bed with a sleeping pill. I'd promised I'd stay with her until her family arrived, and that's how I found myself on the floor of Dani's elegant guest bathroom, my hand over my mouth attempting to muffle my tears, my body shaking, my cell clutched in my hand as the adrenaline seeped and oozed out of me, leaving me hollowed out and exhausted.

There had been times in our long-distance relationship when I'd missed Noah, when I'd needed to talk to him. But there was nothing like this moment, this need. I would have given anything to hear his voice, even for a second. The rational part of my brain knew that he was alive and that he was safe, and that should have been enough, but it wasn't. The part of me that felt nearly paralyzed with terror needed some tangible proof that he'd survived beyond someone else's word. I felt like I was floating in a sea of loss and I needed his touch, his voice, to keep me from drowning.

I clutched my phone even tighter, my knuckles white, the pain breaking through the haze. My heart pounding, I dialed his number again, chanting the same phrase over and over again.

"Please pick up, please pick up."

He answered on the second ring, and with the sound of his voice, I became tethered.

"Jordan."

He said my name like a prayer and a plea, his voice taking on a reverence I'd never heard before.

I tried to answer, tried to gather the courage that had helped me keep it together with Dani, but this time it fled and a sob escaped instead.

"I'm okay."

The words and the fact that he was alive, breathing through the phone, answering me, confirmed what he said. And yet his tone suggested he was anything but.

"I'm sorry I couldn't call you earlier. We aren't allowed to make any calls when these things happen." He paused, and then he broke my heart. "I was flying."

Pain lanced me.

"Noah."

His voice broke. "I was number three. Joker was leading."

There was a lump in my throat that I couldn't get past. He'd been flying when his friend had died. They'd been flying together. It could have just as easily been Noah. And even though he had come back safely this time, how did one even come back from something like that? How would he come back from something like that?

"What do you need from me? What can I do?"

He paused for another moment, and I got the feeling he was gathering his strength, that he was held together by strings, too.

"Have you seen Dani yet?"

"I'm at her house now."

I didn't tell him the rest, couldn't tell him the rest. I couldn't say the words, couldn't explain that I hadn't known if it was him, that I'd been here waiting to hear if the man I loved would come home to me, only to watch as my friend, someone I respected and cared about, lost her *husband*.

Our conversation was more about what we didn't say, than what we did. He seemed hesitant to talk about the accident, like if he did, he'd simply shatter. And I wasn't ready to share the fear that had lodged its way into my heart the second I'd heard Meg say those fateful words:

There's been a crash.

"She's sleeping. One of the flight docs came and gave her a sleeping pill."

It was almost a minute before Noah spoke.

"Can you stay with her?"

"Yes. Her parents are coming out soon. Joker's, too. I promised I'd stay with her as long as she needed."

"There will be funeral arrangements that need to be made. We'll start working on it. And getting the body home." His voice cracked. "We should be returning to Bryer in a couple days. We're trying to figure out the plan now."

I wanted him home. I wanted to put my arms around him, to feel that he was real, that he was whole, that he was safe. And at the same time, I couldn't help but feel the pang of guilt at the fact that I would get my homecoming, that I would get to see him again when Dani would never have that same chance with Joker.

"Okay. Just let me know what you need."

"I will."

Silence filled the line again, the emotion throbbing between us making it almost impossible to speak. It was strange; I'd expected to feel differently. You would think that the fear of almost having lost him would have made me want to tell him how much I loved him, would make me want to say all the things that I might have never had a chance to say. But it didn't. I didn't know if it was the grief of watching Dani lose Joker, or the exhaustion of the day, or the fact that this moment felt almost too sacred to profane with words.

There was nothing I could say that felt adequate, nothing that would describe the pain in my breast or the panic coursing through my body. There were no words you could give to this kind of loss.

So we stayed on the phone with each other for an hour, not really even speaking. I sat on Dani's bathroom floor, listening to the sound of Noah's breath, that reassuring whoosh of air that told me that all was right in my world, that as long as he inhaled and exhaled, I would not come undone. I learned to count time in breaths, that my life could be measured by the flow of air from his lips to mine.

And with each breath, I felt revived.

NOAH

I got off the phone with Jordan, feeling like I'd just come out of surgery, my battered body patched back together with the unique brand of magic only she possessed.

I was so fucking tired.

So fucking empty.

Held together by a girl thousands of miles away.

I headed toward the O-Club, not quite ready for the scene that would greet me when I got there, but somehow needing it just the same.

The entire squadron was at the bar, minus the most important member. It was a gathering like all the ones I'd been to hundreds of times, but this one was completely different. There was a pall over the crowd, as visible as if we'd all been dressed in black.

We'd come to honor one of our own.

I took the shot of Jeremiah Weed that one of the lieutenants handed me, my gaze running over the crowd, searching for Easy and Thor. They stood together yet apart from the group, the grief on their faces a punch to the gut. Thor looked green, as if he would throw up at any moment, his expression ragged. Easy looked destroyed, a version of my best friend I'd never seen before and never wanted to see again.

I headed over to them, my feet lead, my body protesting. I didn't want to be a part of this club, didn't want a piece of the memory we all shared.

We were the three who returned, when it should have been four.

We didn't speak, the feeling too raw. Instead we stood next to each other, shot glasses in hand. I looked down, watching as the liquid trembled in the hollowed-out Gatling gun shell that had been cleaned and fashioned into a shot glass. A gift from Dani and Joker last Christmas. And then I realized the tremor was coming from me. The hand that had always been so steady at the stick shook like a fucking leaf, my knuckles white.

Someone led off a song. One I'd heard sung at piano burn after piano burn, when we all came together to honor those who had made the ultimate sacrifice to the sky. Those moments had always resonated with me. The reality of our jobs, the knowledge that even though we flew as if we were gods, untouchable, we were all too mortal. But now . . .

Now we sang for Joker.

The music filled the O-Club bar, the lyrics the standard fighter pilot fare—plenty of *fucks* dropped, female body parts mentioned—an ode to the world we lived in, to a life on the edge. But even though the lyrics harkened back to wilder days, the tone told a different story. We sang, our voices thick with grief, thirty something voices united in pain and loss.

And as the sound crested, spilling out the doors, voices getting louder, the chant taking on a life of its own, I swore I could feel Joker standing beside me like he'd done so many times before, slightly off key, shot glass in hand.

And so as we came to the end, as we lingered over those last notes as though we were reluctant to let them go, I lifted my glass in the air, toasting one of the greatest men I'd ever known.

And then I shot the liquor back, the bitter taste sending a fire down my throat as I said good-bye.

JORDAN

At some point in the night, I made my way to Dani's guest bed. I woke the next morning, my body stiff from hours spent sitting on the bathroom floor, my heart aching.

I walked into the kitchen, surprised to see Dani sitting on one of the stools at the granite countertop, a mug of coffee in hand.

She looked much as she had last night. Pale. Worn. Devastated.

I walked toward her and gave her a hug, words failing me.

"I always knew," she whispered.

My stomach clenched.

"He talked about getting out in two years." Her voice shook. "I couldn't get excited about it. I couldn't see us in that life. Couldn't imagine him coming home at 6 p.m. in a business suit." A tear trickled down her face. Then another. "I always knew we would end up like this."

I wrapped my arms around her again while she sobbed,

her slim frame shuddering in my embrace. I didn't speak, but then again, there weren't words for this. I didn't know how long we stayed like that, but eventually she pulled back, her eyes red and swollen.

"What time are the jets getting in?" she asked, her voice strained.

I froze. "Dani . . ."

"What time?"

Noah had texted me this morning to tell me that they had the arrival plans sorted out; I was planning on going to the squadron to pick him up. They were working on the memorial service for Joker, and I'd told him I'd talk to Dani about what she wanted to do. It was definitely not a conversation I was looking forward to; I had no idea how to even broach a topic like that. But now we were talking about the rest of the squadron coming home, and I didn't know how to handle that one, either.

"The first cell lands tomorrow at four," I answered, my voice cracking with each word.

"Who's in the cell?"

God. I couldn't make myself say the words. Couldn't push them out. It felt wrong for his name not to be in that list.

Her gaze met mine. "Who's in the cell?"

"Noah, Thor, Easy, and Merlin."

Her whole body shuddered, her chest rising and falling as she sucked in air.

"We don't need to talk about this, Dani. Not now. Don't worry about the landing. We have it sorted out."

"It's Joker's squadron. Those are his guys. I'm his wife."

"Dani . . ."

"I have to be there." She choked out the words. "I have

to be there for him. He would have wanted me to be there. I need to represent him."

I bit down on my cheek, fighting back tears. I couldn't lose it when she managed to hold herself together. I couldn't imagine having the strength to watch those jets land.

$\mathcal{T}$WENTY-FOUR

JORDAN

I gripped Dani's hand so hard our nails dug into each other, our eyes trained to the gray sky. Families held signs, children playing in the grass near the flight line, and despite the fact that this was a homecoming, there was very little happiness about it. No one spoke. No one smiled. We all stood there, tension cloaking us, the knowledge that one less pilot was coming home casting a shadow over the entire day.

And then there was Dani.

She stood ramrod straight, the center of everything.

I didn't know how she did it. I couldn't have done it. There was a grace that flowed from her now. The kind of strength that I didn't even know existed, of enduring the unendurable.

It was a different kind of courage; the kind that didn't get praised with American flags waving in the air, or parades, or people coming up to shake your hand and thank you for your service.

There was no uniform for this, no outward evidence that

she'd suffered an unspeakable loss, that she'd given her life to her country in an entirely different way than those who risked their lives to fight for our freedom.

She gave a whole new meaning to the concept of sacrifice.

I squeezed her hand, and then we heard it, the sound of jets in the sky, everyone's attention riveted to the clouds, searching for the first plane, for the first spot of hope, that while nothing would ever be all right again, at least we could put a tourniquet on our loss, and somehow, impossibly, begin to heal.

My heart pounded as I searched the cloudy sky, as I waited, my fingers gripping Dani's even tighter, tension flooding my limbs until my body felt like it had been filled with lead. Like I was underwater, fighting for breath.

And then the first plane came into view.

It was Noah. He'd told me he would be leading the formation, and I watched as he flew through the sky, three planes trailing behind him.

I released a breath, and then another, tears pooling in my eyes.

We all watched, unable to tear our gazes away from those four jets as they got closer, flying in a tight formation, looking like a flock of birds in the sky, four jets that became one. And then a murmur rose through the crowd and Dani's arms wrapped around me as the second jet in the formation pulled away from the others, flying high in the sky, as if soaring away from earth.

I heard the words "Missing Man formation," felt the way Dani's body quaked against mine, as the squadron gave their own a good-bye in a moment that felt sacred, as though Joker joined all those who had fallen before him. It was beautiful and terrible all at once, and we stood there, a captive audience, tethered to those we loved among the clouds.

I didn't know how to explain it. I wasn't even sure there were words for it. But there was something about watching that plane up in the air, knowing Noah was inside it, that evoked a feeling that simply engulfed me.

I was thirty years old. I'd spent most of my teen years and adult life looking for love while simultaneously guarding my heart, calculating risks, approaching love like it was something I could ensure. And here it was. Bigger than me, than my fears, than anything. There was no guarding against this. No insurance I could take out that would protect me. This was skydiving, free fall, jumping off the cliff with no idea if there were rocks below or how deep the water was.

And whatever questions I might have had, the fear that I'd go splat when I reached the bottom, were carried away with the wind.

His job was dangerous. And I knew without a doubt in my mind that I'd be in for a lifetime of worry, sleepless nights, my phone tight in my hand while I waited to hear if he was safe. And as much as I hated it, I couldn't ignore the possibility that one day I might be in Dani's position, my hand clutched in someone else's, watching jets fly in a formation saluting my fallen pilot.

I hated to say it, hated to even think it, but watching Dani go through an immeasurable loss made it even more real. Made it impossible to ignore the fears I figured would be my constant companion for years to come.

I didn't care.

I was in. All in.

When it was love, capital letters, can't-live-without-you love, there wasn't much of a choice. We were forever, for however long forever lasted.

A rush of adrenaline hit me as I saw the first plane over the runway, as I watched that big metal beast get closer and closer to the ground. It was a moment that felt like an eternity, and I swear I held my breath the entire time, watching as those wheels got closer, closer, and finally hit the ground, the jet heaving a nearly imperceptible sigh as the nose bounced up for a second and then it was taxiing down the runway and I could breathe again.

Dani clutched me a little tighter as the rest of the jets landed and we waited for them to taxi over to the hangars.

En masse we walked onto the flight line, heading toward the hangars, ready to welcome our pilots home. Dani let me go with a squeeze of her hand, her body swallowed up by some of the squadron wives who formed a protective circle around her.

And then I was walking, no, running, toward Noah. I could see him through the canopy, my arms aching to wrap around him, my heart pounding like an intense drum session.

And then the canopy popped up and my heart spilled open.

NOAH

I'd come home from dozens of TDYs. There was always a rhythm to it—a weariness from what was usually a long, tedious flight in a cramped jet, the exhaustion of crossing time zones, the desire to collapse in the comfort of my bed, a beer in hand, game on the TV.

I'd never come home after losing one of our own. And I'd never come home to a girl waiting for me. Not like Jordan.

A different kind of exhaustion filled me now. A different kind of desire.

I felt as though I'd been chopped up into pieces, and try as hard as I could, I couldn't put them back together. Couldn't erase the sound of Joker's voice on the radio seconds before we lost him.

I needed Jordan. Needed her strength to hold me together. Needed her to piece me back and make me whole. I felt as though I was sinking, my hand reaching out, desperate to grab on to something . . . on to her.

She stood next to the jet, her eyes covered by enormous sunglasses, looking so beautiful it hurt. My emotions felt barely strung together, days of trying to take care of the squadron in Joker's absence crashing into me. I didn't know if I was going to cry or collapse at her feet. Didn't know how much longer I could pretend that everything was okay, that *I* was okay, when I couldn't get that night out of my mind. It replayed, over and over again, interspersed with the nagging questions: Could I have saved him? Did I fuck up somehow? Or was it just an accident?

I shrugged my gear off, the pressure in my chest building, and then I was climbing down the ladder, and Jordan threw her arms around me, and for the first time in days, I felt like somehow, impossibly, I just might be okay.

She clung to me, her arms wrapped around my neck, her lips on mine, breathing life into me. Tears trickled down her face, wetting my skin as our flesh felt like one.

"You're home. You're home."

She whispered the words over and over again, her voice pushing them out between sobs.

My body shuddered, any hope of composure lost in the face of her love. Each sigh from her body broke me down and put me back together again.

Minutes passed before we pulled away from each other,

our limbs tangling as we touched each other's faces, as
though we needed the physical weight of each other to ensure that this wasn't just a dream. I needed something tangible to anchor me from a week when I'd felt like I'd been
floating through a nightmare.

Our palms found each other, fingers linking.

We walked toward the crowd of people, toward Dani
standing at the center of it all. I didn't know if it was the
white noise in my mind, or if silence truly did descend over
the crowd, but either way, it felt like all of the sound was
sucked away, my world reduced to the sight of my friend's
widow standing in front of me and Jordan's hand clutched
in mine.

I stopped in front of Dani, words failing me. Jordan had
told me that she wanted to come, we'd all been prepared to
see her, and yet there was no preparing for something like
this.

And then I heard his voice in my mind. Clear as day. Not
the radio calls, not the horrible moment *before,* but I swore
I heard him in the *after*, and as weird as it sounded, it was
impossible to ignore the possibility that maybe Dani had
been Joker's anchor much as Jordan was mine, and maybe,
somehow, he was here inside her.

I hugged her, using whatever strength I had left to fight
the tears rising in my throat. It was impossible to fall apart
in the face of her strength. She didn't cry. She didn't speak.
She just held on to me for a moment, and then I pulled back
and met her gaze through the frames shielding her eyes from
the world.

"I'm so sorry."

"Thank you."

Her voice came out as a whisper, so different from the

last time we'd spoken, when her voice had been a song of laughter and joy.

I ached.

"He loved you more than anything."

She nodded, her voice raw. "I know."

"Anything you need. We're here."

She squeezed my hand. "Thank you. He loved you, too. Loved flying with you. You were a good friend to him. You've been a good friend to us."

I nodded, the lump in my throat even bigger now, the threat of tears even more perilous. Without speaking, Jordan seemed to sense how close I was to losing my shit, and she nudged me along and we moved to the side, watching as the rest of the guys in my cell walked toward her.

Thor came first, his face pale, his eyes red, looking like he was about to throw up. He'd been second in the formation, Joker's wingman. I'd tried talking to him after, knew Easy had as well, but it was clear just by looking at him that he wasn't ready to hear anything we said. I got it. We were alone in the cockpit, the jet ours, and yet we flew as a formation. We were trained to think about the guy on our wing, about our lead. We were trained to think of each other. But more than that, we were bros. Living this life, we all knew that every single flight was a risk that someone wouldn't return. We all knew someone who'd crashed. Especially when you'd been in this job as long as we had.

But living it was something else entirely. Coming home one man down changed you in a way I'd never understood before. The three of us would forever be bound by the memory of this horrible night. It was the worst kind of brotherhood to belong to.

Dani spoke to Thor in whispered tones. He hugged her, his eyes wet. And then it was Easy's turn.

JORDAN

I felt like I should look away, as though I was intruding on an intensely private moment. And yet the moment crested like an aching note hovering above us, and it was impossible to look away.

Easy didn't *walk* anywhere. Ever since I'd met him, I'd watched him swagger everywhere, his long limbs moving in a beat that ensured all eyes were on him and he knew it.

Not today.

He walked like he'd aged twenty years overnight, as though each step was a weighty effort, like a condemned man heading toward his execution. It hurt to watch him walk, each step filled with a palpable pain. He didn't look at her. He didn't look at anyone. He stared down, his shoulders hunched, his body broken.

I could feel the guilt and shame in Noah, had seen it in Thor, but on Easy it was something else entirely. Easy walked like he wished he could disappear, as though he could trade places with Joker, and it would be his body on the ground.

He'd been number three in the formation.

It seemed as though we all held our collective breaths as he stopped in front of Dani.

He spoke, his voice too low to be heard, his words only for her. I sucked in a deep breath as Dani reached out, her hands grasping his face, holding his gaze. They stood there like that, suspended, and I wondered if this was the moment when Easy would simply fall apart, as if seeing her loss would be too much to bear. I would have said he looked like he was held together by a string, but really, even that was optimistic. If it was a thread, it was gossamer. And even that appeared ready to disintegrate.

Except it didn't.

Dani moved forward, her body collapsing into his, and it was as if she gave him her strength so that he could take her pain. Easy's arms came around her, holding her tight, his face buried in her hair. Her small frame shook with sobs, his body still, anchoring her grief.

$\mathcal{T}$WENTY-FIVE

JORDAN

The rest of the day was a blur. I felt numb going through the motions, doing everything I could to support Dani while trying to take care of the guys. While trying to keep it together for Noah. And then we got home and some of the tension eased.

Noah sat hunched over at the edge of the bed, his head in his hands. He'd managed to unzip his flight suit and shrug out of the shoulders, but he hadn't gotten any farther than that, so he sat there, half-undressed, staring at his boots as though he could will them off.

I sat on the bed, my chest pressed into his back, wrapping my arms and legs around him, my body enfolding his from behind.

"Do you want to talk about it?"

I had no clue what to say to him, or if talking about it would even make it better, but I felt helpless, and I hated standing by and doing nothing while Noah suffered. I'd fed him and he'd attacked the food like a starving man. Now he looked ready to collapse from exhaustion, and I didn't know if I was supposed to let him sleep or fix it with sex or conversation.

"I never want to talk about it," he croaked.

His body shuddered against mine, his chest jerking as I held on to him tighter, trying to give him whatever strength I had left, even when my body felt nearly drained.

"The weather was good . . ."

I stilled, the ache in Noah's voice piercing my heart.

"Visibility was fine."

I closed my eyes.

"It was a normal sortie. We were headed home. We were on the radio. I heard him on the radio."

My hold on Noah tightened.

"And then that was it. He was gone."

His body shuddered again and the first tears seeped from my eyes.

"I can't believe he's gone," Noah whispered, his voice cracking.

"I know."

"Seeing Dani today . . ." Noah's voice trailed off as he reached for me, grasping my hand, his fingers squeezing mine.

"I was with her when they told her."

We hadn't talked much about what was going on around us, me so focused on taking care of Dani, Noah working so hard to take care of the squadron and get everyone home.

Noah let out an oath, moving out of my arms to sit next to me on the bed. He cupped my face in his hand, his gaze locked on mine, and I swallowed, more wetness dripping down my cheeks. I'd tried so hard to keep a tight lid on my emotions, to keep him from worrying, to keep it all together somehow. But I couldn't. Not now.

"I'm so sorry," Noah whispered, his voice rough, his lips soft as he kissed my tears away. "I'm so sorry."

"I love you." I choked on the words, a basketball-sized lump in my throat. "So much. I woke up and Meg called me and told me to check the news and I saw that an F-16 had crashed." I couldn't say the rest of it. It was too much, too close to the fears I lived with each time he flew to even give a voice to them.

But he knew without me even saying anything.

"I don't . . ." He swallowed. "Looking at Dani, imagining you . . ."

I leaned forward, resting my forehead against his, our lips inches apart, breathing the same breath.

"I want to get married. I want to go to Korea with you."

None of this was going down the way I'd imagined it. But from the beginning, that was how we'd been with each other. Everything had been unexpected. And so, in a weird way, it sort of felt right. Whatever I'd thought of romance, the reality of it, was something else entirely.

It wasn't the splashy, Valentine's Day, jewelry commercial moments. It wasn't anniversaries or holidays—hell, he'd probably miss his fair share of those anyway. No, now I understood that romance was taking the moments you had—those little, precious, too-short moments—and stringing them together and clutching them to your chest as though you'd always cherish them, and never let go.

Romance, love, whatever you wanted to call it, was the faint smell of jet fuel when he came home from work. It was lying in bed at night, feet tangled, watching TV. It was the smile that took over my face every single time I saw him, as if the sight of him, the mere existence of him, was the best thing that had ever happened to me. It was holding hands, the way he always said "I love you" back, even when he was sleeping, even when it was a nearly unintelligible mumble. It was sitting with your phone clutched in your hand, feeling like your entire world existed in him. It was terrifying and amazing, and it was the kind of chance you hitched your future to. Even without a net waiting for you.

"You want to get married?"

I nodded.

"And move to Korea?"

I nodded again.

"Are you sure?"

"Yes."

I hated that it had come to this, that my memory of deciding to marry him would always be tied to this horrible, horrible tragedy, but maybe this was the best way we could honor those we'd loved and lost. By living our lives to the fullest. By living our lives for love.

"After what happened . . ." Noah's voice trailed off and then he seemed to gather himself. "I understand if it's too much. I don't want to ask you to give up everything, don't want you to ever be in the position Dani's in." His voice trembled. "I love you so much, Jordan. I want to spend my life with you. But I don't want you to give up your life for me.

"I can't give you normal. I can't promise that I'll be there for every holiday or anniversary. Hell, I probably can promise that I'll miss Christmases, and birthdays, and so many times when you'll need me and I won't be able to be there. We might get a good assignment after Korea; we might get a shitty one. I wish I could promise you that this will be easy, that there won't be days that you might regret marrying me. I wish I could promise you that I'll come home to you every day. I can't.

"I should have thought about that when I asked you to marry me before we left for Alaska. I should have thought more about what I was asking you to give up. I didn't. So I want you to really think about this and make sure it's what you want. Because if it isn't, I understand. It's a lot to take a chance on. I understand if it's too much."

"What can you promise me?" I asked, needing to hear the words, knowing he'd give them to me.

He took a breath as though it pained him. "That I love you. That I'll always love you. That I will do everything in my power to stay safe, to come home to you. That I will die loving you, whenever that is. That I will do anything I can to make this lifestyle work for us. That if it comes down to a choice I can make, I will always choose you over my career. I'll give you a family if you want it. I'll spend my life loving you, working to make you happy."

I'd wanted absolutes before, guarantees he couldn't give. I'd wanted an oath signed in blood that this was a risk that would pan out, that I wouldn't get hurt. I'd wanted a big fucking net at the bottom when I leapt.

What I got instead was love, so much love, and it turned out, that was all I had really needed after all.

I reached out, capturing Noah's face in my hands, staring into those dark eyes that looked a little bit lost, drowning in them, wanting to spend my entire life looking at him.

"I love you. I want to marry you. I want to go to Korea with you. I'll go anywhere with you. I don't need anything else. Just you."

He groaned, and then the sound disappeared, lost between his mouth and mine.

Noah's lips devoured me, his kiss both desperate and hopeful, as though we had all we needed to get through this.

My hands found the zipper of his flight suit, dragging it down the rest of the way, and then I pulled away from his mouth and sank to my knees, my fingers working the laces of his boots while he watched me. I removed one, then the other, pulling his socks off.

His flight suit came next, then his worn khaki-colored T-shirt, and finally his boxers, until he sat on the edge of the bed, naked, legs spread.

I settled between his thighs, gripping the base of his semi-hard cock, my hands stroking him as he grew beneath my touch. I dipped my head, licking the tip, and then I took him deep in my mouth as he fell back on the bed, a groan torn from his lips.

I licked and sucked, using every trick I knew to lead him toward orgasm. This wasn't sex; it was resurrection. My attempt at taking his tired body and putting it back together again. His body quaked beneath my touch as I laid siege to all the stress, and fear, and pain that plagued him. As I brought him closer and closer to release with my tongue, and lips, and hands.

Noah's hips rocked forward, taking what I gave and wanting more.

He groaned. "So fucking good, babe. I'm going to come."

I increased the pace of my hands around the base of his cock, my fingers twisting and stroking, my tongue laving the head, sucking him deeper and deeper, harder, faster, until finally I felt him coming, his body shuddering with each thrust. When he finished, his body stilled, his limbs hanging over the edge of the bed.

I got to my feet, pressing a kiss to one of his pecs. Our gazes met, and it seemed like some of the shadows had disappeared from his eyes, as though some of the demons had been chased away.

Maybe blowjobs were a little magic.

I leaned back, but Noah's hand curled around my wrist and held me in place.

"Straddle me."

"Aren't you tired?"

He gave me a knowing look. "It's been over a month. Straddle me."

God, yes.

I was already wet, already turned on to the point where little foreplay was needed. It had been a long six weeks, and more than anything, the past few days had been interminable. I needed him in a way I hadn't needed him before.

Noah moved higher on the bed and I straddled him, taking his cock between my hands—he hadn't been exaggerating, he was still hard—stroking him from base to tip, once, twice, and then I positioned myself over him and sank down, my body shuddering as he filled me. My head rolled back, my chest arching forward, and for a moment I didn't move, just enjoyed the feel of him inside me, and then his big hand came down on my hip, his skin just a touch darker than mine, his fingers molding my flesh, and without speaking, he commanded me to ride him.

It was fast. It was hard. And when my orgasm came on like a freight train, I simply shattered, the remnants of my pleasure met by the beginning of Noah's.

We collapsed together, and before my eyes closed, I prayed that I'd chased away whatever dreams plagued him at night, whatever memories he had of the accident.

I prayed for peace.

NOAH

I awoke to Jordan's body wrapped around me like a vine. To the scent of her perfume, the smell of her shampoo, the feel of her hair tickling my face.

I hadn't dreamed.

I kissed her shoulder, rolling out of her embrace, my feet hitting the floor with a wince. The flight back from Alaska had been a tense one and my body ached from sitting cramped in the cockpit, from looking over my shoulder.

I headed to the kitchen, needing coffee, food, and a moment to get my shit together. I walked past Easy's open door, more than a little worried to see his bed made, no sign that he'd come home last night. Easy out all night wasn't a new phenomenon by any stretch of the imagination, but considering it was his first night back from being gone for over a month, I was surprised he hadn't gotten settled in. Maybe he had wanted to give me some space with Jordan. More likely he was out with some girl. Casual sex wasn't new with him, either, and I didn't blame him; hell, I hadn't been a Boy Scout, but the edge with Easy and the look I'd seen in his eyes did worry me. The whole squadron felt broken, and I had no fucking clue how to piece it back together again. Especially when I was hemorrhaging myself.

I started the coffee, noticing that Jordan had it all set up and waiting for us. And that the kitchen gleamed. As did the rest of the house.

I was definitely getting the better end of the deal here.

The front door opened. I walked out of the kitchen and came face to face with Easy, still dressed in his flight suit from the day before.

He nodded in greeting.

"Do you want coffee?" I asked.

"Yeah."

He followed me to the kitchen.

I poured us two cups, then turned to face him.

"You okay?"

"Are you?" he returned.

Neither one of us spoke, which I figured was answer enough.

"I'm planning the memorial. We thought it would be good if everyone in the squadron said something about Joker. Nothing too long. Just a few words about him. Can you do that?"

Easy's knuckles tightened against the coffee mug.

I hesitated. "I think it would mean a lot to his family." Her name hung unspoken between us.

It will mean a lot to Dani.

"I can't."

My eyes narrowed.

"I just can't."

"You were one of his closest friends."

Easy's gaze met mine, panic in his eyes. "I can't."

Fuck.

"It wasn't your fault."

He jerked back like I'd hit him.

"It wasn't any of our fault," I continued. "They'll do the accident investigation." They'd already questioned all of us. "But you and I know it was an accident."

We wouldn't know for sure until the final report came out—which wouldn't be for a while—but we'd all been flying long enough to know what had happened to Joker.

We called it spatial D, also known as spatial disorientation. It could happen to anyone. And when it did, you couldn't gauge where you were in the air, often until it was too late.

"I love his wife." Easy said the words like he'd confessed to murder, as though the existence of them was his most shameful secret. They tore through the silent kitchen, stunning me.

I knew, of course, and he knew I knew, and still, I'd never heard them spoken aloud.

"I've dreamed of his wife. Wanted his wife. Loved her for a fucking year. And he died. I heard him die. And she hugged me yesterday. I came home and he didn't. It should have been his arms around his wife. Not mine."

"So what, you think you're somehow responsible for his death? That because you wanted Dani, you somehow wished it?"

He didn't answer, which was answer enough.

He fucking thought that.

"That's bullshit."

He wouldn't meet my gaze.

"We can't change what happened. You know that better than anyone. He was a good pilot. But what happened to him could have happened to anyone. You didn't fucking will it to happen. We take our lives into our hands every single time we fly; you're too good of a pilot to not know that, too good of a pilot to blame yourself. The younger guys in the squadron look up to you. Everyone looks up to you. Dani needs you."

He staggered back like I'd hit him as soon as her name left my lips.

"Maybe she doesn't feel the same way you do, but she cares about you, relies on you. You guys have a friendship that matters to her. She just lost her husband. She needs you right now. We all do. You don't get to fall apart, not when she's holding it together."

"You don't think I know that? That I don't want to be there for her? I can't."

"Why?"

"Because it should have been me," he shouted. "I would have traded places with him in a heartbeat. I would have done anything to give her that. For him to have come home."

I'd known it was bad, but somehow I didn't realize it was this bad. We all felt guilty for surviving when Joker didn't; it cloaked us. But to hear Easy admit that he wished he'd died was too much. I'd thought that if I could just talk to him, I'd help him see that he needed to be strong for the squadron and Dani. But now I realized I'd underestimated how much this had fucked him up.

"If you love her, you'll step up and forget this shit. If you really do love her, then you'll be there for her when she needs a friend to lean on. You can't change the past, and wishing yourself dead isn't going to bring Joker back. All you can do is be there for his widow. We owe him that. He would want us to take care of Dani."

"If he'd known . . ." Easy's voice broke off. "If he'd known, he wouldn't have wanted *me* to take care of Dani. He was my friend and I dreamed of fucking his wife."

I didn't know what to say anymore. I'd tried, but I was barely held together myself, and I lacked the cohesion to fix Easy.

"Are you coming to the memorial service, at least?"

"I don't know."

I made a sound of disgust, unable to hold it in anymore. I left him standing in the kitchen, dragged down by his guilt.

$\mathcal{T}$WENTY-SIX

JORDAN

We huddled into one of the giant airplane hangars, seated on metal folding chairs, staring up at a projection screen that showed a video with pictures of Joker's life. Tom Petty's "Learning to Fly" played in the background. I'd never cried so much in my entire life.

There were images of Joker when he was little—clearly his airplane fascination had started young because some showed him wearing pajamas decorated with red and blue biplanes, others with a slightly older, but still adorable Joker, running around his parents' backyard with his arms out like he was flying. Next came the high school years, a boy in a basketball uniform, wearing a tuxedo at prom. Pictures of Joker at the Air Force Academy, going through pilot training, surrounded by friends who had come now for the memorial service. And then came Dani.

They looked so happy in every single one of their photos. So in love. They looked like the world lay before them, theirs for the taking. We watched as their wedding flashed by, interspersed with photos of Joker landing, arms outstretched for Dani. Some were clearly after deployments if the sand-colored flight suit was any indication, others from TDYs, trips like his last one to Alaska. It almost seemed to highlight the one homecoming that was missing.

There were pictures of him as he took over command of the Wild Aces, picture after picture of him surrounded by Noah, Thor, and Easy. It was clear that the four had been even closer than perhaps I'd realized. My heart clenched at the picture of all of them in Vegas, me on the fringes of the photo, my body tucked against Noah's, a smile on my face. It felt like a lifetime ago.

The last image flickered on the screen, a shot of Joker from behind, walking out to a waiting F-16, the sun setting behind him, his helmet bag thrown over his shoulder. It froze there, the image of Joker heading to the sky for one last flight settling over the crowd. And then it disappeared, and it was as though the life had been sucked out of the room.

Noah's hand clutched mine, our fingers twined together, giving each other strength. We sat near the front, two rows away from Dani and her family, in a sea of blue, the squadron wearing their service dress, family members sprinkled throughout.

I hadn't seen Easy.

The video ended and the wing commander rose, heading toward the makeshift podium that had been set up. I'd never met him, but I'd heard enough talk from the guys to know he wasn't well liked. Noah had described him as a "careerist asshole," which I figured was his way of saying that the guy was more concerned with getting ahead than with his people. To hear him speak now, Joker had been his brother, soul mate, and best friend all rolled into one. I caught a few shuffles and barely muffled snorts from the guys, giving the impression that Joker had shared Noah's opinion.

And then he was finished, his speech, which had read like an emotional Mad Libs—insert name here—already forgotten.

There were people here who'd known Joker, who'd loved him, people who felt his loss like an ache in their chest. But that loss almost felt overwhelmed by the other side of this—the part of his death that was more about what he'd done than who he was. Joker had become a clip on the evening news, a post on social media with a picture of the American flag and a comment about how he'd died a hero. And he was a hero. But he was also a man. A friend, a son, a husband. And somewhere in the ceremony of all this, it seemed like that essence of him was overshadowed by his job. I knew people meant well, knew they were proud, but it was strange to see him as a sound bite or a post on social media, to hear others talk about him as though they knew him. To claim his loss as their own. It was the strange dichotomy of being in a world where your life was private and yet it wasn't, really. In a way it felt like his death, like his life, was the military's, too.

And somewhere in all of that, mentioned as a line in articles—*he is survived by his wife*—was Dani. As if this was something she could survive. As if losing the person you loved the most, the person your entire life revolved around, was something you survived.

And for the first time since we'd gotten the news, I realized I was angry. So fucking angry. It bubbled up inside me like a scream pushing to escape my lungs as I sat there surrounded by service members and their families, knowing we'd do this again.

My anger wasn't rational. There wasn't a bad guy here, a villain I could blame or direct my rage at. But it was still here, choking me. It was an accident. A fucking accident. Seconds. Seconds that made the difference between life and death. Seconds that made the difference between lying in bed listening to the sound of your man breathing, the rhythmic song lulling you to sleep, and reaching across an empty bed, the distance feeling like a mile, the silence deafening, stretching on and on into years.

There weren't any words that could make this okay. Nothing could make this okay. And I knew that whatever Dani clung to now, whatever got her through this horrible day, was wrung from the depths of her soul.

How many times throughout the course of my relationship with Noah would this scene repeat itself? How many times would I sit here, my ass cold against the metal, trying to comprehend the incomprehensible? I knew someone had to do to it. Knew that freedom came at a price and that all these men and women surrounding me paid it. Their families paid it. Their children paid it. And the fear that I would pay it, too, that one day I would sit in the seat Dani sat in, was nearly too much to bear. I felt selfish for thinking it. Like the worst person in the world for the part of me that clutched Noah's hand a little tighter, grateful for the warmth of his palm in mine. I wanted to wrap him up in a protective bubble. Wanted to shield him from harm. I didn't care if he was a badass; he was *my* badass. Had become my world. And the idea of losing that . . .

I couldn't.

I gripped his hand more tightly, holding on to Noah with everything I had, as though the connection between us would keep him safe as waves of protectiveness crashed over me like I'd never experienced before.

And then the room got so quiet you could have heard a pin drop, as we all watched Dani rise from her seat and walk to the front of the room.

Noah had told me that it was typical for the widow to speak last, but they'd wanted to spare her the emotion of listening to the squadron tell stories about her husband and then having to stand in front of over a thousand people and eulogize him. So she would go first and everyone else would follow her lead.

She walked up to the podium, the wing commander at her side, which seemed more for protocol and pretense than anything else considering the space between their bodies.

She'd asked me to find her a dress and I'd pulled some strings through the store to get one sent here so she wouldn't have to deal with buying one herself.

She didn't look like she belonged here in this airplane hangar. She looked like an auburn Audrey Hepburn or Grace Kelly, like a throwback to another time and place. This, too, was her way of honoring Joker. Even in her grief, she carried herself with poise, and I couldn't help but think that he was beaming down on her with pride.

Another lump grew in my throat, joining the three thousand, four hundred, and twenty-two that were already lodged there.

I squeezed Noah's hand a little tighter.

Dani stopped at the podium, her hands on either side of the frame. She didn't speak for a moment, staring out at the crowd. Her eyes were covered by large black sunglasses, her hair pulled back in a severe bun that made her look even more fragile.

Another lump.

She took a deep breath as though steadying herself and then her voice rang out over the microphone.

"Thank you for coming today to celebrate Michael's life." Her voice cracked over the words. "Michael was a wonderful husband. He was my best friend. And more than anything, he was a fighter pilot. He loved flying, loved serving with all of you." Her gaze ran over the crowd. "As hard as this is, as much as I miss him, he wouldn't want me to cry up here. He wouldn't want us all to gather in grief, but to celebrate the tremendous life he led."

She swallowed, her voice trembling. "He knew the danger every time he flew, knew the price he could pay, but he loved to fly. And anyone who knew him knows that he went out the way he would have wanted to, flying the plane he loved, doing the job he was born to do. Defending the country he loved."

She paused and the silence stretched on, her hands gripping the edge of the podium as she struggled to continue.

"Michael—" His name came out as a choked sob.

We'd asked her if she wanted anyone to go up with her, but she'd said that it was something she needed to do on her own. We should have insisted, should have realized that no matter how badly she'd wanted to do this on her own, it was too much.

Noah let out an oath beside me.

The wing commander stood off to the side, and even though I doubted he would have done much to comfort Dani, at least it was something. I silently willed him to go stand next to her, to help her get through this, but he didn't fucking move. The silence continued and I waited for her family, for someone, to go help her, and then Dani's gaze jerked to the side, and I caught a flash of blue walking toward the podium.

Easy, wearing his navy blue service dress, his body tense as though poised for flight, strode to the front, his gaze on

Dani the entire time. And then Noah's hand left mine and he stood, walking to the edge of our row, up to the podium. Thor followed.

Easy reached Dani first, his arm going around her waist, looking like he was propping her up. Noah stood next to Easy, Thor on the other side of Dani.

They flanked her, the three men who'd been there for the last moments of Joker's life. Three of his closest friends. They surrounded her like sentries, giving her their protection and support.

"Michael was the love of my life," Dani continued, her voice stronger now. "And I can't imagine my life without him. But I know he is watching all of us, looking down on us from his place in the sky." Her voice warbled, the tears there unmistakable. "He's home now."

There wasn't a dry eye in the hangar.

Dani stepped away from the podium, her arm tucked into Easy's, surrounded by pilots. They walked her to her seat, and then Noah was beside me once again, his hand in mine.

The rest of the service went by in a flood of stories about Joker. Most of the squadron got up and spoke about him, painting a picture of a leader who had been both friend and mentor, who had cared about his people and put them first, even when it meant he had to stick his neck out for them.

When it was Noah's turn, he spoke of the friend he'd lost, and I realized just how difficult this must be for him, and how he fought to keep it together for everyone around him.

I'd never loved him more.

TWENTY-SEVEN

NOAH

The fucking day wouldn't end. It was like that last radio call kept playing over and over in my mind, Joker's voice in my ear, and then . . . nothing. He was just gone.

That was the part I couldn't wrap my brain around, the thing that no matter how many times I told myself, I couldn't make sink in.

Joker was gone.

Fucking gone.

We stood in an open field next to the squadron, all of the Wild Aces in attendance forming a circle around a gleaming piano standing in the grass.

How many piano burns had I gone to? How many times did we do this? How many times did we lose one of our own? And the irony was that our losses didn't come from enemy fire, they came from routine training. From going to work. As the weapons officer, it was my job to ensure that the squadron was tactically proficient, to keep these guys safe by teaching them not to get shot down, to fly better than any threat that could come their way. But there were some things you couldn't prepare for. Some things you couldn't train for.

Sometimes fate fucked you over.

Jordan wrapped her arms around my waist, cuddling her body against mine. I kissed her hair, inhaling her scent, steadying myself.

And then Thor walked to the front. As the official mayor of the squadron, it was his job to preside over all of the social functions. His voice rang out over the crowd.

"Tonight the Wild Aces commemorate the life of Michael 'Joker' Peterson with one of our most closely held traditions—a piano burn. Some of our guests tonight might wonder why we burn a piano. The tradition originated with our British brothers and the Battle of Britain. As legend has it, and I guarantee at least ten percent of this story is true, there was once a British pilot who was the greatest piano player who'd ever lived. He used to fly in combat and then return and play at the O-Club for all to hear. But one fateful day he was killed in action. In their grief, his squadron decided that no one would ever play the piano as well as he did, so they burned it. And so began the tradition of the piano burn."

There were different variations of the story, and as Thor highlighted, hyperbole was pretty much a fighter pilot standard. But this was without question one of our most revered traditions, one we celebrated at major squadron functions, and no matter how rowdy or drunk the crowd was beforehand, everyone always went silent, their gaze riveted to the flames.

Thor went to get the lighter and Easy broke away from the group, taking his usual place at the piano. Jordan's arms tightened around me. He was the only one in the squadron who played, and it never failed to surprise me that Easy was capable of making the sounds he did.

His fingers touched the keys and the familiar strands of a Dos Gringos song filled the air—standard fighter pilot fare. Easy played it like he was sitting in some fancy concert hall performing for guys in tuxes and girls wearing big rocks rather than the motley group we were.

Jordan stiffened beside me.

"Whoa. He's amazing."

I nodded. "Yeah, he is."

I'd have been lying if I didn't admit that Easy definitely used his musical skills to sweet-talk girls into bed. It was just another arrow in his quiver, another tool to get laid. But no one who'd ever seen him play could miss that he loved it, too.

The squadron broke into song, the lyrics as natural as breathing as the piano caught fire, as Easy played and played, the flames consuming the instrument until they grew too close and he had to walk away. Maybe it wasn't the kind of song you expected to hear sung at a memorial service, but fuck it, it was us, and more than anything, it was definitely what Joker would have wanted.

We sang the shit out of that song.

JORDAN

I was emotionally exhausted by the time we walked into Noah's bedroom. It felt as though we'd packed a lifetime worth of grief and sadness into one afternoon and evening, and if I felt that way, I couldn't imagine how Dani must have felt.

I slid into bed next to Noah, my feet brushing against his legs under the covers. We slipped into our usual routine: he raised his arm so that I could lay my head on his chest, my hair brushing against his bare skin, his arm settling over my body, holding me toward him as though I was something he had to protect. Something he was afraid to let go of.

Today had made me appreciate the fragility of life in a way I never had before. Seeing Dani's loss . . . I shuddered. I wanted to stay like this with Noah forever, wanted to know that he would be safe, because it was impossible for me to imagine a world without him. Impossible for me to imagine my life without him now that I'd found him.

"Thank you for being there today," he whispered, his lips grazing the top of my head. "I couldn't have gotten through it without you."

"Of course."

"You okay?"

I wasn't sure how to answer that one. My emotions were a messy gnarl I couldn't untangle. I felt both empty and full, as though everything had been scraped out of me to make way for the enormous grief that pulsed through my body.

"I don't know."

"Yeah, me, too."

My throat tightened, but I figured if we were going to do this, we had to do it right. So I gave him the truth, as much as it pained me.

"I don't want to lose you."

He sighed, his arms tightening around me.

"You won't."

It wasn't enough.

"How do you know?"

"I'm safe. Always."

I believed that. I also knew he was a really good pilot. It still didn't feel like enough.

"Wasn't Joker safe? He'd been flying even longer than you had."

"Spatial D happens. Especially at night. But I promise you, I'll always be safe. You aren't going to lose me."

I didn't want to keep picking at him, didn't want to turn into an annoying nag, but I could feel myself hovering on the edge there. It would be so easy to give in to the anxiety, so easy to tell him that I couldn't do it, that the danger of his job was too much to bear. That I didn't want to spend my days and nights fearing the ring of the phone or the knock at the door. That I didn't want to watch him walk out the door every day for work with dread in my heart, wondering if it would be the day he wouldn't come home.

I wanted to be stronger, wanted to let it go, but I clutched that fear tight in my palm, my fingers wrapped around it, unable to relax and release it. Unable to move past the image of Dani at the podium. And then, just like her image filled my mind, her words came to me:

You'll have to be strong for him. Stronger than you think you can be. Because at the end of the day, his mind can't be on a fight you had that morning or on whatever problems you might be dealing with at home. It has to be on the mission. On coming home safely. Because in their line of work the smallest mistake can be the difference between life and death.

I unfurled my hand and opened my palm.

It wasn't some magical, heightened awareness. It wasn't like I suddenly became zen and equipped to deal with the shit that would come my way. My heart would always clench a bit when the phone rang. And I'd never see the words *"F-16 crash"* and not feel as though the loss was personal.

I didn't want to marry a hero or a symbol; I wanted to marry a man. A man I would grow old with, have children with, spoil grandchildren with. I wanted forever, and because I was me, and I'd been thrust into a world I didn't really understand and probably wasn't equipped to deal with, I wanted guarantees on forever.

But life just didn't work like that.

I'd fallen for the man that night in Vegas. But he wasn't just Noah. I'd recognized it that first moment I saw him in the nightclub, even if I hadn't known exactly what *it* was. He carried himself a little differently than the guys I'd known before him. As though there was a weight on his shoulders—responsibility, dedication, sacrifice. And I couldn't love one part of him and not love it all. So maybe I hadn't wanted to marry a hero or a symbol, but I'd fallen in love with a fighter pilot, so as much as he would always just be Noah to me, I had to accept that there might be a time in our future when it would be his picture in the paper next to a jet, or my name entangled in the phrase "survived by his wife."

And I got it.

As much as I knew Dani suffered right now, as great as her grief was, she endured. She loved her husband. She loved her husband and she wanted him to be happy, wanted him to live his dream. And at the end of the day, that was all we could do. I didn't want Noah to worry about me, didn't want him to be focused on doing anything other than the job he needed to do so he could come home to me.

So I shut it down.

I wrapped my arms around his waist, burrowing my body against his, cuddling into his warmth.

"I love you," I whispered, the words more a vow than an endearment.

I love you. I will always love you.

"I love you, too."

I heard the promise there; felt it in the way he held me, like he would do everything he could to protect me from harm. Like I was his everything the same way he was mine.

Noah was silent for a while, his hand stroking my back in lazy strokes. My eyelids fluttered as I struggled to stay awake.

"Do you want a big wedding?"

That woke me up.

"What do you mean?"

"I was just wondering if you wanted a wedding like your sister's. And how much time you would need to plan."

I shrugged. "I don't know. Honestly, I haven't really thought about it. And with everything going on right now, I figured a wedding was pretty low priority."

Noah shifted so we were both on our sides, facing each other. His hand skimmed my hip in a habit I doubted he was even aware of.

"Our wedding is definitely not low priority. I know the timing sucks. I hate that I didn't give you the big proposal and that the memory of losing one of my closest friends will forever be linked with the memory of us getting engaged. I'm sorry for how complicated all of this is. But no matter how difficult our lifestyle is, I definitely want to marry you and I want you to have the kind of wedding you deserve."

I thought about this for a moment, wondering what kind of wedding I even wanted. I wasn't kidding; right now things like weddings didn't seem all that important. The marriage, yes. But the rest of it? He was scheduled to report to Korea in a little over a month. I wanted to spend my time with him, not obsessing over seating charts, and menus, and arguing with my mother over the color scheme and whether the invitations were elegant enough.

"I want to marry you. I don't care how, or where, or when. As long as it's you and me promising forever, the rest is just details."

"I thought those details were important to girls."

"They can be. But after everything that's happened, it's hard for me to care."

"I don't want you to regret—"

I silenced him with a kiss, and then inspiration struck.

"Can you get leave for next weekend?"

"To get married?"

I nodded, excitement bubbling up, threatening to spill over. It was the perfect place for us to get married. Romantic, and meaningful, and absolutely perfect.

"Where are we getting married?"

I beamed back at him.

"Vegas."

$\mathcal{T}$WENTY-EIGHT

JORDAN

It was totally surreal to be landing in Vegas with my fiancé. Hell, I still couldn't believe that Noah was my fiancé. Last time I'd made this descent, I'd been with my sister and her bridesmaids, never imagining how much one weekend would alter my life.

Besides Sophia, we didn't tell anyone we were getting married. I told her on the same day we had a conversation about her buying out my half of the store, something I had worried she would be opposed to, but it turned out she completely understood. That was the thing about being partners with your best friend—more than anything she just wanted me to be happy. And that was Noah.

I'd played with the idea of inviting Meg, knew Noah had considered asking Easy to come out. In the end, it had somehow seemed right for it to just be the two of us. Dani had gone home for a few months to stay with her family, but considering the loss she'd suffered, I didn't want to make a big deal of our marriage. I knew she'd be happy for me, but it felt wrong to ask her to attend the wedding. And there was something romantic about it just being the two of us, a memory we wouldn't share with anyone else. Maybe later on we'd have a party with our families or something, but for now I had everything I wanted.

The wheels hit the runway, the plane bouncing slightly in a way that had me gripping the armrest and Noah smirking and muttering under his breath about bad landings. Flying with him had been an experience. I was a nervous flier, the type who jumped at every bit of turbulence, my stomach rolling every single time the plane hit a bump in the air. Noah was bored by the whole thing, but I figured when you flew like he did, anything else seemed pretty tame. I'd asked him inane question after inane question, occasionally gripping his hand when the moment called for it, until the captain announced that we were beginning our initial descent and I realized the whole flight had passed by without incident.

In booking our wedding weekend, I'd had the idea to re-create the weekend we'd met as much as possible, so when we checked in to our hotel, we ended up staying at the Venetian in the same suite where we'd first had sex.

Who said I didn't have a romantic side.

Noah lifted me up in his arms, carrying me over the threshold with ease.

I grinned. "I think you're supposed to do that after we get married."

His mouth found mine. "I'm practicing," he mumbled between us.

I leaned back slightly, fluttering my eyelashes, my tongue darting out to lick my bottom lip. I'd put a moratorium on sex the night before the wedding, but that didn't mean we had to start just yet.

His eyes flared.

"In that case, I definitely think we should practice the wedding night."

His hand settled on my ass, cupping, squeezing . . .

His voice sent a tremor down my spine that had my nipples tightening and a low pull settling in my belly.

"That sounds like a great idea."

After we'd christened our room, we got dressed up and hit the Strip.

We'd decided to get married tomorrow to give ourselves a day to recover from the travel. The wedding might have been spur of the moment, but that didn't mean I didn't want to look my best. I had the perfect dress, and an appointment to get my hair and makeup done at the hotel.

Noah took me to dinner at a fancy restaurant at Encore, where we ate a fabulous meal, complemented by an even better bottle of champagne. The whole night felt magical, and I realized how badly we'd needed this break from reality, how much we'd needed to make some time just for the two of us.

Afterward, he took me to Tao.

I grinned as we walked through the entrance. "Returning to the scene of the crime?"

He gave me a heartbreaking smile. "I'll never forget seeing you dancing here. You were so beautiful, so full of energy. You looked like fun and trouble, and I knew instantly that I wanted to see that smile thrown my way."

"I thought you looked like a badass," I admitted. "A hot

badass. There was something about you. The way you walked through the room like you knew exactly who you were and wouldn't ever apologize for it. You looked like a man and it made me think that I'd been dating boys the whole time."

He led me out to the dance floor, taking me to the exact spot where I'd been when we'd first seen each other. I was shocked that he remembered with that kind of detail.

"I thought you were the Chupacabra," I told him, the confession escaping before I even realized what I'd said.

The corner of his mouth tipped up and my heart lurched. God, he was beautiful, and even more than that, it just felt good to see him smile after everything we'd been through. I'd dedicate my life to making him smile. To taking care of him. Loving him.

"Excuse me?"

His voice dripped with amusement.

"The Chupacabra. Legendary mythical beast indigenous to Latin America."

His grin deepened. "You thought I was a beast."

"A sexy, needle-in-the-haystack beast."

"Well, that makes it better, then."

My eyes narrowed. "Are you mocking me?"

"Never."

"'Cause it seems like you're mocking me."

"I am honored to be relegated to a tale told to scare children."

I laughed. "Something like that."

He pulled me into his arms. "I love you."

My heart still tumbled and sputtered at those three words falling from his lips, my mouth breaking out into an enormous grin.

Would it always be like this between us? Would time temper the feelings inside me? Take the love bursting through me and turn it into a steady stream rather than an explosion my skin couldn't contain? Or was it part of our life together—the uncertainty of it, at least—did the craziness of his schedule, of deployments and danger, make us hang on tighter, feel more, love deeper?

Yes.

He released me, taking a step back, and then he was on his knee.

We were getting married, so the proposal really shouldn't have been that much of a shock, and yet, some part of me that had once thrown weddings for my dolls and worn my T-shirt inside out over my head like a veil trailing behind me felt a freaking flutter taking root and spreading through my limbs.

This was the moment. The moment I'd thought about as a little girl. The moment I'd thought would never occur when I endured bad date, after bad date, after worse date. We'd put the cart before the horse, but right now I didn't care. Every single romantic bone in my body and a few I didn't even know I possessed were focused on the sight of Noah kneeling in the middle of a crowded Vegas nightclub—the exact spot where we'd met—offering me the world.

He pulled an immediately recognizable little blue box out of the jacket he'd worn to dinner and my heartbeat kicked up a notch.

And then he flipped open the lid.

It was a classic setting, a round solitaire diamond that was the perfect size and full of sparkle.

Noah swallowed, his expression intent, his gaze on mine. "I know this hasn't been the most romantic engagement. And I'm sorry that you aren't getting to have the big, fancy wedding. With our lifestyle, it'll be like this sometimes, but I want you to always know how much I love you." He flashed the cocky grin I'd fallen in love with. "Will you marry me?"

I laughed, tears filling my eyes as I gave him a shaky nod, holding out my hand so he could slide the ring onto my finger.

NOAH

"We're not having sex tonight."

I skimmed a hand up Jordan's leg, my fingers reaching the hem of the sheer black lace nightgown she'd put on that had me questioning the sanity of our decision not to fool around the night before our wedding.

I groaned as I traced the line of lace against her skin, my fingers itching to go higher, to sink between her thighs.

"Just a little bit?"

She laughed. She lay on her side facing me, her body on gorgeous display, her lips so fucking tempting.

"It's bad luck to have sex the night before your wedding."

I made a face. "Says who? I'm pretty sure I've never heard that particular superstition."

"Says everyone."

She cuddled closer to me, her tits pressing into my chest, making the ache in my cock even worse.

"Let's make our own luck," I whispered, hoping my voice came off as tempting and not needy as hell.

Our sex life had changed since the accident, since I'd returned from Alaska. What had been fun and playful between us had become a thing of need, a desperate race to fuck. It was good. Mind-blowingly good. But part of me missed the playful sex, the ease of it that drained the tension from my day and replaced whatever shit was going on with a smile. I wanted to get back to normal, or whatever our normal was anyway. And I *really* wanted to get underneath her lace.

"What about just the tip?"

She snorted. "What are you, sixteen?"

"Feels like it."

She laughed. "It's been like six hours."

"It's been eight."

"Let me get this straight, you can't remember what I asked you to pick up from the grocery store when I give you a three-item list, but you can remember exactly how long it's been since we last had sex?"

I fingered the lace, wishing I was fingering something else, moving my hand just a few inches higher.

"It's a gift. I also remember what you were wearing and that you sat on my face."

Jordan shoved at my chest, her palm resting over my heart. "Why do I love you again?"

"Because I'm naturally amazing, and if you let me, I'll make you come your brains out."

The fingers on my chest stroked my skin.

"Really?" she purred.

We have liftoff.

Her fingernail scraped at my nipple, sending a tingle down my spine, my balls tightening.

"What about fooling around?"

"Is this a variation of just the tip?"

I rolled over until she was beneath me. Her legs spread and I settled my cock between her thighs, my boxers a barrier I was desperate to shed.

"Maybe," I murmured, my mouth finding the spot in the hollow of her neck that I loved. I nipped her skin there, my tongue following the bite. Her hips arched beneath me.

I slid my hand between us, trailing my fingers up the inside of her thigh, each touch teasing a shiver from her skin.

"Am I going to get an orgasm out of this?" she whispered, her breath hitching as I slid even higher, hovering there.

"Definitely."

I leaned down, claiming her mouth, taking her tongue into mine, sucking on it, my teeth scraping at her pouty lips. If she didn't want to have full-on sex before our wedding, I'd respect that, and if her version of fooling around meant I'd have her lips wrapped around my cock later, then I was all in.

My fingers stroked higher, her legs parting wider, a sound somewhere between a moan and a sigh filling the air around us as I hit the right spot. I teased her flesh, gliding over her pussy, her arousal coating my fingers. She shuddered beneath my hand.

My thumb found her clit, and she arched forward, her tits in my face a temptation I couldn't resist. My free hand reached up and slipped under the lace, cupping her, my thumb finding her nipple, rubbing the tight point back and forth while my other hand worked her clit.

God, she was gorgeous. So fucking gorgeous. There was something so sexual about her. She wasn't shy about what she liked, her gaze hungry, and I knew immediately what she wanted. She wasn't chasing an orgasm, she was hoarding them, knew that with her no-sex challenge the gauntlet had been thrown down. Maybe I couldn't make her come with my cock, at least, not with my cock inside her, but I'd make her come every other way. First with my fingers and then while I fucked her tits.

I leaned forward and captured her other nipple between my teeth, tugging lightly while she squirmed against me, her pussy clenching around my fingers, drawing me deeper. Jordan's hands threaded through my hair, pulling me down, offering more of her body up to me.

I fucked her with my fingers while my mouth teased her nipples, moving from one breast to the next, her skin flushed from my lips, tongue, and teeth. Her hips circled my hand, taking what she wanted, doing everything she could to get herself off until I increased the pressure on her clit, my strokes faster now, and then she arched her back, her hair falling against the pillow, moans escaping her lips, as I watched the unforgettable sight of Jordan coming.

When the last tremor left her body, I rolled to the side, my arm around Jordan, until we lay in bed facing each other, our bodies still joined by my hand between her legs. My fingers slid out, stroking her soft skin, covered in her wetness. Jordan sighed, her gaze on mine, a happy smile tugging at her mouth.

Her gaze went molten as I sucked her off my fingers.

I grinned. "Sweet. I can't decide which part of your body I like to taste more."

My hand turned greedy, and I couldn't resist playing with her rosy nipples, the sight of them tight and wet from my mouth and hands making my dick ache.

Jordan groaned, moving out of my grasp, her voice teasing. "No. More. Orgasms. At least, for the next five minutes."

I leaned back against the pillows. "Weak sauce."

Jordan arched an eyebrow at me. "Are you challenging me to see who can take more? Game on, fighter boy."

She tossed me a naughty grin, her naked body sliding down mine, all hips and boobs, until her mouth disappeared between my legs.

"My turn," she purred, her throat vibrating against my dick.

Best time not having sex I'd ever had.

$\mathscr{T}$WENTY-NINE

JORDAN

With everything that had happened in the past few weeks, I hadn't had time or really even thought about getting a wedding dress. Luckily, Sophia had amazing taste in fashion and access to designers, and she hooked a sister up with a dress that had needed minimal altering and stole my heart the first time I saw it.

I adjusted my boobs, pulling the bodice up with a sigh. Strapless was iffy with double Ds. On the one hand, I knew Noah would appreciate the show; on the other, I'd be waging a losing fight with gravity for most of the night. Whatever. It would be worth it to see Noah's expression.

The dress was hands-down the prettiest thing I'd ever seen. It was cut in a mermaid style, the fabric a gorgeous lace that looked like it had been hand-sewn by monks who'd taken a vow of silence or something like that. The bodice was a sweetheart neckline. The hem had a hint of tulle under the lace that gave the illusion that I walked on a cloud.

It hugged my curves, giving me killer cleavage, a hidden

corset sucking in the parts that needed to be sucked in, highlighting my hips and ass.

I'd have been lying if I didn't admit that through various times in my life I'd wished I were skinnier or had a little less boobs, a little less ass. And then somewhere along the way, I'd stopped caring. This was me, and I liked it, and Noah liked it, which was an added bonus considering I doubted I had the patience to put up with a guy who was going to give me shit about my body.

I loved that Noah loved me exactly the way I was. I realized now how many of my dating years had been spent trying to be someone I wasn't, never understanding that if I had hooked a guy, it wouldn't have meant anything because he wouldn't have known *me*. There was no substitute for finding the guy who loved you for you.

I picked up the pink bouquet, inhaling the scent of roses, peonies, and a few other flowers I didn't recognize. Five minutes to show time.

I'd done the bridesmaid thing enough times to see bridal nerves in action—my friends crying because the flowers in the church were screwed up or freaking out over a glitch with the seating chart. I hadn't thought a lot about what kind of bride I'd be on my wedding day, but then again, even if I had, the reality of today was so different—so unexpected— that I doubted I could have even come close.

I wasn't nervous. At all. No second thoughts—I'd been to those weddings too, one where a friend had almost been a runner—my body was free from tension. I was excited. Ready to start the next chapter of my life, ready to claim my future with Noah. Maybe it was all we had been through in the past few weeks, but I liked that we'd stripped all the trappings and excess away, and while I wasn't having the glossy magazine wedding, we'd gotten down to the essentials.

Him. Me. Forever.

"Are you ready?"

I turned toward Sharon, the wedding planner, hovering near the open doorway.

"Yes."

I slid my engagement ring—I couldn't stop staring at it—to my right ring finger in preparation for Noah slipping on the band that would make me his wife.

My bouquet in one hand, the hem of my skirt in the other, I did a last-minute beauty check in the mirror. I'd splurged and had someone from the hotel salon come to the room and do my hair and makeup and she'd done an amazing job. With how casual the wedding was, a big veil had seemed kind of silly, so I ended up with a short wisp of netting that covered the side of my face and was attached to the most gorgeous headpiece of crystals and feathers.

It was amazing.

I followed Sharon out of the room, the first flutter taking root in my stomach.

This was it. This was the beginning of the rest of my life.

I walked forward, each step feeling like it took me closer and closer to where I belonged, and the music hit me first. And when I realized the song he'd picked, a smile spread across my face, a laugh escaping, then another. And then the tears came.

Elvis Presley. "Can't Help Falling in Love."

It was the perfect song for Vegas, the perfect song for the love that had swept us up and turned our lives inside out. And it was Noah, big, badass, fighter pilot Noah, giving me romance.

My feet hit the aisle runner as Elvis crooned around us, at the exact moment when the Bellagio fountains shot up over the Strip, the Vegas sun setting in a gorgeous sky of pinks, and reds, and oranges. But the thing that made me stop in my tracks for a moment, stealing the breath from my chest, wasn't the scenery or the unabashedly romantic air enfolding us. It was the sight of Noah standing at the end of the altar, dressed in a formal blue uniform—elegant jacket that looked like a military version of a tux, crisp white shirt, navy bow tie, and blue trousers that highlighted how tall and masculine he was. The medals on his chest gleamed in the dying Vegas light.

I'd been wrong when I'd said I liked Navy uniforms best. This was something out of a fucking fairytale. He looked like every prince I'd read about when I was a child.

Total Chupacabra.

Our gazes locked across the aisle and the look on his face was so close to the one he'd given me the first time he saw me, like I was everything he'd ever wanted, and it hit me so hard that I gave up on trying to fight the tears and crossed the distance to my future.

NOAH

I would never forget this moment as long as I lived.

I was a guy, so it wasn't like I'd spent a lot of time thinking about my wedding. I'd wanted Jordan to be happy and have the kind of day she'd dreamed of, hence the wedding package at the Bellagio, and the mess dress, and the fancy dinner reservations I'd made for later on tonight. A part of me worried that I'd cheated her out of the big wedding, so I'd tried to make up for it as best as I could, knowing that this wouldn't be the first time I couldn't give her everything she deserved.

The blinding smile on her face told me she didn't care.

A lump filled my throat.

I was asking a lot, and a part of me kept waiting for her to tell me that it was too much, that she couldn't handle the move to Korea. And yet here she was. Standing in front of me, ready to give me her future, trusting me to do right by her.

I was thirty-three and I'd known plenty of women, but anything before paled to this. It wasn't just the sex—the way her body welcomed mine, the way sliding into her tight heat felt like heaven. It was my ability to see a future with her, the knowledge that this was forever.

Who would have guessed that I'd find forever in a night-club in Vegas?

My gaze swept over her, the initial punch staggering. I didn't know how she did it, how she managed to stun me, and yet she did. There was just something about her. Something beyond the mouthwatering cleavage and curves I couldn't wait to explore later; it was the spark of her, the promise in her eyes that said she'd take you on the ride of your life. The smile that told the world she'd wring every last drop out of life. It was the way she'd stood by us all when Joker died, thrown into a world she didn't understand, a world so far out of her depth. She grabbed life by the balls and it was impossible not to be impressed by such a feat.

Impossible not to be impressed by her.

I was a guy, and more than that, I was kind of a simple guy. I didn't have poetry for her or pretty words, and I wasn't sure I was even all that great at romance.

But while this life might have molded me, chiseled my edges, hollowed me out of whatever frivolity I had left, it had taught me the value of a promise. Had taught me how to stick through the bad times, how to hold on to the good times with a tight grip, to live the hell out of life, and to spend my life serving something greater than me.

So maybe I couldn't give her the window dressing of love, but I gave her my heart and soul.

It was like breathing.

Our gazes locked as she started her walk down the aisle. Tears swam and then spilled down her cheeks.

The lump grew bigger.

I felt like an electric charge vibrated through my body, like I was a powder keg waiting to go off. It was a short walk to the altar, and still, I felt some irrational desire to close the distance between us, and take her hand in mine.

And then she was there, right in front of me, looking up at me with a blinding smile on her face.

Christ.

"I love you so much."

I groaned the words out, past the lump, through the pounding in my chest.

Another tear slipped down her cheek, and I reached out, swiping it away, the pad of my thumb lingering on her skin.

I took her hand in mine, holding on to this moment, some part of me afraid that she'd slip through my fingers, that it wasn't possible to be this happy.

"I love you, too."

It escaped her mouth like a vow, one I clutched tightly to me.

The officiant cleared his throat and then he began the ceremony. My voice shook as I spoke the words that bound us together, a tremor running through my fingers as she slid my wedding band over my knuckle, as I did the same to her.

We stared into each other's eyes the entire time, an entire conversation between us.

I'll love you forever.

I'll follow you anywhere.
I'll spend my life trying to make you happy.
All I need is you.
Only you.

And then it was over, and Jordan threw her arms around me, a laugh escaping her lips, her mouth on mine, kissing the hell out of me.

I was hers and she was mine.

Forever.

JORDAN

We didn't have three hundred guests, or spend ten thousand dollars on flowers, or dance our first dance in some fancy country club. It wasn't the wedding I'd imagined when I was a little girl playing with my dolls. It, like my relationship with Noah, was a whirlwind.

Like so many monumental days, the reality of it was like a photograph with blurred edges. It would come back to me in pieces, flashes I would remember for the rest of my life.

Our first dance in front of the Bellagio fountains. Laughter. So much laughter. Kissing Noah on the Strip until onlookers started shouting things like, *Get a room.* Noah stripping my wedding dress from my body when we got back to our room and bringing me to orgasm after orgasm until we collapsed in bed, exhaustion overtaking us.

It was messy, and chaotic, and unexpectedly amazing.

It was perfect.

It was us.

Turn the page for a sneak peek at
the next Wild Aces Romance book,

INTO THE BLUE,

coming from Berkley in July 2016.

BECCA

I walked into the bar, already feeling about ten years past my prime. Columbia was a college town, especially the closer you got to the University of South Carolina campus, and while Liberty Tap Room managed to straddle the line between students and young professionals fairly well, tonight the place was packed with fans celebrating the Gamecocks' latest football win.

I pushed through the crowds wearing garnet and black, my gaze peeled for my friend Rachel's distinctive red hair. I neared the bar, spotting a flash of red through the crowd. Rachel and her friend Julie sat on barstools, locked in conversation with three guys.

Whoa.

Two of the guys had their backs to me, but the view was pretty spectacular. They were both tall with impressive muscles that tapered down to lean waists. The third was something out of a magazine ad—tall, blond, tan, panty-dropping blue eyes, and a shit-eating grin with a body to match. He leaned into Rachel, whispering something in her ear, bracing his muscular forearms on the back of her chair.

In all the times we'd come to Liberty, we'd met some cute guys, had our fair share of successes, but this was something else entirely. This was like an alternate reality. This was karma making up for one failed engagement that resulted in my heart as emotional road kill and the series of less-than-spectacular relationships that followed.

Rachel spotted me, her lips transforming into a wide smile that gave me a pretty good indication of how the night was going.

I lived in my hometown of Bradbury, South Carolina, population twenty-five thousand, and while I loved it there, most of my friends had married long ago and started families. At thirty-one, I was one of the few singles left, so when I needed a night out, I made the hour-long trek to Columbia and Rachel. We'd met at a law school alumni mixer a few months ago, and she and her friends had adopted me into their group.

She waved me over, the guys turned, and my ovaries exploded a bit as three sexy smiles flashed back at me. Rachel closed the distance between us, leaving the hottie behind at the bar. She wrapped her arms around me in an enthusiastic hug that suggested I had some catching up to do.

"Ohmigod, Becca. You got here just in time. We hit the jackpot," she hissed in my ear.

I grinned. "So I noticed. Which one isn't taken?"

"The dark-haired one in the blue sweater."

I pulled back slightly, studying the guy who was apparently "mine" for the night. Cute, and not in the same intimidating way the blond was cute. The dark-haired guy shot me another friendly smile and my heartbeat kicked up a notch.

Rachel led me over to the group, making the introductions, her voice nearly at a shout to be heard over the conversations around us and the pop music blaring from the speakers.

The blond guy introduced himself as Easy, the other one as Merlin, and the dark-haired guy who was "mine" told me his name was Bandit between pulls of beer.

I blinked.

Boy band? Professional wrestlers? Guys reliving their high school years?

My gaze swept from Rachel to Julie and back again, wondering why I seemed to be the only one concerned about the fact that a group of thirty-something-year-old men had just introduced themselves by such bizarre monikers. Were they part of some preppy motorcycle gang?

"Umm . . ."

"They're fighter pilots," Julie announced with a grin, her body angled toward the one called Merlin.

Oh, hell to the no.

Considering Shaw Air Force Base was only an hour away from Columbia and two hours from my hometown, I'd always considered it a stroke of good fortune that I'd managed to avoid meeting any of the F-16 pilots who called South Carolina their temporary home.

Apparently, my luck had changed.

I'd known one fighter pilot in my entire life, and since that experience had left me completely and utterly fucked—and not just in a screaming-orgasm sort of way—once had been enough.

"Why don't you sit next to me?" Bandit asked, patting the seat of an empty barstool.

Rachel and Julie flashed me encouraging smiles. One of the great things about making new friends was the fact that they didn't know your every failure or all your flaws. But that meant they also had no clue that this was basically my own personal version of hell.

One night. I'd just wanted one night to go out, have fun, meet a cute guy, and maybe get laid. Okay, so sex was definitely off the table considering lady town had gone into lockdown mode at the phrase "fighter pilot," but that didn't mean I still couldn't have a good time. I mean it wasn't like Eric was *here*. And how many F-16 pilots could there be in the world? Maybe they didn't even know him.

I climbed up onto the bar stool, a lead weight settling in my stomach. I'd stay for a drink. Then all bets were off.

"Can I get you something?" Bandit asked.

"That's okay. I'll get it." I turned and caught the bartender's attention, ordering a glass of wine for myself, feeling like I'd brought the group's mood down considerably. Everyone was in full-on flirt mode, the couples clearly paired off for the night, and I felt bad for the one they called Bandit for getting stuck with me.

I turned back to face the group while I waited for the bartender to pour my glass of wine, pasting a smile on my face.

"So how long have you guys been stationed at Shaw?"

"I've been there for a year." He gestured toward Easy and Merlin. "They're visiting from Bryer Air Force Base . . . here for a buddy's bachelor party last night . . ."

I heard Bryer and my world came to a crashing stop.

Motherfucker.

The world really was way too small.

I wasn't one of those girls who kept in touch with her exes—not *the* ex, at least—the one who took my heart and shattered it, then ran over it with his car, and for an encore set it on fire. We weren't friends on social media, everyone who knew me from before, who'd known *us*, knew better than to bring him up with me. But at the same time, we were both from a small town, and even though he hadn't come home for the better part of a decade, he was the local boy who'd hit it big, the troublemaker who'd turned it around, joined the military, and become an officer and fighter pilot. So I'd heard that Eric was living in Oklahoma. That he flew F-16s there. And despite all my best intentions not to keep tabs on him, he was frequently in the back of my mind. I'd waited for years, my heart in my throat, wondering when someone would mention in passing that he'd gotten married, mentally steeling myself for the inevitable blow that ultimately didn't come.

Then again, he'd made his choice clear a decade ago when I'd lost out to a hunk of metal. Maybe he didn't wear a wedding band on his finger, but he'd promised 'til death do us part all the same.

It was on the tip of my tongue to ask if they knew Eric—I figured the fighter community was pretty small, the F-16 community even smaller, and Bryer its own little world—but I wasn't sure I wanted to know the answer. On one hand, didn't everyone want to win the "who's doing better" contest after a breakup? I didn't want him to be suffering or anything, but if he was desolate in my absence, had developed a weird fetish where he'd stopped clipping his toenails, and had lived a hermit's life for the last decade, I wouldn't exactly shed a tear.

"We were going to Tin Roof to see if there's any music playing. Want to come?" Bandit asked.

I considered his offer for a moment. "Yeah, maybe I'll come for a bit."

I could just casually mention him. No big deal, right?

"We're just waiting on our buddy, Thor," Bandit whispered

in my ear, a flirty smile on his face. I had to give the guy some credit—I had the personality of a wet mop tonight and he was still looking to score.

"Okay." I took a sip of my wine, making an effort to smile, feeling a little guilty for ruining this guy's shot at getting laid. Would it be weird if I casually mentioned that nothing was going to happen? It would give him a chance to find someone else for the night, at least.

But what should I say? *I'm already in a relationship* was a blatant lie that Rachel and Julie could easily debunk. And I didn't want to hurt his feelings and make him think it was something wrong with *him*. And, *Sorry, but you have the same job as my former fiancé who I have not managed to get over in a decade*, sounded really fucking sad.

"Listen—"

"There he is," Bandit interjected.

I would later appreciate the irony as Taylor Swift filled the bar, singing about a guy being trouble, at the exact moment—

I swiveled in my chair, my world stopped, and my wine-glass hit the ground.

Eric—heart-crushing, would-rather-slide-inside-a-jet-than-me, one-that-got-away Eric stood in front of me, his arm draped around the shoulders of a stunning blonde.

He was just as tall as I remembered—tall enough that it was an effort to look up at him. His reddish blond hair was the same—or was it just a touch lighter? His blue eyes seemed more intense than I'd remembered, which was just stupid because of course they hadn't changed—maybe it was just me and my reaction to him. Or that the way he looked at me had changed. Before, his gaze had been heated and affectionate; now, it just looked . . . I didn't even know. His shoulders were broader, his body much more impressive than I'd remembered, but I figured that came with the territory and his job.

He looked good. Really good. Better than the mental image I had kept tucked away in the recesses of my mind, which was a pretty impressive feat considering I'd had some good memories to keep me company in his absence.

His hair fell over his forehead, his gaze boring into me, and his teeth sunk into his bottom lip—a lip I'd sucked over and over again—and a little wave of light-headedness hit me. Or maybe it was the sexual drought finally hitting me full force, or the wine, or the loud music, or the fact that my heart hammered in my chest.

More likely, it was the force of Eric. Six-feet-two-inches of Eric.

Fuck me.

THOR

No fucking way.

I blinked, convinced I'd somehow hallucinated her, that Becca Madison couldn't possibly be *here*, standing a few feet away from me, Bandit's arm brushing against her side.

The sound of breaking glass shattered the haze, everyone around us scrambling to pick up her dropped wineglass. *We* didn't move; it was like time stood still for the two of us while the world went on.

"Becca?"

I had to say her name, as though somehow that would confirm that this wasn't a case of mistaken identity or a dream, that she was really here, in front of me.

She looked different and somehow the same—maybe

that was the effect of ten years. Her dark hair was up, exposing the curve of her neck and highlighting the deep vee between her breasts. Glasses perched atop her nose, dark frames that somehow complemented her deep brown eyes and made her even more beautiful. She'd never been in-your-face sexy; instead, she'd cornered the market on the sexy librarian fantasy, the good girl who you wanted to play with until she turned bad.

And considering how many times I'd had her naked, my body sliding into hers, drowning in her tight, wet heat, I knew just how mind-blowing the sex could be.

"Do you guys know each other?" the girl next to me—Mandy or something—asked.

"Yes."

"We used to," Becca answered at the same time.

I took a step away from Mandy, still feeling like I was in a dream.

"I can't believe it's really you."

She didn't answer me, her gaze unwavering, assessing. I struggled not to flinch under the weight of her stare, the measure of all that I'd lost.

"How have you been?"

Had it really been ten years? Did it feel like less because there hadn't been a day when I didn't think of her? When I didn't wonder where she was or what she was doing?

And now she was here, looking up at me with those big brown eyes that I was helpless in the face of, her presence a punch in the gut and a knee to the balls as she knocked the wind out of me.

Finally she spoke, her voice making me ache.

"Good. Great, actually," she squeaked.

"Good. Good." I swallowed, losing a bit of myself as I stared at her. "You look great."

A flush of color spread across her cheeks. "Thanks."

I heard Easy calling my name, felt the blonde tugging on my arm, watched as Bandit slipped his arm around Becca as though he could somehow claim the girl I'd fallen in love with when I was seventeen fucking years old.

I wanted to reach out and hold on to her, wanted to keep her in front of me even as I felt her getting ready to pull away, wanted to fall to my knees and fix the mistake I'd made a decade ago.

I swallowed again, trying to steady my voice, wondering if I sounded as desperate as I felt.

"Do you want to get out of here—"

"I'm going to go." Becca lurched off her chair, her gaze darting around the group, looking everywhere but at me.

Look at me. Please. Give me a chance.

"Becca—"

She didn't look at me, didn't react. It was as though I hadn't even spoken, and after a hasty good-bye—swallowed up by the white noise rushing through my ears—she was gone as quickly as she'd crashed back into my life, her brown hair gleaming, bobbing through the crowd until even that disappeared and I was left standing by the bar, feeling like I'd just been hit by a Mack truck, surrounded by six pairs of curious eyes and one pissed-off blonde.

LOVE

ROMANCE NOVELS?

For news on all your favorite romance authors, sneak peeks into the newest releases, book giveaways, and much more—

"Like" Love Always on Facebook!

 LoveAlwaysBooks

M1063G0212